Praise for the work of *USA TODAY* bestselling author

JENNIFER GREENE

Also available from

JENNIFER GREENE

and HQN Books

Blame It on Cupid
Blame It on Chocolate

JENNIFER GREENE

Blame It on PARIS

ISBN-13: 978-0-373-77278-0
ISBN-10: 0-373-77278-5

BLAME IT ON PARIS

Printed in U.S.A.

Dear Reader,

I've been to Paris only once, but I've never forgotten it. It's a mesmerizing, magical city like none other—a city of lights and legends, of sights and smells and sounds just made for fantasies and lovers.

Over the years, those memories kept brewing in my mind... just waiting for a story to weave around them...and finally it came.

I needed a special man, the kind of man who could make a girl want to throw away all that was safe and sure, everything she thought she believed about herself...just for the chance to be with him. And I needed a special woman, the kind of woman who could challenge and entice a man to be more than he was, more than he thought he could be...just for the right to be with her.

So I created Kelly...who meets the wrong man at absolutely the wrong time. And then I found Will...who has such a code of honor that he can't possibly seduce Kelly, much less become involved with her.

But in Paris, what seems wrong anywhere else can be impossibly, wonderfully right—if my two lovers will just take that huge risk and leap off a cliff together.

I loved writing this story...and love having the chance to share it with you. Hope you enjoy it!

All my best,

Jennifer Greene

To my Lar

For being MY Paris

Blame It on PARIS

CHAPTER ONE

GUILT WAS so much fun.

Kelly Rochard grabbed her shoulder bag and bounded down the cracked porch steps of the centuries-old bed-and-breakfast. She couldn't wait a second longer to inhale all the sights, smells and sounds of Paris in the springtime.

Who'd have thunk it? That a gregarious, nosy, hopelessly open person such as herself could possibly have managed to keep a secret this big?

No one even knew she was here.

Of course, in a week, she'd go back home to South Bend, confess everything to her new fiancé, never tell another fib again as long as she lived, and probably do penance for two or three aeons. As her mother loved to say, you could take the Catholic out of the girl, but you were stuck with the guilt for life.

But today, she just plain didn't care. Guilt or no guilt, she was thrilled to be here.

Blithely she stepped off the curb—and a dozen horns shrieked at her mistake. She backed up fast, heart pounding. A couple taxi drivers yelled as they passed by—something about *connarde* and *ballot* and *une tête de linotte*. She was pretty sure the insults were aimed at her specific genetic heritage, with a few general references about her being an American scatterbrain, as well.

Okay, okay. So she was suffering jet lag, not at her brightest, and it was going to take her a while—and a map—to figure out how to get around…preferably without getting herself killed.

The small inn where she was staying didn't seem located in exactly the newest, safest part of town, but the neighborhood still exploded with color.

Three street vendors in a row tried to woo her into taking a bouquet of fresh flowers. The next one sold *café*—which she fumbled with her brand-new euros to buy, and then sipped as she ambled on. Pedestrians bustled past, clearly on their way to work. All the women looked so savvy—their clothes not necessarily expensive, but even basic styles jazzed up with an interesting scarf tied the right way. A man winked at her. She gawked at an open-air grocery, where the smell of fresh fruits mixed with a luxurious array of fresh flowers.

The grin on her face just kept getting bigger and sillier. She was free. This was Paris. In May. The city of romance. The city of lights.

Her father's city.

The open door of a bakery drew her inside. A single look at the croissants and baguettes made her realize she was starving to death. Euros were exchanged—too many, she was positive—but the first taste was better than sin, and well worth whatever the baker had cheated her out of. The pastry was buttery, light, a puff of sweetness on her tongue.

Juggling the pastry and the coffee and her bag, she stepped back into the throng of pedestrians... when a stranger suddenly grabbed her arm.

Initially Kelly reacted with more exasperation than fear.

When the mugger tugged, she tugged back. And no, tangling with a thief wasn't the wisest thing Kelly Nicole Rochard had ever done—particularly when the jerk was a good half foot taller than her five feet five inches and easily outweighed her by fifty pounds. But, as her mother had noted during labor, Kelly was as naturally stubborn as a goat.

Her roll went flying. Coffee splattered everywhere. She was so busy struggling just to keep her balance—and free herself—that she didn't originally realize why the mugger was yanking so hard on her arm. But then she did. Fast. Her engagement ring *did* tend to glitter in the sun, which was probably what caught the jerk's attention. He yanked on her finger so hard she almost cried, but that was just pain.

When he managed to wrestle off the ring, Kelly let out a war cry worthy of a marine. "You give that back, you rotten son of a flea-bitten scumbag!"

She couldn't finish because the mugger suddenly

jerked her around and yanked her tight against his chest. Her courage suffered an instant and complete crash. She forgot the ring. Forgot the dazzling day and the wonder of Paris.

When the bony arm cut off her windpipe, she forgot just about everything.

Faces and storefronts blurred. Sounds muted to a distant cacophony. She'd never tasted fear this acid, this consuming. Her entire consciousness was zoned in on her thief. The man wasn't huge, but he was still a ton bigger than she was, and he stank of drugs and desperation. His breath blew fetid on her neck, his body reeking of old sweat. He hissed something to her in French.

Four years of high school French didn't seem to address his particular choice of vocabulary. Still, she was ninety-nine percent certain that she understood him. He seemed to feel that her mother lacked morals, that she herself was a worthless bitch and that her life wasn't going to be worth dog breath if she didn't give up her purse.

She was more than willing to.

Almost.

"Look," she said desperately, and then stopped. He tightened the choke hold on her throat. She couldn't breathe. She couldn't think. She was panicked enough to suffer a heart attack. Or pee in her pants. Or hurl.

Or possibly all three.

At the same time.

Her mugger hissed another command, this one angrier and more urgent than the first.

She got it, she got it. She didn't have an hour or two to think up a plan. Either she released her death grip on her purse, or just maybe he was going to break her neck.

"Look," she blubbered. "You don't understand. You can have all my money. I don't care. You can take every euro, every dollar. And all the credit cards. Everything. My passport—you want my passport? You can have that, too. But I really need some papers in that purse. You couldn't possibly want those papers. Please, I—"

On her last gulp of oxygen, her voice quit. Completely quit, like a cell phone with no battery. She tried to tell herself it didn't matter. He probably couldn't speak English, so why was she even trying to reason with him?

It was just...there were some very old, very private letters in her purse. They were her father's. The only thing she had, or would ever have, of her dad's. They were the whole reason she'd made this impulsive trip to Paris. She couldn't give them up. She just couldn't.

His other hand clamped on her left breast and squeezed. Hard.

She dropped her hold on the purse faster than a hot coal.

The mugger grabbed it and then shoved her, hard.

She toppled on the cement walk, stunning both her knee and elbow when she crashed on the hard surface.

It had all happened so quickly. The mugger disappeared into the crowd. Some pedestrians kept on walking, acting as if she were invisible, but a few rushed over to her, jabbering sympathetically in French. Someone yelled for a gendarme—she understood the word for police, but by then she didn't care. It was too darn late for that.

She was fine. Her heart didn't know it yet; she was still gulping down air like a panicked beached whale…but really, she knew she was okay. Her engagement ring, her passport, her money—losing all of it was a nightmare, but she was alive and the jerk was gone.

Everything was survivable except for the loss of those letters. No one even knew she had them, even her mom. Especially her mom. And no one would likely recognize the ratty old envelopes as remotely valuable, because they weren't.

To anyone but her. Unfortunately, they were irreplaceably valuable to her, and the loss hit her like a blow.

"Mademoiselle…" A mustached man in a uniform pushed through the onlookers, bent down to her. A cop. But what good could he possibly do? Find a thief in this kind of city traffic? The guy was probably at the Eiffel Tower by now. And when he got around to opening her purse, he'd undoubtedly take the loot

and credit cards and passport and throw out everything else.

Like the letters.

A raw, rusty sound came out of her throat. Kelly told herself to get a grip and turn back into her usual strong, sturdy self, but man, somehow she couldn't find the on switch. Caving was totally unlike her. She'd always been a go-to woman, the kind of woman who could cheerlead through a tornado, who saw problems as opportunities rather than crises. She never had meltdowns. She wasn't the meltdown type.

But *damn*. The loss of those old letters really, really, *really* hurt.

"Mademoiselle," the cop repeated, and reeled off some questions in French.

She pushed a hand through her hair, struggling to understand, flunking, struggling again. She could see he was getting impatient. Hell's bells, so was she—with herself. But she was shook up, and the gendarme was speaking so fast.

But then…somewhere in the sea of strange faces and confusion, she heard an American accent.

An American Midwestern accent like hers.

A man.

"Hey," he said, "are you in some kind of trouble here?"

Her head shot up. One glance gave her a jolt. The guy was tall and lean and blond, with a Matthew McConaughey angular face and come-on baby-blue eyes. He wasn't just killer good-looking. He was to die for.

But that wasn't what snagged her attention. His clothes did. Filling out a Notre Dame sweatshirt were brawny wide shoulders.

The logo wasn't for Notre Dame, as in the French cathedral. But as in Notre Dame football. As in the golden dome. As in South Bend, Indiana.

As in *home*.

She fell in love so fast it made her head spin—of course, her head was already spinning. And it wasn't like she thought it was *real* love…but it was real enough for that moment.

She pushed toward him, never losing eye contact, and said breathlessly, "You can't imagine how much I'd appreciate some help. I know a little French, but not enough to communicate, at least as fast as I need to. If you'd play translator for just a few minutes…it couldn't possibly take long…."

WILL MAGUIRE, at age thirty-one, had done all the bailing out and damsel saving and white-knight crap he ever intended to do in this lifetime.

But hell. He had noticed the commotion from all the way down the block, and when he heard the sudden, sharp, panicked yell—obviously a woman's voice—he instinctively hustled toward the sound. The instinct wasn't heroic. It was lunatic.

He'd lived in Paris long enough to know getting

involved in a tourist brouhaha was complete lunacy. Yet still he came closer.

It took only seconds for him to interpret the scene. She'd been ripped off. Moments before, a gendarme had shown up, and typical of Paris, so had every busybody bystander. Most of them figured an American tourist, being an American tourist, had done something stupid. A few wanted to whine about the danger of Paris streets these days. The gendarme was trying to question her about exactly what happened.

In those same few seconds, he snared a quick look at her.

Very quick.

But that was all it took for him to feel a potent kick in the gut.

He didn't get it. A pale purple sweater cupped her small boobs. Dark pants fit snug enough to clarify that she had skinny legs and no ass. Since he'd always tended to like more breasts and less bone, there was nothing below her neck that should have rattled his hormones. Yet his pulse was kabooming like a freight train.

Heightwise, she came up to his chin. And that was where she stopped being ordinary. The eyes were mesmerizing, almond shaped, tea-brown, looking right at him. The details included a small, thin nose; pink mouth; and a sweep of almost-shoulder-length brown hair. Only brown wasn't an accurate description of the color. The sixty-five-degree morning was drenched in sunshine, and that's how her hair looked—lustrous, full of light, shiny in the sun.

Okay, so she was adorable. But that alone didn't explain the kaboom thing. There were fabulous-looking women all over Paris.

There was something else about her, something he couldn't define. A zest. A glow. A female thing. Will didn't need to identify it to know it was a serious problem.

Ever since he'd devoted himself to a life of decadence and vice—that'd be the last four years—he'd fine-tuned his sonar to beware of women who meant trouble.

She meant trouble.

On the other hand, all she'd asked him to do was translate for her for a couple of minutes. How could that possibly be any kind of risk?

"Sure," he said. And immediately discovered that helping her wasn't going to be quite that simple.

The gendarme shot him a look as if a savior of the universe had just shown up. The bystanders kneed in closer, all hot to participate. Everybody claimed to have seen the thief close-up. One said he was tall and burly. One said he was lean as a stick. One said he had a beard, like a homeless person, and another said he'd just been a guy walking down the street who suddenly sprang into this deviant behavior, far too fast for anyone to stop him or come to the girl's aid.

Still, for all the confusion, it didn't take forever to get the basic questions asked and answered. Her name was Kelly Rochard. She was twenty-seven. From South Bend, Indiana. Here for ten days. Vacation.

Something flickered in her eyes when she said "vacation," but Will just dutifully translated—it wasn't any of his business whether she was telling the truth or not.

"So the thief took off with your purse," he said. "Can you give the cop a list of the critical stuff in the bag?"

Hell, she said, her whole world was in the damned bag. Passport, money, credit cards. Oh yeah, and then she got around to mentioning that the thief had also taken off with her engagement ring.

"What?" she said, when Will and the gendarme exchanged a quick look.

Will didn't answer. It was obvious that the cop had immediately thought the same thing he did. What sense did it make for a beautiful woman to be traveling to Paris alone in the spring? Her so-called fiancé was either a jerk or an idiot. Probably both.

"…and there were some private papers in the bag, too. That's the worst. That those records are probably gone forever. I have no way to replace them, no way to…"

"Hey," Will said gruffly. Tears suddenly magnified her eyes, making them look extra huge and exotic. "Take it easy there. It'll all get straightened out."

Well, it wouldn't, of course. Losing a passport in

a foreign country was a guaranteed nightmare. Times fifty.

The cop heard about the "private papers," but he was tuned to the same practical channel that Will was. It didn't really matter what Kelly had lost, because the mugger was long gone. She'd still need a police report, which was a pain for the gendarme to fill out when there was about zero chance in a zillion they'd ever find the guy. But he'd get her one so she could pursue a replacement passport.

That wasn't going to happen overnight.

"Je sais," Will said drily. He knew. American bureaucracies and French bureaucracies—even if the French didn't like to think so—were kin. Ghastly. Time-consuming, inefficient, frustrating, etc., etc.

The cop had some questions for him to translate… Did Kelly have enough funds to survive, someone who could wire her money, a way to live until the paperwork got sorted out, what was the address where she was staying. All that yadda yadda.

"You're from South Bend, too?" She motioned to his sweatshirt.

"Yeah." Like it mattered? He suffered a gulp when he heard the address for her hotel. She was damned lucky she hadn't been ripped off there, too.

"Oh my God. The key to my room was in my purse, too. I can't even get into my room." She'd been doing okay, or reasonably okay. But now the more she realized how much she'd lost, the more panicked she got. "I don't have *anything*. I don't even have money to buy lunch. Or dinner. Or enough to buy another hairbrush. Or lipstick. Or even to wire home. I don't even have my coat—"

The more panicked she got, the faster the gendarme talked. "What does she think we can do? We can't even get a clear description of the perpetrator. You know these Americans, now she'll be saying nothing's safe in France. I'll file a report, of course, but God—" he crossed himself "—couldn't get her a replacement passport this instant. Where was her common sense, to have all her money in one place? And a bag she was carrying on her besides?"

Kelly was on a completely different track. "I carried those letters on me all the time," she said mournfully. "They're all I ever had of my dad. I don't care about the rest...."

Will fished in his pocket for a tissue. Came through. But after she blew her nose, she looked at him expectantly.

As if there was some insane kind of magic between them, he found himself looking back. At those eyes. That mouth. That glow of hers.

He told himself firmly to look away.

He told himself that the gendarme would transport her to the embassy or consulate or wherever she needed to go, and the rest of her mess wasn't his problem. She'd be okay. That's what embassies and consulates and cops were for, taking care of people.

It wasn't his problem. She couldn't possibly, remotely, be his problem.

He told himself that his sisters had irrevocably taught him to steer clear of damsels in distress. At the same time he was analyzing her looks again. Her hair was this glossy mass of loose dark waves, not a style exactly. It just looked all soft and silky. Naturally sexy.

"Monsieur?" The gendarme growled at him impatiently, as if he'd asked him a question a few moments ago and Will had failed to pay attention.

Which was possible.

Possibly she'd been talking, and he hadn't been listening to her, either.

And then he made his third mistake of the day—this one far worse than stopping to help, far worse than failing to pay attention.

"She can't very well just stand here in the street," he told the gendarme. "I'll take her."

The instant those three words came out of his mouth, Will realized that he'd completely lost his mind. "I mean for a little *while*. I'll go feed her. Lunch. But you have to promise to get the police report done pronto, so she can go to the consulate for her passport."

"Bien, bien," the gendarme said. He probably would have promised anything now that he was off the hook.

He disappeared faster than lightning. Ditto for the bystanders.

And Will was left alone with her.

CHAPTER TWO

"I'M ENGAGED. I told you that, didn't I?" Kelly asked him.

"Yup. About three times in the last half hour."

Now, that couldn't have been true, because Kelly knew she hadn't been nervous a half hour ago. It was only now, as they turned down his street and were aiming directly for his place, that her nerves started suffering major hiccups.

Earlier, it seemed like a superb idea to leave the scene of the crime with a nice, tall, big, tall, strong, tall, protective guy. Especially when the guy was a fellow American. Her judgment had nothing to do with his being cute. Or sexy. It was only about her feeling terrified out of her mind from her mugger experience.

Only now, approaching his front door, her judgment didn't seem to be quite the same. It was a cool front door. Old, old oak. Shaped with an arch. The handle was a weathered brass lion. Like Will. Not the weathered and brass part, but the tawny lion part. "I have to admit, it feels a little weird, being here," she said with a laugh. "For one thing, it's just crazy for you to feel stuck with me, someone you don't know from Adam."

"Kelly. You're not worried this is a pickup, are you? The only reason I suggested coming here was because it was nearby. It was the fastest we could get you to a place where you could put your feet up, have a cup of coffee in one hand and a phone in the other. It's not like there isn't another way to handle this, but you've got a bunch of calls to make, no easy way to do it on the street."

"And you're from South Bend besides."

"And I'm from South Bend besides."

"Which practically makes you like family."

He stuck a key in the lock and pushed open the door so she could enter first. She did, grazing his arm as she walked past him, thinking that Will would feel like "family" when it rained cats.

She knew perfectly well she'd been blathering on like a goose. Another time she'd feel embarrassed or guilty, but the truth was, she'd started shaking about fifteen minutes ago and hadn't stopped yet. It wasn't every day a woman got mugged. She kept remembering the creep's stinky breath and body odor, the feel of his arm choking her neck, and that started the shakes all over again.

They were just little shakes. Not big ones. It wasn't that she was a wimp or anything. At least she never had been before this, and Kelly kept telling herself she was mighty grateful that Will had offered to help her. Being suddenly penniless and without ID in a foreign country would have been pretty darn daunting if she'd been alone.

Yet she only caught a single glance at the inside of his apartment before some silly instinct made her whirl around and back out again—or try to back out. Will was still standing in the doorway, blocking her escape. Her nose was suddenly an inch from his chin. She was only a breath's distance from those killer blue eyes. And those shoulders. And those disreputable blond whiskers.

"I'm engaged. Did I mention that?"

"Yeah, you did. What's wrong now?"

"Nothing. Nothing. You've really got an interesting place." But *interesting* wasn't the word for it. One look, and she labeled it *bachelor lair.* The whole place shouted *single guy on the prowl.*

His flat took up the second floor of an old building. She could only see so much from the narrow hallway, but there seemed to be a bunch of rooms, all small. The main living area, off to the right, had long, thin windows; old, rich woodwork; carved tin ceilings. He'd left the French doors open a crack, leading to a step-out balcony. The sunlight and erotic, exotic breeze drifted through the open door.

Well, possibly it was just a plain old spring breeze, and possibly her mind had totally invented the erotic, exotic thing, but Kelly didn't think so. Reality was that sex appeal poured off Will in sheets.

She tried to concentrate on being nosy, which should have been natural for her. The living room was tiny, with a soot-stained corner fireplace and an elegant tiled hearth. The couch was old leather, all wrinkled and soft. The Persian rug looked seriously ancient, thick and fringed, in reds and dark blues. One wall had built-in shelves, with books heaped to the ceiling.

The dust wasn't more than half an inch thick, and Will swooped a shirt off a chair. "Look around, make yourself at home, okay? The bathroom's off to the left. I need to call work, and I'll start some coffee. Then we'll concentrate on what you need to do from here."

He squeezed her shoulder as he ambled past—an erotic, exotic squeeze, totally inappropriate for an engaged woman.

Or more likely it was her response to him that was inappropriate. Splashing her face with cold water right then seemed a great idea, so she took off for the bathroom.

Naturally, she nosed around. The toilet had an antique pull chain from the ceiling—interesting, once she was sure she could make it work. The white pedestal sink and tub were the old-fashioned kind with feet. He used a straight razor, she noted. Didn't have much in the medicine cabinet but deodorant and first-aid stuff and one medicine. She thought it was for colds, nonprescription and more than two years old; he should have thrown it out. It was outdated.

Her conscience chided her for being so shameful, but really, nosing around was better than musing that the tub was big enough for orgies. Not that she'd ever participated in an orgy. Or spent a lot of time thinking about them. Or planned to take up thinking about them.

Impatiently she splashed her face with cool water, then grabbed a navy-blue towel to dry off. The towel was almost the size of a bedsheet. A thick blue rug covered most of the marble floor. No question that Will liked the color blue and his creature comforts.

She opened the door, which gave her away with a telltale creak.

Will immediately called out, "Across the hall and one door down. I'm in the kitchen."

So…it wasn't her fault she got to see more of the apartment en route. To the left, an archway led to an alcove. Impossible to guess what the odd-sized space was for, but Will had squished in a small desk, lamp, chair, laptop, so it worked as a miniden. Still, it wasn't ordinary. The walls had some kind of linen-like finish; the carved ceiling looked hand done. Everywhere, the creaky floors were covered with old Oriental rugs. Nothing seemed new. Everything about the architecture seemed older than a few centuries, practically older than America. Will's love for blues and comfortable textures followed through everywhere. And he might not be into dusting, but he was basically a put-away tidy kind of guy.

"What? Did you get lost?" He stepped out of the kitchen.

"No. I'm just dawdling around. No amount of guilt ever seems to stop me from being nosy. And I love your place—it's really interesting." Looking around had also given her a chance to catch her breath. Maybe she didn't have a full-bore grip yet, but the adrenaline had finally quit pumping. "Will…thank you for helping me. Really, thank you."

"Yeah, well, I stumbled around plenty when I first moved to Paris. Might have gotten into real trouble if a few people hadn't offered a hand. Anyway…" He turned away, started pouring steaming water into pottery mugs. "Did he hurt you?"

She blinked. His tone was so casual that she almost missed it, but then Will wasn't an in-your-face kind of caretaker. Instead he was subtle, found a way to slip in a disturbing question and get it out of the way. Most strangers wouldn't have cared, much less made the effort to steer into a potentially awkward problem.

She thought that just maybe her attraction to him was more than ordinary old sex appeal. Damned if he wasn't coming through like a seriously good guy.

And then she tried to answer the question. "I'm bound to have a few bruises show up tomorrow, maybe even a nasty one on my neck. But I don't need a doctor. Nothing serious." Yet suddenly she needed to snug her arms tight under her chest. "I have to admit, though, that I keep feeling…weird. I was never mugged before, never had anyone touch me with the intent to hurt me. I can't seem to shake it off. There's just a high…ick…factor."

"Sit. I was going to make coffee, then figured that was stupid. You need caffeine like a hole in the head. So it's tea. French-style. With a bunch of sugar. Sugar for shock, right?"

"Actually, I never need an excuse to use sugar, but that'll do."

The kitchen was mostly copper and blue, with white trim. There was no dishwasher, and no place for one, she noticed with shock. The sink was messy, but cleaned fairly recently, and the counter just looked typical of a guy, dishes reproducing since the night before. Her scrutiny kept picking up details. A small fridge, a couple bottles of unopened wine, the luxuriously sexy smell of fresh bread, a heap of fresh fruit in a bowl. The eating table only had room for two chairs, was hardly big enough to put plates on, but it overlooked the boulevard below, the whole view of thick, old trees, the steady snake of cars and street traffic. Sunlight ribboned through fresh green leaves.

"Ever since I got here," she murmured, "I keep seeing the same things I could see at home. Cars. People. Buildings. Spring flowers and smells. But somehow it's incredibly different."

"It's Paris," he said, as if that explained everything.

And maybe it did. Heaven knows her response to

Will was unlike her response to any other stranger. She couldn't seem to pin down a reason. Maybe being mugged had just thrown her normal reactions off-kilter. Maybe shock and fear just made her senses more acute, inflamed her emotions.

And maybe burning her tongue on the hot tea would distract her from these idiotic thoughts about him.

"Better," she pronounced, after she gulped down three long sips of the strong brew.

He leaned against the counter. "Okay, I figure we'd better organize a plan of attack here. Obviously the first priority is getting you a new passport. Somewhere, do you have your original passport number, and other ID like a birth certificate or driver's license?"

"Well, I *did* have. But that stuff was all in my purse."

"Okay. But did you leave that kind of information with someone back home? Like a copy of your passport?"

She nodded. "I left some obvious information in an envelope with my mom—the address where I'd be staying, copies of credit cards, a copy of my birth certificate. I've never traveled outside the country before. It didn't occur to me that I'd need to do more than that."

"Normally, you wouldn't. So the first thing you want to do is call your mom, get her to fax that information here. By then we should have the police report. That's the stuff we need to take to the consulate, get the process going to get you an immediate temporary passport."

She frowned. "Temporary?"

"Well, if you want a regular passport, it'll take a while. The bureaucracy here is no faster than it is in the United States. But you can fly home right away with a temporary, no waiting or hassle."

"And that would be great," she said slowly, "but I don't want to go home immediately. Will, it wasn't my fault this happened. And I didn't come here on a whim. I've waited a long time for a chance to make this trip."

"Okay...well..." For a long moment, he studied her, as if suddenly realizing she hadn't come here to Paris just to do the tourist thing. "The way you'd attack a new permanent passport takes basically the same steps. Get the ID records, then the police report, then go to the consulate. If I remember right, a regular replacement passport'll cost you around eighty-five, ninety bucks. But I'd be amazed if the paperwork went through for that in less than two weeks, and it could take longer."

"But as long as I could get money wired here, replacement credit cards and all that, there's no reason I couldn't stay?"

"I'm no expert, Kelly, but my understanding is that, yes, you'd be fine as long as you stayed in France. It'd probably be pretty dicey to leave the country without an active passport in your hand."

"That's okay. This is the only place I wanted to come to." When she swallowed the last sip of tea, she realized that the adrenaline had quit pumping; the shakes had disappeared. Talking to Will, being with Will, she'd forgotten the mugger. Yet, when she met his eyes, her heart rate still seemed determined to heat to an edgy simmer. "You know a lot about this," she said.

"Not a lot. But I lost a passport once. And I've been living in Paris for the last four years, so naturally I've learned a few survival tricks." He shot her a wry grin. "You can take it to the bank—from replacing credit cards to getting money wired to getting the cop report and the application, you're going to learn a whole bunch of French swearwords over the next couple days."

She chuckled, but she thought it was about time to stop gazing into those sexy blue eyes and move her butt. For Pete's sake, right now she didn't have a brush or deodorant or even the means to buy herself lunch.

Will had been a hero, but he certainly owed her nothing. He'd already gone the long mile to help her out. "Okay," she said brightly. "If you'd just let me use your phone…"

He gave her a look she didn't understand. Then he steered her into the room with the balconies and the high tin ceilings, handed her a phone and left.

She appreciated the privacy. But twenty minutes later, she was pretty close to curling up in a ball under a couch. Any couch.

Will showed up in the doorway. "Not doing too great?"

She sighed. "I couldn't seem to make a direct connection, so I had to use an operator. She didn't speak much English. Or want to."

"Yeah. You're in France."

"Got past that. But my mom wasn't home. I tried her landline, her cell. Twice. Left messages. Twice."

"Okay." He scratched his chin. "I thought you said you had a fiancé."

She straightened. "I do."

He looked at her. She wasn't sure what he was thinking, why a sudden silence fell between them, but whatever wheels were turning in that interesting brain of his, he suddenly seemed to come to a decision. "Come on. We're getting out of here."

FOUR HOURS LATER, Will still wasn't sure what he was doing. She wasn't his problem, he kept telling himself. And once she brought up the fiancé, he'd normally have backed off faster than lightning.

It had taken him a long time to cultivate an irresponsible, don't-give-a-damn, love-'em-and-move-on kind of lifestyle. Poaching was a bad idea. Not because it was right or wrong but because it was inviting trouble.

Only this was different. Really. The thing was, Kelly kept bringing up this so-called fiancé, but the infamous fiancé wasn't the one she wanted to call for help, wasn't the person she'd left records with, wasn't the person she wanted to ask for money.

As far as Will could tell, if the fiancé existed, he was in the toad class.

Maybe that didn't totally explain how they ended up at Pont d'Alma on the Left Bank, with Will forking over major euros at the ticket counter, but by then the day had been so irretrievably awful that *he* needed a pick-me-up.

"A boat ride?" she questioned.

"Neither one of us has had food all day. You have to be hungry by now."

She was intently trying to read the signs. "This is for a riverboat cruise of the Seine?"

"Yeah. One of the worst tourist traps in the whole city. But we were close." A complete lie—he'd driven forty minutes out of his way. But she didn't know that, and who cared, anyway? "It'll get your mind off the rest of the day. That was quite a scene at the your hotel."

The understatement of the year, he thought. When he realized her lodging was in the 20th arrondissement, he almost had a heart attack. Times three.

"Well, I thought I'd researched places to stay quite intensively on the Internet. This one looked clean in the pictures. And it was the cheapest I found, for sure. And when I looked up the area, it said the place was going through a major renewal, so I just didn't expect it would be quite so…"

"Rough." He put it in spades as he ushered her up the gangplank of the riverboat.

"It was okay. Mme. Rossarde seemed nice enough

last night." Kelly lifted exhausted eyes. "Not like this afternoon."

"In French, we'd call her...*un peau de vache.*"

She thought. "The side of a cow?"

He chuckled. "Well, literally, it means hide of a cow, I guess. Meaning...tough. Unyielding. A bitch," he clarified. The fiasco at her hotel kept replaying in his mind. He was still on a steam. The damn woman hadn't wanted to give Kelly her clothes or anything else unless Kelly came through with a week's worth of rent. This, after being told Kelly's passport and money had been stolen.

Will had intervened. Kelly had a major conniption about his paying all that rent for her, but she obviously had to have her stuff. And whether or not she realized how bad the neighborhood was, he did. The other boarders looked like they were fresh out of jail or rehab. By contrast, Kelly looked milk-and-honey fresh. Leaving her there would be like leaving a kitten in a jungle.

So now all her gear was in the back of his car, safe enough, but she'd just gotten more agitated as the day wore on.

"I have to call my mom again. I have to reach her. And then I promise, I'll return all the money I borrowed from you immediately."

"This may be killing you, Kelly, but it's not killing me. And I know you'll return the loan. Quit having a stroke."

"But I don't borrow money. From strangers. From anyone."

"Think of it from my perspective. If I were in a bind in a foreign country, I'd like to think someone would step up and help me."

"But not like this. You've given up the whole day. Your work. Your place. And you're still stuck with me."

"You know what? You need a drink. We both do."

She opened her mouth as if she were going to object to that, too, but then...for the first time... she suddenly seemed to open her eyes. Forget the all-consuming anxiety that had been eating her up.

A few moments later, he wrapped her hands around a glass of wine. A Syrah from the Rhone Valley, red as a ruby in the fading daylight.

She took a sip without looking, likely without tasting.

The boat had just started moving, the buzz of Paris traffic and tourists fading away. The other cruisers fell silent, too. No one could seem to help it on these Seine riverboats, even the Parisians. Paris really was the city of lights...and as dusk fell and the monuments lit up, so did all the ancient bridges. Those diamonds of light glittered in the Seine.

They passed the Musée d'Art, but all the good stuff was a distance away yet. The guide would do his tourist thing, identify the Jardin des Tuileries and the Louvre and all the usual great historical stuff…but that was later. Dinner was now. Wine. The lights. The textures and sounds of Paris.

At some point he accepted being in just a wee heap of trouble. Denial wasn't doing any good. You couldn't pretend you weren't in a swamp if you were knee-deep in mud. He wasn't in mud. He was just suffering from a mighty, mighty pull toward her.

He'd get over it, he assured himself. He'd just met her, for Pete's sake. What was the harm in an evening together? So he liked looking at her. Liked the itchy charge of chemistry. Liked those liquid brown eyes of hers. So?

Once they were seated for dinner, she did all the tourist-sucker oohing and aahing for the Tour Eiffel, Jardin des Plantes, the Louvre, Saint-Germain-des-Prés.

Notre Dame was on Île de la Cité, though. And he knew she'd get into Notre Dame because of being a South Bender. But by the time they'd passed the real Dame, he'd ordered a second bottle of wine, a Puligny-Montrachet from 2002, and they were almost finished with the fabulous flammenkueche.

"What is this dish again?" she asked.

"Well…it's kind of a cross between a pancake and a pizza. It's got cream and herbs and ham and cheese. You like it?"

"You've watched me gobbling it down and you have to ask? It's to die for. Like nothing I've ever tasted before. But I think one taste of escargot is enough for me."

"Hey, you came all the way to France. You might as well try all the French things you can."

"True," she murmured.

Everyone on the cruise was more dressed up than them. They'd never had a chance to change. Hell, Will hadn't even come up with the impulsive idea to do the cruise until late in the day. But now, as they wandered back on deck—Kelly wanted a clearer view of the cathedral on shore, and God knew, they were both stuffed from dinner and needed a walk— she shivered in the sudden damp night breeze.

Her pants and thin V-necked sweater weren't warm enough. Her throat was bare, no jewelry at all, just her skin glowing in the moonlight and distant city lights.

He didn't put an arm around her, but he shifted closer. Close enough so their shoulders and arms touched, a way of simply offering some of his body warmth. But his heartbeat thought there was an implication because his pulse leaped like a pole vault.

Or maybe the leap was caused by the way she suddenly looked at him.

Music from the live trio playing inside drifted back to their part of the boat. He heard it, but like the buzz of other passengers' conversation and bursts of laughter, all sounds seemed to be coming from miles away. Every nerve ending in his body focused on her.

"I can't believe I'm really here, really seeing this."

"You mean the real Notre Dame?"

She chuckled. "The one in South Bend is real, too. Which is funny, because we're here, yet this is the one that seems like a fantasy. It's all so…magical."

The old cathedral wasn't remotely magical, he thought, but she was. And when another spring breeze whisked at her hair and made her shiver again, she didn't fight his arm scooping around her shoulder, nudging her closer.

He knew at that instant they would sleep together.

"You said you'd been in France around four years now? So all these monuments and museums are old to you. You've probably been inside Notre Dame a zillion times."

"Museums, yeah. But Notre Dame, I've never been there."

"Really? But it's so beautiful."

"Yeah, well, might as well get this right on the table. I'm allergic to churches. Especially Catholic churches. My dad had two career goals for me. One was to become a priest, which he must have realized was highly unlikely when he found me sleeping with the babysitter when I was fourteen. I'm pretty sure that incident set off my Recovering Catholic phase. I'm still in it."

"Hard work, this recovery?" Humor glinted in her eyes.

"You can't imagine. I've had to be really vigilant.

Guilt sneaks up on you when you're not looking. You see a nun, you get this instinct to stand up and recite catechism. You have to fight it all the time."

"You're so funny," she murmured.

"Yeah, so they say."

She cocked her chin. "I'm a rebel in a different way."

"Yeah? What way?"

"I stayed with the Catholic fold. Have to admit that. But my senior year, I was suspended from school, almost didn't graduate. Kind of staged a party at a friend's house. The party got a little out of hand. Ended up with a car in the swimming pool in the backyard."

"Uh-oh."

"A major uh-oh. My friend was the dean's daughter."

Will winced on her behalf.

"Yeah," she said. "So don't be thinking I'm a saint."

"Oh, no," he assured her. "I took one look at you and thought, Now there's a wild woman. A hard-core rebel."

"A lot of others don't seem to recognize it."

"Imagine that." A strand of hair drifted across her cheek, mesmerizing him, for no reason that he could imagine. "I attended Notre Dame, actually. The university. Since we're confessing sins and all."

"That's quite a biggie."

"It was my dad's choice of school. Naturally. Played tight end." He added, "That's an offensive football position."

"Like there could be anyone raised in South Bend

who didn't know that. Only darn, we can't talk anymore now that I know you're a god."

"Not. Team didn't do well in those years."

"Ah. And that was all your fault?"

"Probably. I know it's sacrilegious to admit it, but I wasn't that into football. It was just a way to get a scholarship, so I could pay my own way."

"A scholarship? To Notre Dame? There's another wow. I'm impressed."

"Good, good. No one else is, so I'm glad you are." He still hadn't brushed away the silky strand of hair on her cheek, but he was thinking about it nonstop. The moonlight. Her cheek. Her eyes. That strand of hair. "It was an athletic scholarship, not an academic one."

"I get it. You don't want to take credit for having a brain, just brawn."

"Actually, the only thing I wanted credit for was paying my own way, however I could do it. Didn't have to jump for anyone else's strings that way."

"Who was trying to pull your strings?"

"Are you always this nosy?"

"Always," she warned him. "It's what I do for a living."

"You make money being nosy?"

"Yeah, that's me. I've got a title. Forensic accountant. Sounds like I do taxes for the dead, doesn't it? But no. My job's tracking down credit card fraud. To most people, I suspect it's not too thrilling. Some might even call it tedious. But if you're really, really nosy, and like prying into people's lives and stuff that's none of your business…well, it's probably the perfect job."

"Okay." He lowered his head.

"Okay what?"

"Okay, I've waited as long as I can possibly stand it."

"Waited for what?"

"To taste you," he said. And then did.

With his first taste of her, the first kiss…Will heard the music. It was a woman singer with a low, smoky voice belting out a haunting ballad. All the other sensory details around him suddenly came into focus. The endless lights of Paris rippling in the black waters of the Seine, the waves lapping at the boat. He turned to Kelly, as if he were spinning her in a waltz. And kept turning. With his lips glued on hers.

She tasted like the rich, warm wine they'd been drinking.

And like innocence.

Her hands climbed up, up his arms, then up around his neck and hung on, as if she were dizzy from all the spinning. Or from him.

Will thought this had to be the stupidest thing he'd ever done…and then went back for another taste.

CHAPTER THREE

SWALLOWED UP. That's how she felt. Wrapped in Will's arms, absorbed in his kiss, the scent of him, taste of him, look of him.

In some part of her brain, Kelly recognized they were still on the boat, that the music had stopped playing, that the engines had quit, that the other passengers were noisily gathering their belongings and descending the gangplank.

And still, she seemed to be dancing with Will. To unheard music.

To scents she'd never experienced before. To textures she'd never imagined—like his tongue.

His wicked, wicked tongue.

Her fingers fisted around his neck, not clenching so much as holding on. Her balance felt increasingly threatened, as if she was precariously a blink away from falling, awash in silver dizziness.

The image of silver dizziness almost made her laugh. How ridiculous was that? She'd never been fanciful. She'd always been practical, the kind of woman who ran her life on facts, numbers, reality.

For darn sure, she didn't go around looking to do wrong things. She suffered enough guilt day by day trying to do the right things.

Only just then her conscience couldn't seem to scare up any sense of doing wrong.

And the silvery dizziness made perfect sense to her.

And so did kissing Will. Being taken in by Will. The scent of him swarmed her, surrounded her, mixed with the silky black water of the Seine and the lights of Paris and just him. Her stranger. Her clean, warm, sexy stranger. Her exotically sexy stranger...

"Monsieur? Mademoiselle?" A staff member patted Will on the shoulder. His expression was tolerant, gentle, as if he was used to regretfully interrupting lovers—this was Paris, after all. The vision of two people lost in each other was nothing new to him.

But it was new to Kelly...and judging from the dazed, dark look in Will's eyes, it wasn't an everyday occurrence for him, either. Finally, Will stopped moving, as if realizing that the only two people still swaying to music were them.

The night had turned downright chilly, midnight chilly, except when she was circled in his arms. And when he dropped his arms, he still didn't look at the uniformed guy, but only at her. His voice was thicker than smoke, lower than blues. "We're going back to my place."

"Yes," she said, as if it were the only word she knew, the only word she could say.

Even at that moment, she knew he wasn't referring to her having no other place to stay. He wasn't offering her his couch.

And she wasn't leaping to offer excuses—too much wine, too much dinner, too much of an exhausting, terrible day, too much Paris.

She knew what he was inviting.

She knew what she was saying yes to.

Where it had taken almost an hour to get to the port where the cruise began, it seemed only minutes before they were back at Will's place, hauling her suitcases from his trunk. He'd left no lights on. She plunked one case right inside the hallway; he dropped the other two. He'd barely closed the door before leaning her against the hard surface and leveling another kiss on her. This one happened to be a whole-body kiss, involving his chest, his knee, his tongue, his hands, his erection. His soul.

And hers. It wasn't totally her fault she couldn't stop kissing him. Lonesomeness poured off Will in waves. This just wasn't about horniness or chemistry or that kind of nuisance stuff. He tugged at something in her, something huge. A loneliness. A yearning. A need to *be* with someone—someone who filled up the emptiness. Someone who mattered. Someone who touched her. Not on the outside, on the inside.

He did stop for breath once, but only to grumble, "If you say no now, you'll kill me."

At that moment, her thin sweater was flying somewhere over her head. His right shoe was gone. Her knee had regretfully connected with a wall. Neither had turned on a light yet, but the glow of streetlights below was starting to infiltrate the darkness. She could see the fierce shine in his eyes. Feel, see, the tension in his body, in his face.

"What if I want to say no?"

"Then say it. Just know, you'll kill me."

"And what if I say…take me right here, right now, Will. Only love me like no one has ever loved me, or don't mess with me at all."

He muttered a curse word. Or a prayer. "Not a smart thing to say if you want a guy to stop, Kel."

"No?"

"No. So don't say it to any other guys. Ever. Okay?"

Well, hell. He didn't give her a chance to answer. Next thing, he was walking her backward down the dark hall, stopping once to yank his shirt over his head, then to heel off his other shoe. Eventually they bounced off enough walls to pass the bathroom, past all the rooms she'd seen before, into one that she definitely hadn't. Still, even in the dark she knew it was his bedroom. It smelled like his soap. Like the fresh air blowing in the cracked window, like…like him.

Like an exotic, sexy, unbearably masculine man. A fantasy man.

A lover.

She didn't get naked easily. There'd only been Jason for her, and it had taken him four years to talk her out of all her clothes. Her procrastinating hadn't been about morality so much as prudishness. She liked her clothes on. She didn't like messiness.

All in all, she'd long figured out that she just didn't have that big a sex drive. Everybody couldn't, after all. She thought sex was important—like meat and potatoes. A staple of life. Needed. A serious thing.

But certainly nothing on a par with cyclones and tsunamis.

Yet that seemed to be how it was with Will. All explosive risk and wicked need and unbelievably soft romance.

He kissed a slow path all the way down to her toes, then trailed back up again, lingering between her thighs—and embarrassing the devil out of her. He gave her no time to work up a royal prudish fit, which she'd always been very good at.

The feather bed was all rumpled and warm, like him. Beneath, the mattress was hard as a board—maybe it even was a board—but thankfully there were all those soft covers to melt into. Or possibly that was Will she was melting into.

"Maybe you better hold on to the headboard, Kel. I think this could get a little wild."

"Um. Did I mention ahead of time that I only do good-girl sex?"

"I don't think you mentioned that today yet, no."

A breeze fluttered in the dark room, chilling her overheated skin when he flipped her on top of him.

They weren't joined yet, but she could feel how it was going to be. Scary. Delicious. "You get a thrill on roller-coaster rides?" she murmured.

"Nope. But I'm going to get a thrill when I ride you. You ready?" He raised an arm, fumbled in the bedside drawer.

"Condom?" she asked. And got the first serious tone from him she'd heard in hours.

"You don't have a problem with that, do you?"

"Hey, don't insult me."

A flash of a smile in the dark. And that was it…the last time she had a coherent thought.

A zillion sensations bombarded her senses. The sterling shadows on the wall, the profile of him riding her, the strength and bold, primal sexuality of him. How she felt…beguiled…spun into a whispery web of touch and taste and need. The texture of their skin, shiny as wet varnish, silky with sweat. Her lungs gasping for breath. The howl of a siren outside. A flash of lights inside, deep inside her, when this crazy, lofty, silver-sharp climax took her over, took her under.

When it was over, he fell back, pulling her half on top of him as if refusing to be separated even for an instant. She lay there, slaked, eyes closed, still trying to catch her breath. She felt him pulling up the covers, the stroke of his hand on her back, the cuff of his knuckle when he tucked the sheet around her neck, sealing all the airholes. He murmured something silly and throaty and low, like, "Who knew?"

As if he never expected she'd be such a red-hot mama.

Before dropping off to sleep, she remembered thinking, *Damn, I was. I really was.*

At least with him.

SWEET, WARM RAIN DRIZZLED down the windows. Horns and sirens heralded the new day below. A child's laughter echoed from the street. Beneath the feather comforter, she couldn't remember feeling snuggled so safely, so securely. Her cheek seemed embedded in Will's shoulder. Her arm was loosely, possessively, draped around his bare waist. His chest hair nuzzled her very warm, very bare breasts.

But none of those things were what woke her up.

Guilt woke her up.

Huge, sharp, ear-drumming, shame-sucking heaps of guilt.

Silent as sin, she inched out from under the covers—praying not to wake Will—and then tiptoed, shivering, into the hall. Her two suitcases and carry-on were still lying in a jumble by the front door, but right then, she only had one thing on her mind and it wasn't remotely her stuff.

Grabbing a towel from the bathroom to cover herself, she hustled into the living room, grabbed the telephone and found a spot to sit upon the carpet behind the couch.

She dialed Jason.

The phone rang.

And rang.

And then rang some more.

She hated using Will's phone, partly because she'd have yet another bill to clock up on Will's balance sheet, and partly because it just seemed the height of wrong. But without her purse or her cell phone or any of her phone cards, there was no other choice. And this call wouldn't wait another minute. Another second.

But there was no answer, even after seven rings. She hung up, bit her lip, then dialed the number all over again.

It was seven hours earlier in South Bend. That meant it was somewhere around two in the morning there. Heaven knows, she didn't want to wake Jason up, but she needed to reach him. Now. And at this hour, he simply had to be in their new apartment, asleep.

Where else would he be on an early Saturday morning? Even if he'd gone out with the guys, he'd have been home hours before this.

On the ninth ring, she clicked off again, frustrated and anxious, but she just couldn't quit. Surely he was just sleeping hard. Sooner or later he'd hear the ring.

She started punching in the numbers again until she suddenly noted a tousled blond head peering at her from over the couch. "I don't know if the customs have changed in America, but over here, we're allowed to sit in a regular chair to make a call," Will said, his voice thick from sleep. She could hear his amusement.

"I was trying not to make noise. I didn't want to wake you up. I was just calling…" She almost said *my mother,* but the lie stuck in her throat. She'd committed enough sins in the past twenty-four hours. She couldn't add another one to the mound. She sighed. "My fiancé."

Will's eyes narrowed as if he were sighting in a rifle. "I thought I recognized that strange expression on your face. Guilt. Which is completely wasted, Kelly. Whoever that guy is, you were never going to marry him."

"I was. I was."

"See? You said it in the past tense. You already know he wasn't remotely right for you."

If she wasn't a lady—and if she wasn't struggling with both hands and a phone to keep covered by the towel—she'd have smacked him. "But I thought he was right. Last week."

"Can't help that," Will said heartlessly.

"Even two days ago I thought he was!"

"Can't help that, either. Good thing you found out, though, huh? Before you got tied up with a guy who was totally wrong for you?" His face disappeared from sight. "I'm headed in the kitchen to make some coffee, so you're welcome to the shower first. By the time you're done, I should have some scrambled eggs ready. That is, assuming you're not still hiding behind the couch."

"I am *not* hiding."

A few minutes later, when she was locked in his bathroom, standing under the shower, which was more a sultry trickle than the exuberant water pressure she was used to in the U.S., she was still feeling defensive.

By the time she'd rinsed out the shampoo, though, her mood had metamorphosed from defensive to morose. Truth was, she would have liked to hide behind Will's couch indefinitely. At least for a few weeks. She didn't know what was happening to her. It was totally impossible that she'd cheated on Jason. It was even more impossible that she'd just made love with a stranger.

More confounding yet, something in her heart, deep down, kept beating the quiet, sure pulse that something about Will was right. Really right. In a way that nothing had ever been this right in her life before.

By the time she'd stepped out of the shower and was pulling on fresh clothes…fresh, wrinkled clothes, straight from the suitcase…she was thinking herself into circles.

Maybe Will wasn't right. Maybe, instead, a massive flaw in her character had just shown up. Maybe somewhere deep inside her, she'd always been a cheater. A piker. A moral-less slut. And the potential had just never shown up before now.

God. It was enough to send a girl into a deep depression.

WHEN KELLY WALKED into the kitchen, Will took one look at her expression and mentally sighed. She looked adorable. For a woman with no boobs or butt, she gave off an amazing amount of feminine-ismo—the girl version of machismo. She was just so pure female, from the arch of her shoulders, to the way she walked, to the way she tilted her head. But she'd opted to wear a summer skirt and top, and the pale top was noticeably buttoned to the neck, the denim skirt noticeably oversize. She wasn't in any hurry to look at him, either.

Last night they'd rocked the walls. Will couldn't remember more stupendous sex. Yeah, she'd started out shy, but that had been fun to coax out of her. Once her engine was started, she was high performance all the way, knew what worked for her and let him work damn hard to give it to her. Talk about delicious.

Not that he wasn't a major fan of sex before—and any sex was better than none—but the good stuff just never happened until you were into a relationship, where the woman knew you well enough to bring down the inhibitions and go for it.

With Kelly, he couldn't explain or understand it, but it was as if they already had that kind of gut-level trust, had known each other forever. He'd gone to sleep wanting her again. Woken up wanting her. Found her hiding behind the couch and suffered yet another hard-on just looking at her.

Given her cover-up clothes and shyness now, though, she clearly didn't feel the same. Either he'd flunked in her bed-scoring class, or…or…or hell, he didn't know what.

"You need coffee," he said, hoping to ward off conversation. Particularly the kind of conversation that was going to be some kind of rehash of what last night had meant.

"I need to call my mother again."

"I know you do. You've got a whole list of have-to's waiting for you. But it's the weekend. Hopefully you're going to reach your mom, get the paperwork going, get some money. Maybe we can even pick up the police report. But unless someone who's worth a few billion is dying, the embassy and consulate will be closed tighter than a drum until Monday. So you might as well have some coffee. Some breakfast. And after that…"

"After that what?" she asked, as warily as a rabbit in a fox's lair.

"After that, we might as well do more Paris."

He didn't exactly have a plan, other than knowing she had to get the stolen-passport business moving or she was going to go nuts. The other major fret on her mind was her mom. Will pretty easily pictured her mother as an independent type, who could easily have shot off to see a friend or do a shopping spree for a couple of days, because Kelly kept saying there was no reason to worry just because her mother hadn't answered her messages; sooner or later her mom would call back. The lack of response meant, though, that Kelly was still dead broke, still financially dependent on him.

And that was killing her. Will tried to keep up a hustling pace to get her mind off it, but initially they only ran into more frustration instead of less. Their first stop was the specific commissariat—the police station. There, of course, the bureaucratic bullshit began. In order to obtain the required *récépissé de déclaration de perte ou de vol*—proof she'd been through a theft—she had to get two separate sets of receipts. One was for the passport papers, and one for any other type of stolen valuables. Everywhere there were lines.

Because Will knew the system, he figured he'd stay cool, but by noon he was coming apart at the seams, like Kelly was. The solution was obvious. Get the hell out of Dodge. By midday Saturday, there was no real chance of getting business done anyway, so there was no reason not to aim for some fun.

He picked Île de la Cité first. The island, located in the middle of the Seine, was sardine packed with history and monuments, a guaranteed attraction for tourists. Hell, even the locals loved it. So did he.

It seemed the ideal place to get her out in the fresh air, removed from everything to do with the trauma of the mugger—and whatever else was haunting those wet-velvet brown eyes.

That was the theory.

The reality turned into something else. Getting her out in the fresh air pepped her up just fine. Only then she opened her mouth and never shut it again.

"I'm *sick* of thinking about me, talking about me. God knows, it's your turn. What's your job, Will? Why'd you end up in Paris? You're not planning on living here forever, are you?"

That nasty line of conversation started when they were in sight of the Notre Dame Cathedral. He'd figured it was the one place guaranteed to brighten up her mood...and it did. Only after thirty seconds of awed, respectful silence, she turned her attention right back to him, waiting for a barrage of answers to her endless questions.

He could only duck so far. *"Fromage,"* he said finally.

"Fromage?" From the depths of her schoolgirl French, she suddenly remembered the word. "Cheese? Your job here is about cheese? Are you kidding?"

He sighed. "It's hard to explain."

"Why? What's hard to explain about cheese?"

The drizzling rain had stopped. A watery sun poked through the tufty clouds. Tourists, as always, were out in droves. It was spring, after all. Paris.

And Île de la Cité had more old stone and romantic history than anyplace in the universe. She should have been entranced. They should not have been talking about cheese.

"I came here originally to…well, to loll around. Play. Live my life. The idea was to take any job I could find that would support me, but otherwise, I wasn't looking for *career* work. There's no way I'll ever be driven the way my father is. I'm not about to be chained to an office or living just for money."

She stopped dead, as if a lightbulb suddenly dawned in those far-too-smart brown eyes. "Oh my God, oh my God. Will…I know you said your last name was Maguire, but you're not…" She gulped. "You're not one of *those* Maguires, are you?"

"Don't go there," he warned her.

"Holy mackerel. You're Aaron Maguire's son? Good grief. Good heavens. Your family's practically a dynasty in South Bend. Everybody knows they're wallowing in money. Practically drowning in it." She hustled in front of him on the sidewalk, walking backward to look into his face. "I'll be darned. I've seen his picture a zillion times in the paper. You look just like him, except that he's tall and distinguished, of course. Where you're more on the plain old adorable side."

He rolled his eyes, than yanked her next to his side. Walking backward, she was creating an obvious hazard for the other pedestrians, not to mention herself. French drivers knew no mercy. Especially for Americans.

"Could you focus on the important stuff here? We just passed the Palais de Justice. Couple blocks down, we'll be at Saint-Michel, and after that we'll be standing in line to get into Notre Dame like every other idiot tourist in the city. Notre Dame. The real thing. You're supposed to be thrilled."

"I will be. In just a sec. I'm still having a heart attack over your family. I think you should tell a girl before you sleep with her when you're part of a dynasty like that."

This time he narrowed his eyes. Give the girl a little sleep, and she was all sass and sparkle. He hooked an arm around her neck, and it wasn't an affectionate gesture. "You know, you're not the only one who gets to be nosy. It's about time you answered a few questions yourself. Like how you hinted that you weren't in Paris just for a vacation."

"I wasn't hinting. There's no secret." She didn't seem to mind the stranglehold he had on her neck. At least she wasn't trying to break free from it. "Actually, I guess there is a *little* secret, because I didn't tell anyone back home what I was doing. But that was because it was no one's business. I came here on kind of a private quest. I wanted to find some information about my father."

Now there was a word guaranteed to stop him dead. "Oh. Fathers."

"Yeah, it wasn't hard to guess we both had father issues...but in my case, it's because I never knew my dad. He was French. From Paris. And he died when my mom was pregnant with me. So I never knew him or had a chance to know anything about him. That's just the way it was." Tears suddenly glistened in her eyes. "That was partly why the mugger upset me so much. I had some old letters in that purse, letters he'd written my mom way back when...."

Hell. He loosened the grip on her neck. She was still talking. He'd figured out that when she started, it was like trying to plug a dike. Better not count on the flow stopping anytime soon.

"Years ago, my mom threw out the letters when she married someone else. A man named George. That marriage only lasted a few years—but anyway, I was just a kid, saw her throwing out the letters and I saved them from the trash. There were only a few, but they were all I had of my dad's. And on the envelopes, they had a return address, from where he grew up in Paris."

The little glisten in her eyes was one thing, but now a big, fat tear trickled down her cheek. Alarm started drumming through him. They were in the middle of a crowded street. There was no place to run.

"So...that was my plan when I came here. I just wanted to see the house, the neighborhood where he grew up. I can't imagine anyone would remember him after all this time...but I still wanted to do it. Just walk that street. See it, feel it, smell it. I don't have any other way to know him. And the whole idea popped into my mind when I got engaged. I mean…suddenly my whole life was going to change. And I just wanted to know more about who I came from."

He tried to steer her to something practical and solvable, so the tears would dry up. "So now you've lost the address? We could find a way to track that down, Kel—"

She blinked. "Oh…no, no need for that. I've had the address memorized for years. What upset me was losing the letters. His handwriting. The words. It was the only thing I ever had of his. I never cared about losing my passport or money or anything like that. But darn it…"

"Don't cry again." This time Will made it a stern order.

"I'm not."

"You are. Quit it." He fumbled for another diversion. "Okay, so what's your father's old address?"

She reeled it off. The street was in the 7th arrondissement, which was the name of the absolute last suburban area he expected her to say. "Are you sure?"

"Absolutely." She cocked her head. "What's wrong? Is there something odd about the address? Or the neighborhood?"

"Not exactly," he muttered, and sucked in an uneasy breath. This was getting mighty complicated.

She was mighty complicated.

Will didn't do complicated. Didn't, wouldn't,

couldn't. Yeah, he felt this wild, insane pull toward her—didn't know why, didn't care why, was just more or less enjoying it. He sure had enjoyed making love with her the night before.

But now, he wanted to extricate himself before he got any more embroiled. Particularly when he sensed she might have a world of hurt coming—nothing to do with him, nothing he could do about it. But there was no point in two of them lying down on a train track if one of them could get out of the way.

"Something's wrong," she insisted. "Just say it. Whatever's on your mind."

"Nothing."

"Yes, there is. You looked tense all of a sudden."

"Well, yeah. The weather's gone south on us fast."

Now there was an understatement. The morning drool hadn't been bad, but the sun just couldn't seem to stay out for long. Temporarily it was just misting hard, but from the look of the dirty clouds, they were minutes away from the day turning into a soaking deluge. A crack of thunder echoed his forecast.

Kelly looked up, startled, and then simultaneously seemed to realize their heads were damp, rain sluicing off their jackets. How long had they been oblivious to the weather? She suddenly started to laugh.

And darn it, because her laughter was so infectious, he started to laugh, too.

Then, of course, they found their wits and ran for shelter. Or that's where he thought they were running....

EXHAUSTED, LAUGHING, soaked to the skin, Kelly burst into the flat as soon as Will unlocked the door. Although it was only early evening, the apartment was midnight dark. Outside, the sky was still grumbling with thunderclouds. Traffic hissed on the wet streets below. Streetlights swayed in the wild wind.

"Good grief! I feel kin to a fish!" she yelped, as she pushed out of her soggy shoes. Pulling off her light spring jacket made rain spatter everywhere, including on Will, who jerked upright when he heard her sneeze.

"We've got to get you to a shower before you catch your death."

They both seemed to reach the same decision—that it was better to peel off their soaking clothes right there, in the dark, not waiting. There was no point in dragging the ocean of wet stuff all through the apartment. And Will's teeth were chattering as hard as hers were.

Still, she was exhilarated. "I can't believe how much we saw!"

"Yeah, well, I should have listened to my better sense and dragged you home hours ago."

"But you said you were stuck doing some work tomorrow. And even if it's Sunday, I still have to push through the passport nightmare. And this way, we had the whole day for you to show me Paris." Her mind was still reeling with the wonders. Île Saint-

Louis and the Hotel de Ville. Sacré-Coeur. The Eiffel Tower. The Jardin du Luxembourg.

"You *don't* see gardens in the pouring rain, not if you have a brain."

"But it was perfect. All rain-clean. And nobody else there but us—oomph." Her fanny seemed to connect with his elbow. It would have helped if they both weren't fumbling to get off wet things in the cramped foyer.

Her head shot up at the same time he tried to get out of the way. And then her head seemed to somehow bump into his chin.

They both let out a responsive howl, and Kelly was inclined to convulse in laughter again. She'd shucked off both shoes, where he still had one on. Both their jackets were draped and steaming on chairs. She'd managed to pull off her damp sweater, but she couldn't wait to get the clammy wet socks off, and it was impossible to do anything fast. Both of them had chilled-clumsy fingers, and every time they bent down, they seemed to collide again.

It was such an easy problem to solve.

All they had to do was turn on a light.

Move into the larger space of the apartment.

Instead, in their shivering, laughing scuffle, there was an instant—at least for Kelly—when she suddenly remembered the night before. Remembered him as a lover, naked, evocative, demanding, challenging. Lusty.

It wasn't as if she'd forgotten that for a second all day.

It was just that all day she'd been good at blocking it out.

Denial was a learned skill. She'd practiced her whole life. And she was safe, she'd thought, because neither of them could possibly be in the mood. They were both cold and tired and had sore feet. He couldn't possibly want her. She looked like a drowned rat.

And she was about to sneeze again.

Then in the blink of a second, his eyes met hers.

There was a second of silence. A second when the laughter died. A second when the shivers and exhaustion and rain pelting the windows in torrents seemed to fade out, as if they were all background colors in an old picture.

He was all foreground. Even in the shadowy foyer, she caught the clear shine in his eyes, heard his breath catch, could swear she actually saw the sudden arc of lightning between them.

She didn't mean to suck in a breath, but he seemed to take that as an invitation.

Maybe it was.

She was in his arms like that. As if she'd die if she couldn't touch him that very minute. As if she'd die if she couldn't have him. As if nothing in her life had created need like this, fire like this, a hunger to live like this. Until him.

She surely accumulated a dozen bruises navigat-

JENNIFER GREENE   65

ing the hall toward his bedroom, and him probably more. Darkness and dampness were only two of the obstacles. She refused to stop kissing him—to stop being kissed—refused to be severed from him for even a second.

"We're going to kill ourselves," he muttered against her mouth.

"You can always say no."

And then, when they finally reached the bedroom, when she finally had him naked, he mentioned, "You know, we don't have to go this fast."

"You want slow?"

"No." His voice turned thick, just like that. Thicker than honey. Thicker than molasses. Thicker than a bluesy sax on a hot night in Paris. "I want you now. Totally. Every which way. Total dominion over you."

"You got it," she murmured, in a voice that wasn't hers. Kelly—the Kelly Rochard she saw in the mirror every day—had a voice meant for a church choir. A voice that giggled with children, that played family diplomat in touchy moments.

The woman's voice talking to Will was a slut's voice. A bad, bad woman's voice. Conscienceless. Greedy. Wicked.

It was all a trick, she thought. A trick her heart was playing on her. A trick that made it okay to be a brazen hussy—not in life, not in general, but with him. Will Maguire. Here. Now. In Paris.

And that was the last coherent thought she had.

CHAPTER FOUR

SOMEWHERE AROUND ten the next night, they both woke up, hungry. It wasn't the first meal Will had brought back to bed. This time he made melted cheese sandwiches, and carted them in with chips and cookies.

She laughed, knowing they were going to sleep with crumbs, not caring any more than he did. Still, something was different when she woke up this time.

It was as if, in the past twenty-four hours, she'd been Will-drugged. Still was, when he carried in the tray, buck naked. The man didn't have a modest bone in his entire long, strong, deliciously male body. But suddenly she felt different. Different enough to tuck the sheet securely under her arms. It seemed silly, when he'd obviously seen every inch of her body in exquisite, thorough detail, but somehow she felt the odd need to hide all the love bites and nuzzle marks he'd left.

He plunked down beside her and they dove into their makeshift meal. She didn't try talking until she'd devoured a second sandwich, but after that, she swiftly ducked under the sheet, pulled up his fluffy comforter and snuggled into the pillow.

"Will…" Outside, it was still pouring, lightning spearing the sky, wind howling through the cracks. "What are we going to do?"

"As soon as we're both done eating, I'm guessing we're going to sleep. You wore me out, woman."

"That's what I've been trying to grapple with. It's not possible that we've been doing this. That I've been doing this. It's seriously wrong." She recognized that her entire behavior had led him to believe otherwise. Hell's bells, her entire behavior had led *her* to believe otherwise, but there it was. Reality seemed to have shown up out of nowhere. Or maybe she'd finally caught a couple seconds where she wasn't sucked under by all that wicked, powerful passion.

He lowered his empty plate to the floor, switched off the lamp and eased down next to her, pillow to pillow. He didn't brush her off. He could have. Didn't roll his eyes at her sudden attack of regretful guilts, either, and for damn sure, he could have done that.

"Just for the record," he said, "I've never gone near a woman who ever took me under before. Not like this. I mean it. Ever."

"Yeah, well. It's totally my fault, not yours."

But he wasn't playing scorekeeper on the guilt record. "I don't do guilt. It's one of the best things about giving up Catholicism. Truth is, I don't think people need guilt to keep them in line anyway. Most people seem to get up every day, trying to be the best people they can be at that moment in time." He ran his fingers through her hair, looking thoughtful, as if confused how that bit of philosophy had sneaked out of him. In other ways he was being careful, like in not touching body parts. More, he was keeping in touch, with that finger-light caress. "So I don't know how to draw conclusions about what's going on with us…except to say that you and I seem to fit. To be right together. I wasn't looking for it, wasn't expecting it. But that's sure how it is. At least for me."

"For me, too." Since he was doing that finger-caress thing, she did, too. On the slope of his shoulder, gleaming in the rain-light. "In fact, that's exactly what's scaring me. What's confusing me. I've never done casual relationships. Ever. It's not possible. If you just knew me…"

No smile. But he suddenly loomed over her, an expression on his face that she'd never seen. Tenderness. And something else. Something…that invoked a soft shiver all through her.

"I do know you," he said. "I know you like this…."

And he showed her.

WILL FIGURED it had to be around three in the morning. If there was a fire, he doubted he could find the energy to move. Not that he'd say it out loud, but he'd always considered himself a good lover. Certainly he'd never had a problem with some eloquent sustaining action, so to speak.

But they'd made love how many times?

His legs were limp. His body was limp. Even willie was limp. He could have slept naked in a snowstorm. He was that wiped. His eyelids were too tired to open.

But Kelly was still talking.

"Okay," she said. "So self-discipline didn't work for us. Or denial. Or pretending this wasn't going to happen again. Or guilt. And I know *you* don't do guilt, Will, but I do. And it doesn't seem to make a lick of difference. I still want to be here, right here. With you."

He managed to find the energy to open one eye. "Do you have to sound so miserable?"

"I'm *not* miserable. That's the whole problem." She shifted on top of him, her elbows digging into his shoulders, using his body for her own personal mattress. But then she bent down and kissed him. And even though willie was wiped, even though he was too tired to breathe, he felt her soft skin from breast to tummy to thighs, layered against him. As if she had the right. As if he did.

When she lifted her head, her lips still just inches from his, she murmured, "You know what you taste like?"

"What?"

"Hot sex. Love. Wonder. Magic." She sighed. "I can feel him. You'd think he'd be tired by now."

"He is, he is."

"Yeah, right." She let out a long-suffering sigh, but there was something in her eyes. A gleam. A wickedness. The way she wiggled her hips was hardly the act of an inhibited, guilt-ridden, goody-good kind of woman. And then she took a nip out of his neck. Not a big one. Not drawing blood or anything like that. Just a nip. With her teeth, then her lips, then her tongue. She whispered, "You'd better hold on to the headboard, because I think this could be a real rough ride."

He said primly, "I don't do bondage with women I barely know."

"You'd do bondage with any woman who'd let you get away with it," she corrected him.

Well, hell, she already had his number. There was no point in fighting with her, when making love with her was so much more fun.

WHEN THE ALARM CLOCK BUZZED at seven, the word *work* entered Will's brain…welcomed on a par with tetanus shots, cavities, the flu. It couldn't be Monday morning. It just couldn't be.

He pried open one bleary eye. Then the other.

There seemed to be a naked woman standing in front of him, holding a steaming mug of coffee. Hazelnut. He could smell it. He lurched out of the bed, nose-first, realizing at that instant that he was hopelessly in love.

The first sip of joe confirmed it. "I can forgive a woman anything who makes outstanding coffee," he told her.

"Oh, good. Then you don't mind if I empty out

your bank accounts, trash your place and decorate your living room pink?"

"You're going to still make the coffee, though, right?"

She chuckled. There was no way, no possible way, she could be this perky. Neither had had any sleep. Her hair was messy, and she was sashaying around the room naked as if she had the cutest boobs, the sassiest butt, the skinniest legs this side of the Atlantic.

Which she did.

Damn, but she did.

"What'd you do with all your Catholic guilt?" he asked her a few minutes later…which was after a shower, after he'd finished the first cup, after he'd yanked on a starched shirt and pants and found—ye gods—breakfast waiting for him in the minikitchen.

"It hasn't disappeared. I just figured this whole thing out."

"Uh-oh." He didn't mean to say that aloud, but it slipped out. He wasn't thinking that coherently when he saw her lift the skillet and plop a light, fluffy omelet on a plate for him.

"I'm just going to be part of your life until the money gets all straightened out. And my passport. The stuff I have to have to survive again."

"And then…" He motioned, waiting for the next part.

But apparently there was no next part. "That's it. The end of the plan. You're in Paris. I'm going back to South Bend. We're not hurting anyone if no one else ever knows anything about this. I mean, you and I could hurt each other. But it's just about you and me. No one else."

He took another bite, but he was watching her bright eyes. She'd pulled on a shirt by then. His shirt. A blue one. It made her look like the most feminine bit of fluff ever born. Times ten. Something made him want to argue with the plan, but he couldn't put a frame on it. It should be exactly what he wanted— sneaky, free sex—yet somehow, the last bite of delectable omelet didn't want to be swallowed.

"You're going to shake the fiancé when you go back." Will didn't phrase it like a question, although it was. For whatever reason, he needed to know.

She bounced up to refill both their mugs. "Well, that was my theory, too, when I tried to call him on Saturday morning. But now I think that stinks. It would be plain wrong and cowardly to try to say anything serious to him in a phone conversation. So there's nothing I'm going to do about Jason until I get home."

He put down his fork altogether. "But *then* you're going to shake the guy."

"Hey. This is the deal. You and I are going to be our own personal Vegas. What's between us this week stays between us. But there's no point in doing before-and-after analyses. I mean, you're not coming home to South Bend, right?"

"Right," he affirmed.

She nodded, as if to say they were both in agreement. Only they weren't.

Will couldn't very well babysit her all day. She had a ton of stuff to do, all of which was fraught with peril—for a tourist, an American, an adorable woman who was an American tourist, and specifically for Kelly, who didn't seem to have the directional sense of a stone. But he left her maps. He left her lists. He left her money, his cell phone, his telephone number at work and instructions to check in every two hours so he'd know she was okay.

At the doorway, when he was leaving for work, she interrupted all his considerate help to say mildly, "You really think you're a lazy, live-for-today, happily irresponsible, completely recovered Catholic, huh?"

Which just went to show, he thought when he climbed into his Citroën, that you could make love to a woman for three days straight and still, she didn't know you at all.

Twenty minutes later, he parked the car—feeling victorious when he fit into a spot smaller than a dime—and ambled into the office with a lazy stride.

The building was older than the guillotine, dark, crowded and drafty. *"Bonjour, m'sieur,"* said Marie, of the Antoinette temperament. She ran the place, something he'd realized the day he applied for a job here.

He greeted her, then the office staff in the bull pen, then Yves, the owner. His boss was a prince of a guy, devoted to his family, but he both looked like and had the temperament of a high-strung terrier. Talk about a worrywart. He sprang up the instant he saw Will.

"You managed to connect on the Wisconsin thing yesterday?"

"Yup. No problems. All fixed." Except for having to do that wrangling on a Sunday, but not like doing a few phone calls at home killed Will.

"Several calls came up early this morning, backup on shipments. Catalog proofs are on your desk. Looks good to me, but if you can get to that today... and that advertising affecting Lucerne and Copenhagen..."

Will listened a while longer, took it on, then aimed for his office—such as it was. A trailer closet was bigger than his cubicle. There was just enough room for him to drop to the desk chair and wade into the five pounds of files and samples and folders and debris.

Kelly wasn't here, of course. If she saw the place, she might leap to the conclusion that he was a hard-core workaholic, busier than a one-armed bandit in a bank vault.

That would be the wrong conclusion, of course. From the minute he'd arrived in Paris, he'd committed to become the laziest, most irresponsible slacker on the planet. That was what he wanted to be.

That was what he'd been *trying* to be since he left South Bend.

THE MOMENT Will left the flat, Kelly felt her smile deflate like a needled balloon. The apartment felt alien and lonely without him.

Still, it wasn't as if she didn't have a full day of complications to deal with. As soon as she poured a last mug of coffee, she addressed crisis number one by dialing her mom. And this time, *finally,* Char Nicole Rochard Matthews answered.

"*Mom!* For Pete's sake, where have you *been?*"

"Out gallivanting." The sound of her mom's chuckle was as familiar as sunshine. "You were gone, and I had nothing on the agenda for the weekend. Mary and Ann and I got to talking and next thing I knew, the three of us were off on a road trip to Mall of America. We were only gone for three days. What a place that is…."

Her mom babbled on for a while, as if calling from Paris were as cheap as calling from next door, but eventually she wound down. "Okay, your turn. I can't wait to hear how Paris is, what's going on…"

Kelly may have misled her mom about the reason for the Paris trip, but there was no way she could hide her current mess, so she spilled. She made as light of the mugger business as possible and clearly outlined what she needed from her mom—faxing the passport copy, to where, how, wiring money, where and how much, the whole complicated rigmarole. "I *hate* asking you to do all this junk, Mom, but—"

"Don't be silly, you goose. I'm so glad you're all

right. The rest of this is just details, and as soon as I hang up, I'll start getting it all cooking...." Her mother hesitated, her whole tone changing. "You know, nothing like this would have happened if you'd waited for Jason to make the trip with you."

Just hearing Jason's name put a fresh nail of guilt in Kelly's coffin of a conscience. She sucked down another sip of strong coffee. "Jason didn't have the time off right now, and I did. Besides which, he never wanted to go to Europe."

"So why go at all then? I never did understand why you were so insistent on this trip. Spending money you could have put into the apartment. Or your lives together." Char sighed, then switched gears, both of them well aware they'd already argued about this several times and had gotten nowhere. "Jason's mother called me. We're going dress shopping together next week. Neither of us can make up our minds whether we want to go short or long, or what colors, and we don't want to clash, so we figured going together would be fun...."

Another nail of guilt stabbed Kelly. "Mom...don't you think you're rushing it? We exchanged rings. But we haven't even talked about setting a sure date—"

"I know, sweetie. But you've known each other forever. And Gaynelle and I have been talking—behind your backs, of course—for years. We're just having fun—"

"Mom, *wait*."

Finally her mother seemed to hear the serious note in her voice. But when Kelly tried to talk, her throat seemed stuffed with cotton wool. She could hardly get the words out. "Mom, would it kill you if I changed my mind? About marrying Jason. About—"

Her mom laughed before she could even finish the thought. "Oh, honey, I've been waiting for the jitters to hit you. I'd have been amazed if they didn't. Sweetheart, you've loved that boy and he's loved you since you were in third grade. Weddings are just nerve-racking, that's all. Don't be scared if you get a few panic attacks. Every bride has them. You're going to look so gorgeous."

Kelly sank into a corner of the couch, rubbing her forehead. Her mom was on a tear. It'd be easier for Congress to reform health care than get a word in edgewise for quite a while.

"...and your Aunt Willa was talking about getting you an Oriental carpet. Wouldn't that be a fabulous wedding present? And Susanna called me again. She's still scandalized that you two have already found an apartment together. I told her, get a life, what century was she living in, anyway..."

By the time the call ended, Kelly's mug was sitting cold and her stomach was kneading guilt into lumps like bread dough. Will's face flashed into her mind. She replayed his face, their lovemaking, this crazy, wild encounter she seemed to be having.

Her life—her real life in South Bend—all came back at the sound of her mother's voice.

In *real* life, she couldn't possibly be sleeping with a stranger. The *real* Kelly Rochard could never be in this apartment. Couldn't possibly have turned into a brazen, lusty, amoral hussy, much less with a stranger.

Only she had done all those things.

She wanted to look in a mirror and see if she recognized the face, because she no longer seemed to be Kelly Rochard. She wasn't sure what woman had suddenly taken up residence in her body, or where the totally responsible, serious Kelly had gone. She felt angry with herself. Ashamed. Confused.

Yet when she thought it would have been so much better if she'd never come to Paris, never met Will…

Her heart clunked as if a mountain had crushed it.

Maybe she was being terribly, terribly selfish, but she couldn't regret a single moment with Will. Couldn't give him up. Not now. Not yet.

And before she could further tangle herself up, going down that impossible emotional road a minute longer, she rose from the couch, figuring on getting dressed and taking off. Then she stopped, sucked in a breath and dialed Jason.

She didn't really want to talk to him, didn't want to pursue any kind of serious conversation with him on the phone. But if she didn't call, he'd worry and start wondering why she hadn't called. And since she was already miserable, she figured another heap of guilt couldn't make any difference.

Jason should have been home from work by about then, yet his voice mail kicked in after four rings. She left a message that she was fine, hoped he was, and she'd catch up with him soon.

All right, she told herself, that was enough trauma for one morning. Instead of driving herself crazy, she had a new plan. To visit her father's old address, the whole reason she'd come to Paris to begin with. And yeah, of course she had the whole mugger mess to work on. Her mom was faxing copies of her ID records to the consulate, then wiring money to the bank Will had suggested. But one way or another, she was going to make something positive of this day.

As she pulled on pants and walking shoes and a cream hoodie, it struck her as mighty ironic that the loss of identity was a double whammy. The mugger may have stolen her paperwork ID, but the identity she'd really lost had nothing to do with paperwork.

Hopefully finding out something about her father would help her with that.

Will's phone rang just as she was chasing out the door. It was Will.

"I told you I'd check in. You haven't been mugged in the past hour, have you? No more crises? No more questions? You know where you're going, how to get there? I left you enough money?"

It was flabbergasting. How the sound of his voice sent a sizzle straight to her nerve endings.

In one second, she was a guilt-ridden, ashamed, responsible young woman who'd grown up on the straight and narrow.

And the next she turned into a sappy marshmallow, smiling at the sunshine, high from the inside out. "Will," she said, not wasting time answering any of his ridiculous questions. "You're a wicked, dangerous man. Did I remember to tell you that this morning?"

So she left the place, humming, skipping down the boulevard, high as the spring breeze. Yes, of course, she had to deal with the extremely serious chaos she'd thrown herself into. But temporarily, she focused her attention on Will.

He wasn't lost, the way she was.

But he had twists and secrets in his personality, too. All the big money in his family, yet his denial of it. His claim of being lazy, when his place was neat to a fault. His claim of being irresponsible, when he'd stepped up to take care of a complete stranger— and an incorrigibly nosy stranger, besides.

Why *was* he living here instead of home? And how come there wasn't already a woman in his life? Parisian women couldn't all be crazy.

Not that his love life was any of her business, of course. Nor were his family or career, for that matter.

She wouldn't interfere for the world.

IT HAD BEEN a long day and looked to be turning into an even longer night, Will thought. The waiter had just brought the wine and left menus when Kelly started in. "So…what's the real story? Why are you living here instead of back home?"

Will wanted to shake his head. She looked so sultry and sexy, in slinky black slacks and a red silky top, something kohl-dark on her eyes and something shiny sex-red on her mouth. Nothing about her resembled an elephant, but damned if she didn't have a memory like one.

"You remembered that question from early this morning?" he asked in disbelief.

"Of course. And we've been talking about me nonstop. I'm sick of me. It's your turn."

It was true he'd grilled her on her paper situation from the minute he got home from work. Nothing miraculously fast had happened, but she should have her own cash by tomorrow, which was exactly how she'd talked him into going out to dinner, as payback for his being so good to her.

Of course it was on his tab, but she ardently promised that she'd be paying back every dime. And in the meantime, she'd pored through her tourist books and come up with a list of restaurants.

He'd tried to talk her out of that list. He'd specifically tried to talk her out of this one, but she had heart set on it. The name was L'Alivi, a restaurant famous for its interesting decor and Corsican cuisine. It *was* good. But the food definitely wasn't for every taste. When he caught her reading the menu with a sudden frown, he said, "I tried to warn you."

She flashed those brown eyes up at him again. "Warn me about what?"

"This place. The guidebooks never tell you the whole story. I'm pretty sure you're not going to be happy."

"Hey. I'm not remotely fussy. I can eat anything. I'm just having a little trouble reading the menu." Then, like a hound who couldn't quit worrying a bone, she went for a perky tone. "So, what's the *real* deal on your doing the expatriate thing?"

She'd planned this, he thought. Not the restaurant. The inquisition. She'd planned it when she put on that red top and the slinky slacks. The top, she'd worn braless. He hadn't been initially aware of that until they'd got here. Someone had decided to keep the restaurant around thirty degrees. Her nipples were puckered up like bitsy soldiers standing at attention.

"I'll tell you what," he said. "I'll answer the questions. But let's order first. I'm starving. Okay?"

"Sure…" Again, her gaze dropped to the menu. Again, she frowned. When she glanced up again, Will promptly jerked his attention from her frozen nipples to her face.

She wasn't fooled. "Be good," she scolded.

"I *am* being good. At least until after dinner."

"Well, dinner's exactly the issue. I thought I wouldn't

have any trouble translating food words, but apparently—" she motioned "—I just have to be wrong about this. I mean sardines? Fresh sardines?" She started to laugh, then looked at his face.

"Fresh sardines with fennel."

"So I was translating it correctly."

"Afraid so."

"Really. Oh, well." She gulped, looked again and let out another short, uneasy laugh. "Okay, I have to admit my school French is turning out to be useless, but on the second line down, they couldn't *really* mean pigeons stuffed with figs, could they?"

"Afraid so."

"Pigeons? They'd kill pigeons? I mean…pigeons coo. And they walk right up to you in a park. They make a mess, I know, but they're so sweet and friendly. I can't even imagine anyone killing pigeons to *eat*."

He sighed. "We're not going to end up eating here, are we?"

She had another restaurant on her list. It was one more place Will tried to talk her out of, but not for long. The more time they spent together, the more he got the big picture. Kelly had the memory of an elephant, the stubbornness of a hound and the absolute capriciousness of a woman.

"I *have* to prove to you that I'm not a fussy eater now," she insisted. "Normally I really can eat anything. I love to experiment and try new stuff. Honest!"

Uh-huh. This round, they got as far as the outside of

the restaurant, where a menu was posted in the window. She looked at it for a long time, while she stood there shivering in spite of his jacket around her shoulders.

"It's a very famous restaurant," she began.

"Uh-huh."

"The food is undoubtedly fabulous. It's listed in every single guidebook."

"Uh-huh."

She sighed. "It's the black," she admitted in a small voice. "It just seems…unappetizing…for all the food choices to be black."

"Is it the black truffle pizza that got to you or the black hors d'oeuvre plate?"

"Both."

He grinned, tucked her inside his shoulder and said, "My turn to pick. You're out of votes."

She'd forgotten about the personal questions, he thought. But God knows that didn't mean she'd run out of conversation.

"I don't quite get the difference between a bistro and a brasserie."

"Well, a bistro's just a little restaurant. Usually it's owned by a family, and a bistro tends to serve regular meals, you know, lunch, dinner. But *brasserie* is the French word for brewery. You can usually get some kind of food in a brasserie, but it's a guarantee they'll serve beer and wine. And both kinds of places are informal."

He ushered her into his choice—Le Petit Saint-

Benoit, in the Saint Germain. It was distinctly a French place, not so touristy, more a place that the locals guarded for themselves. It was a night spot, with a good share of tables set up outside, even though it was ball-bustingly chilly by then. Still, the decor inside was from the thirties, and the food was basic French, which meant damn good if not outright fabulous. They had all the basics. Shellfish. Good wines. Filet mignon so tender it could melt in your mouth.

"All day, everywhere I went, the women were wearing scarves," Kelly, who'd already proved she could talk and look at everything in sight at the same time, noted. "And what really irritates me is that they all know how to tie the scarves to look really chic. I mean, the *real* chic, not the cliché chic. I stick out like a sore thumb, don't I?"

"Sore thumb, no. Uniquely attractive woman, yes."

"You don't have to butter me up. We're already sleeping together. And I meant, I stick out because I look like an American. Not like a Frenchwoman."

He started to loosen his tie, then remembered he didn't have one on. It was the question that was constricting his airflow. "I don't know. Would that be a good thing or a bad thing?"

She chuckled and pointed a shrimp at him. "Are you afraid to answer the question, Maguire?"

"Of course I'm afraid. When women ask certain questions, a guy tends to feel like he's stepped in cow manure. No matter what he answers, he's gonna be in trouble."

"But you're not going to step in cow manure if you tell me what the big deal is about your living in Paris. I realize I'm prying, but come on, what possible difference could it make if you tell me? I'm not telling a soul. You can get it off your chest. No one'll ever know."

"There's nothing to get off my chest."

"Fine," she said. "Be a martyr."

The waiter returned to pour more wine. He took one look at Will's face and brought another liter. "Did I know before sleeping with you that you could be a complete pain in the butt?"

He thought it was a pretty good insult, but she only chuckled. "Hey, I'd have 'fessed up to being a pain in the butt if you'd just asked. But it's okay. You can keep your secrets. I was just thinking of all the reasons why you might not want to go home. A warrant out for your arrest. Like for a murder rap. Or drugs—"

"Oh, for Pete's sake. It's nothing like that." He reached for the bread at the same time she did. Naturally the bread was fresh out of the oven, still warm, still wonderful. But every other woman he knew fretted whether stuff like bread went straight to their thighs. Kelly inhaled it faster than he did.

"My dad and I don't get along. Think of two quarterbacks from opposing teams," he said finally.

"Opposing quarterbacks play together every Saturday," she noted. "And you already told me that you and your dad have a really conflicted relationship. But it's still a stretch from not being close to feeling you have to live a whole continent away."

Hell. It went on. Past the bread and salad. Past a liter and a half of wine. Past the filet mignon, and then, when she saw the pastry tray, past watching her salivate as she made her choice.

Correct that. Choices.

"I've got three sisters. No brothers. So I'm the only male. My dad started Maguire's, built it into a monster-size corporation. But now he wants to retire, and he wants to do it by my taking it on."

"But pretty obviously you didn't want to, so you told him no."

"I've been telling him no since I was old enough to talk. He's heard it. He doesn't give a damn. Aaron Maguire wants me to do what he wants me to do." Will pushed away the plates, went for the demitasse. "And back when I was a boy, I really cared. I did everything but stand on my head to win his approval, his respect."

"But it was impossible?" she asked gently.

"Oh no. I got it just fine. As long as I do exactly what he wants, everything's always been hunky-dory. And that's the point. He doesn't just want me to run the company. He wants me to do it *his* way. Eighty-hour workweeks. Him involved in all the decisions. And then there are my sisters."

"Your sisters work at the company, too?"

"No. That's exactly the point. They don't. They want to live in the style he's let them become accustomed to. Lots of money, no responsibility. Bail them out whenever they lift a finger or run up a credit card bill or want a trip to Goa."

He wished she would look at him with a little more sympathy. Instead she kept asking more questions. "So you told your dad how you felt about that, too."

"I've talked to him about all this fifty ways from Sunday. I also always met him more than halfway—like going to Notre Dame because he wanted me to. That was a smooth stretch, but the minute I graduated, the pressure started up again about my coming into the company with him. He wouldn't give up. He won't give up. And I just plain got tired of fighting all the time."

She fell silent, which was damned scary. She never shut up if given the opportunity to talk. By then she'd finished three desserts—three—explaining that they were pastries, after all, and she was only in France for a short time, and anyway, she couldn't help herself.

He found the crumb of Napoleon at the corner of her mouth and grinned. She just did everything so two hundred percent. And he was bringing her back here tomorrow, if he had anything to say about it. In the meantime, she claimed he'd have to carry her out of the place, because she was that stuffed.

He drove them back to his place, but then, instead

of going in, he suggested taking a stroll down the boulevard. It was midnight by then. He had to work tomorrow, he knew. But it was a starry night, and even though she'd nagged him into talking about stuff he really didn't appreciate, he still didn't want the evening to end.

"A walk sounds good," she agreed.

So he wrapped his jacket around her shoulders and stuffed his hands into his pockets. They walked, hip to hip, working off dinner, doing a boulevard loop.

Finally, when they were almost back to his place, he said, "All right. Spill it out. I can't take much more quiet."

She obviously caught the long-suffering teasing tone in his voice, because she chuckled and deliberately bumped hips with him.

Then she answered. "I think you need to find a way to solve this problem with your dad. Because you're an American, for heaven's sake. You can't want to give up your country."

"Hey. I'm not. I wouldn't. I never said I was going to do anything like that."

"Okay. But then it means that you intend to come home, not live here forever. And *that* means you have to find a resolution with your dad."

There was a reason he never talked about this. With anyone. He was a grown man, had been for a long, long time. When you were a kid, talking about problems sometimes helped. But when you were an adult, talking often simply meant giving someone else the power to interfere. And somehow it thorned even deeper because Kelly seemed to think he needed to be interfered with.

"For now, this *has* to be the resolution. Moving a serious distance away was the only way to stop the constant war with him. I didn't want my mom upset all the time. And I won't and can't live the life my father insists on."

She said firmly, "And that would be fine, if living here was working for you, but it isn't. You're camping out here. You can't commit to a relationship, get married, have kids, set up house—not if you really don't want to stay here. So you've set yourself up in limbo. It sucks."

"Hey. It's not exactly a hardship to live in Paris," he said drily.

"It wouldn't be. Except that in the meantime, you don't get to see your family. Your sisters, your parents and friends. All the people and things you loved. How much pressure could your father possibly put on you?"

He said flat out, "Twenty million bucks' worth of pressure. Not counting compound interest and a few spare assets here and there."

Finally, something that took that wind out of her sails. "Whew. Okay. I have to admit that's some fair-size pressure." He heard her take a big, long breath.

"But even so, that's just about some stupid money. It's not about anything that matters."

They seemed to be back at his front door. In the shadowed arch, he dug out his key. While she waited, Ms. Hardcore-Idealist lifted her head, taking the moment to smell the fresh spring leaves, to savor the crescent moon cradled in a wisp of clouds. She was relaxed and happy, now that she'd scratched all his emotional allergies.

"Did anyone ever tell you," he said, "that maybe it's easier to give advice when you've never had to walk in their shoes?"

"Oh, yes. Lots of times. I've ticked off reams of people with my nosiness and my opinions. Zillions. Hordes. Trust me, I've just irritated you this time. If I really got going, I could probably tick you off enough to throw me out forever—"

There seemed only one way to shut this down.

He moved her against the old brick, in the shadow of the doorway. When her head shot up—mouth still open, of course—she stilled, just for a second, when she saw his eyes.

Then he bent down and took her mouth. Feasted on it, more like. For a kiss that was clearly intended to communicate some annoyance and impatience and maybe even a little temper, it somehow turned out wrong.

It turned out tender.

Damnably tender.

She looped her arms around his neck, closed her eyes and sank into him on a sigh.

He couldn't understand it. One minute he was ticked off at her. The next, she was his whole world. Times ten. He couldn't kiss enough, taste enough, touch enough.

He fumbled with the key, groped to turn it, not severing the connection to her mouth for even a second. The door finally creaked open, then crashed against the far wall. He kissed her in, kicked the door shut, kissed her down the hall, kissed her into the velvet shadows of the bedroom, kissed her as he started peeling off layers of clothes. His. Hers.

The clothes fell in a matching heap.

And so did they.

CHAPTER FIVE

SHE STIRRED the next morning before Will. Half-awake, she slowly became conscious of the pale sun filtering through the screen, the first horn on the street, a tufty breeze, the sounds of a sleepy Paris coming to life. She stayed cuddled up to Will, not wanting to move, not wanting to think, just wanting to absorb the feel of her lover...until she felt his gaze on her face.

"You're awake," she murmured.

He was studying her, not with sleepy eyes but with an ultraquiet expression. "You're still feeling guilty," he said.

She didn't try lying. Didn't have to lie, not to Will. "That's my life," she admitted. "By everything I've ever believed this is wrong." Yet she added softly, "But I've never even remotely felt this way about anyone. Just you."

"So does that make it wrong or right?"

"It makes it something I can't walk away from." She felt his thumb brushing her cheek. Her eyes wanted to close, to absorb the simple intimacy. "How about you?"

Suddenly he sat up. "Oh, no. We grilled Will for dinner last night," he said wryly. "It's gonna be all about you today."

Before he went to work, she got a complete, complex list of instructions. Directions. Money. Key. Food. Stuff she could do, stuff she couldn't. Places she could go, places she needed to steer clear of. "This is a city, remember. You can't go smiling and saying hi to strangers on the street."

On and on. "All these orders," she grumped.

He chuckled, but he stopped smiling at the door. He knew her schedule for the day. To pick up the wired money from her mom, then to head for her father's old neighborhood. It was the latter that clearly bothered him. "Kelly, the neighborhood where you're going…it's more than safe. You won't have to worry about that. But maybe you should wait to do this until I get home from work."

"Heavens, no."

It was the second time Will had expressed uneasiness about Kelly visiting her dad's old neighborhood alone. She did all her chores, felt enormous relief when she had her own money in her hands, fumbled around with public transportation, picked up a sandwich from a French bistro and made it to her father's old house just before noon.

When she stepped out of the taxi at the corner, Will's uneasiness shot back into her mind. It seemed especially crazy, once she saw the neighborhood.

She'd expected…well, anything. An old house, some kind of neighborhood where families raised kids, schools close by, maybe a corner grocery store.

She'd never expected…elegance.

Her step slowed and then stopped when she reached the exact address. Architecture wasn't her thing, but she was pretty sure the style of the Rochard house was Beaux Arts. Long stone steps led up to a multiple-arched doorway. A couple of lions framed the entrance. It wasn't the Smithsonian. It wasn't even a castle. But it was a darn fancy house, three stories of marble and stone.

She stood there, bewildered, racking her brain to make sure this was the correct address. Without the old letters, she couldn't be positive—but she was. She'd read and reread those letters a zillion and a half times.

All she'd really wanted to do was see the house, see the neighborhood. Maybe in the back of her mind, she thought she'd find someone to talk to, someone who could tell her about the Rochard family…or that she might be able to walk around, see the school her dad might have walked to, see the church he might have attended on Sunday.

Now she took a step toward the house…stopped again.

Suddenly it wasn't so easy to simply go up and knock on the door, but then she noticed the carved emblem on the door. An intricate vine shaped into the letter *R*. Her lips firmed. Maybe they'd throw her out, call the gendarmes, slam the door in her face. But she'd come all this way, and no matter what happened, she couldn't just turn away.

She marched up the steps, took a breath for courage and knocked softly. Then knocked again.

She was about to knock a third time, when a man opened the door. The look of him startled her so much that her jaw must have dropped ten feet.

He looked around her age, give or take a few extra years. Rich brown hair, thick, with a little unruly wave. Tea-brown eyes. Slim to the skinny side, fine boned, medium height.

"*Bonjour*," she began in her schoolgirl French, telling herself she had to be an idiot to think they looked so much alike. "I'm sorry to bother you. *Je m'appelle Kelly Rochard. Je sais*…this sounds… odd…but the thing is, my father—*mon père*—grew up at this address. His name was Henri Rochard. I wonder if there is any chance someone in the house might have known the family or anything about him…."

Her voice trailed off.

She'd expected her stumbling language to be a problem…. Instead, her appearance seemed to provoke the man in an entirely different way. She didn't stop talking because she ran out of things to say, but because he started to look so…angry.

Red flushed up his neck to his cheeks—the same

icky-splotchy red that happened to her when she was overheated or upset.

And then he let loose a torrent of words, far more than she could possibly keep up with. She caught *menteusse*, which she was pretty sure meant *liar*. When he yelled, *"Ça va barder,"* Kelly was pretty sure there was going to be trouble, and instinctively started backing up.

She recognized another term—*les couilles*—that in another universe might have made her laugh. She believed he was suggesting that she had balls, which wasn't just an anatomical impossibility, but a curious thing to insult her with besides. He spewed out a few other choice words, all in the same angry tone. *Vache. Chameau.*

She'd backed up four more steps when another man, about the same age, showed up in the doorway, clearly curious about what all the commotion was about. They talked to each other, a mile a minute, for a few seconds, and then the second man looked at her. Really looked.

And suddenly no one was talking.

WILL HEADED HOME, wiped from a killer workday and annoyed by the frazzle of traffic…yet still feeling his pulse jump when he finally parked in the drive-way, knowing he was going to see Kelly.

The damn woman. In just a few short days, she'd managed to irritate him, challenge him, exhaust him.

She poked her nose where she wasn't wanted or invited. She could outtalk a magpie. She was the last kind of woman he even wanted to be near.

But he couldn't wait to see her.

He'd connected with her twice that morning, so he knew she'd gotten the wired money, knew she was headed on her "dad quest" after that. He'd intended to catch up with her in the afternoon, but business nonsense kept intruding on his time.

He always intended to spend a lazy workday with his feet propped on the desk. But his boss was such a...well, such a baby. Yves had come from the country with big hopes of selling his gourmet cheeses—some so outstanding he'd caught the attention of several famous chefs. Yves had outstanding products but no clue what to do about them.

He'd needed a brand. A marketing strategy. A manufacturing and production and advertising and distribution plan.

That was what Will discovered when he first took the job. It wasn't *real* work. It paid the rent; it was easy. Mostly he just had to set stuff in motion and then sit down with Yves, explain what to do, where to go from there. There was nothing about the job tying Will down. The stuff was stressful for Yves, a guy who could be reduced to tears by the simplest business decisions—who could figure? But occasionally, like today, Will was forced to exert a little serious energy.

Calls had come in from Canada, Germany, Denmark. Then something had gone wrong with a shipment arrival. Then certain packaging decisions had to be made. Yves got upset at that kind of thing.

Didn't bother Will. It was just business, but he was still fairly wrung dry by the time he vaulted the steps and pushed open the door.

"Kelly?"

He stopped almost immediately. Something was wrong. The place looked the way it had before Kelly showed up here. It was all…tidy. No lights, no smells, no messes, no sounds. No ultragirl perfume invading his space.

Alarm stole the smile from his face. "Kelly?"

He dropped the newspaper, his jacket. Poked his head in the living room, thinking maybe she was outside on the balcony and that's why it was all so quiet—but no. He checked the bathroom, thinking maybe she was taking a long soak in the tub, but she wasn't there, either.

"Kel?"

"I'm in here, Will."

He saw her even before he heard her voice. That single glance, though, made a double dose of alarm quicken his pulse.

Kelly wasn't *quiet*.

She was curled up in the desk chair in his mini office. The alcove was about the only place in the whole flat that was windowless and dark, nothing nice about it. It was just a hole to locate his computer and work with no distractions. At a glance, he could see she wasn't crying. She was sitting absolutely still in the dim light, with her legs tucked under her.

Motionless…Kelly. Quiet…Kelly. No animation, no wild zest for life, no heart hanging out there for any fool heart-thief to take advantage of. Like him.

Hell. The look of her hurt Will like a stab in his gut.

"What happened?"

He hunkered down next to her, wanting to be at her eye level. Her expression reflected that something had seriously shaken her.

She said, "I met my father."

"The one who's dead?"

"Yeah." She gulped. "It was quite a shock."

"Well, hell. I imagine it was for him, too."

She looked startled at his humor, but then the shocked stiffness seemed to loosen in her shoulders and she let out a little laugh. Very little, but still a laugh. "Oh God, Will, I'm so glad I had you to come home to, you to tell."

He lurched back to his feet, fetched glasses, a wine bottle, the opener. He could have opened it in the kitchen, but that would have taken a minute or two. He wasn't willing to leave her for that long, so he carried it back to the office and immediately started working on the corkscrew.

"I was afraid of your going alone there," he admitted.

"Why? You couldn't possibly have known—"

"That your dad was alive, no. Of course not. I don't know anything about your family. But when you told me the address, I was kind of taken aback. That neighborhood is known for money. Big money. No piddling millionaires. I mean the serious, major-fortune people." He wrenched the cork free, poured a glass for her, handed it over. "Nothing bad about anything in that picture. But somehow I didn't think you were expecting…"

"A fortune in the family history? You've got that right. You know what else? I've got two brothers. Two half brothers, anyway. Who hated me on sight. I didn't pick up all the language, but I'm pretty sure they immediately concluded that I was a gold-digging, lying bitch. Well. Either a bitch or a camel. I've always gotten those two words in French confused for some reason…."

Will forgot all about pouring his own wine. The idea of someone, anyone, hurting Kelly put a growl in his throat. Growing up with three sisters, he'd gotten over any desire to save damsels in distress. Chivalry was nothing more than a land mine. It was designed to heap trouble and responsibility on a guy's head until he sank from the weight of it, so the sudden instinct to bash Kelly's half brothers was disturbing. He hadn't slid into his old, bad habits for years now.

"Maybe you'd better start at the beginning," he said.

"That's just the problem. I thought I *knew* the

beginning. The story my mom told me was that my parents met when my mom was in college, doing a year at the Sorbonne. I thought they fell in love, got married, moved back home to South Bend. I thought my dad made a trip back to Paris to see his parents when my mom was pregnant. I thought there was some kind of train accident. That he died along with his parents. That there were no Rochard relatives left."

Will wanted to wince on her behalf. "Hmm...I take it a few of those things aren't exactly true?"

"Will?"

"What, honey?" He couldn't believe he was using the word *honey*. As if they'd known each other a bunch of years. As if he were into comforting her, instead of having a red-hot illicit affair. Yet, what the hell. He got up, took her—and the wine—and settled them on his lap in the office chair.

"My mom and dad weren't married. They were never married. In fact, my father—the one who's still alive—already had a wife. Not now, because she died about four years ago. But he was married to her way back when, which is exactly how I have two brothers who are older than me."

"Uh-oh," Will murmured, and stroked a hand through her tumble of hair. "A little shock. Finding out you're illegitimate?"

"Cripes, I don't care about that. This isn't the Middle Ages. Mistakes happen. So I was a mistake. That's all right. But it's killing me that I didn't know

I had a father all these years...that my mom lied to me all this time."

"A pretty big lie," Will admitted.

"She slept with a married man."

"Maybe she didn't know he was married."

"Maybe she didn't. But she knew he was alive. She knew I had a living father."

He couldn't say anything to that.

"My brothers... Well. It seems my father has a ton of money. And he's developed a heart condition. His two sons were visiting him today, that's how they saw me, although I'm pretty sure I'll have to come up with DNA for them to believe we're related. But I think they knew the truth, because for damn sure, *I* knew, the minute we looked at one another. We have the same eyes, same hair, same mouth, same coloring. Will?"

"What, honey?"

"They thought I was showing up because I was after my father's money."

"It's a shame your brothers are stupid. You must have gotten all the IQ genes from your mom."

"Don't make me laugh. This is awful. They didn't want to let me in the door, just started yelling at me in French right off the bat. In fact, it was the yelling that brought my father from somewhere upstairs in the first place, to see what was going on. He took one look at me—"

"Listen. No crying allowed here. We talked about this before, remember?"

"He didn't get it. Until I mentioned my mother's name. Then there was this look on his face. He knew. He *knew* I was his daughter."

Will winced again. It didn't take a super brain to figure out the cretin had hardly greeted her with open arms.

"It was such a *mess*." Kelly dragged a hand through her hair, turned to him with tear-blurry eyes. "Obviously his sons never knew there was a sibling from the wrong side of the blanket. They started yelling at him, then. I couldn't stay. Couldn't leave. Didn't know what I was supposed to do."

"So what did you do?"

"I gave him a piece of paper with my e-mail address and asked for his. I couldn't give him my cell-phone number because that was stolen, and I didn't want to give him my mom's address in South Bend for obvious reasons. But I wanted some way to contact him, and where he could contact me. Even though I don't think he will or wants to."

One gulp of a sob, so big it scared the hell out of him. He splashed more wine in her glass, spilling a bit on her jeans and his.

"But right then…he needed to talk to his sons, you know? I mean, he had more to sort out than just *me*. And I didn't know what else to say, anyway—*I'm glad you're not dead, even if you happened to be a coldhearted adulterer who left a pregnant woman alone to fend for herself?*"

"Probably that would have been a tough thing to communicate with your French, cookie."

Again she looked startled at his irreverent humor, yet again she laughed. Another weak one, but a laugh nonetheless.

"Then I came back here. Didn't know what else to do. I wanted to call my mother and ask for an explanation, yell at her for lying to me all these years. But more than that…I keep thinking that I'm not *me*, Will. Three weeks ago, I had a job, an apartment, I was engaged. I never doubted who I was. I thought I understood my mom, how she felt after losing my dad, the one man she really loved, turning into a single parent. Now…"

"Now what?"

"Now," she said slowly, "it's not just that I was lied to. It's that everything I knew about myself suddenly seems to be in doubt. I thought I had the genes of a quiet-professor type who was good in math—not the genes of a tycoon. I thought I came from this tragic, romantic history, not from a plain old sordid affair. I was raised to believe honesty was everything. That was another lie. I thought I was mostly like my dad, or the image I had of my dad. But that's all a sham, too. I feel totally confused. Nothing about my life is what I thought it was."

Will put down her glass. His. She was already curled up in a ball in his lap, with her head under his chin. His right thigh muscle was falling asleep. He didn't care.

"Maybe," he said, "that's really why you came to Paris."

"What do you mean? I couldn't possibly have known about my dad."

"No. But you had questions about your life, right? You were looking for something. You knew something wasn't right at home." Like the fiancé, Will thought. But she'd gotten touchy when he brought up the creep before, so he didn't want to mention him again.

"Maybe I did. In fact, I think you're right."

"Ye gods. A woman who admitted a man was right?"

She cocked her head back, nearly cracking his chin. "Don't rub it in. You're next."

"What do you mean, I'm next?"

"I mean…maybe I landed in your life at this specific time for a reason, too."

"Yeah. Fabulous luck."

She kissed him. Clearly reluctantly. But she couldn't let the compliment pass, and even after a long, long lip suck, that elephantine memory came back. "Maybe fate brought us together because we were both meant to solve our father issues."

"I'll go along with the fate thing. But I think fate had incredible sex on its mind. That we'd find each other for this moment of time. And it'd be earth-shatteringly fantastic."

"Okay," she murmured. "That, too." And did the lip-suck thing again. "Will?"

"What now?"

"I'm so hungry I can't think. And it's been an awful day."

"So you want to—"

"Make love," she finished, as if that made perfect sense to her.

It did to him, too.

WHEN KELLY WOKE up the next morning, the impossibly bright sun matched her mood perfectly. In spite of everything, she'd slept like a child, one of those healing, safe sleeps that renewed her spirits.

And that was a good thing, because nerves promptly gnawed on her conscience the instant she sat up. What should she do about her father? How was she going to handle Jason? What should she say to her mother? What should she do next? Why had her mom never told her the truth? Was there one thing in her life that made sense anymore?

So much for a restful night's sleep. The whole mess was overwhelming. She sank back against the pillows and pulled the sheet over her head.

A few minutes later, though, she felt the sheet being tugged off her. Will was standing naked with a skillet in his hand. The aroma reached her even before she saw the contents. Technically, breakfast was just scrambled eggs, but he'd added herbs and cheese. "Coffee, too."

"Am I still dreaming, or did you turn into a hero while I was sleeping?"

"You're not still dreaming. It's me. Your hero." But he looked at her hard before teasing any further. "Yeah, I figured you'd be chewing your fingernails before even getting out of bed, Ms. Guilt Queen. So come on. I'm serving breakfast on the balcony. And after that, I have a plan."

"I'd follow that cute butt anywhere," she told him.

"Don't embarrass me before breakfast."

"You're walking around naked. Is it even possible to embarrass you?" It was easy to tease him, yet Kelly still felt a headache threatening behind her temples. Her whole spirit felt trounced from yesterday's revelations. Or maybe from the whole week of traumas. Five days. She'd been in Paris five days.

In those five short days, she'd lost her identity—physically and emotionally. She'd been mugged. She'd lost the life she'd had. She'd taken an irrepressible, unforgettable lover, when she'd never been the kind of woman to "take lovers." Or even to find lovers.

Will set down the tray on the metal table on the bitsy balcony before he even seemed to think about putting on clothes. She grabbed a robe before stepping outside. "I told you I was the repressed type, didn't I?"

"Yeah," Will said. "I think you mentioned it. Just before we fell in bed the first time."

"You want to hear about my fiancé?"

"No."

"I think I should tell you," she said honestly, as she lifted the carafe to pour coffee for both of them.

"Nope. No interest. You're with me. When you're in Paris, you're with me. When you leave Paris…" His gaze shot to her eyes, so hot and blue. "Then there's nothing I can do. You'll be there. I'll be here."

"That was the agreement," she concurred.

"But you do need to shake that guy. He's not right for you."

"Now, come on, Will. You really have no basis to know he's not for me."

"I'm three hundred percent sure. You're going to break it off when you get back to South Bend." Will made it sound more like an absolute statement than a question. The sky was blue. Her broken engagement was a given.

Kelly didn't respond. Thinking about Jason and going home just tangled her up again. She was tangled up enough.

Besides, just below their balcony, Paris was waking up. An old man was hawking the morning newspapers. Another vendor was pushing fresh flowers— he stopped below, saw her and raised a bouquet to her, peeling off a whole speech so fast she couldn't follow.

"What's he saying?" she asked Will.

"He says if you'll come down, he'll give you a bouquet for free, because you are a beautiful woman, a darling, where I am but a *canard* for hiding you from the world up in this apartment. He wants to kiss your hand. He wants to adore you. He wants you to be with a man who knows how to love a woman—a man such as himself."

"Oh." Tugging her robe closed, she bent over the balcony and threw the flower man a kiss. *"Merci, monsieur! Je vous aime! Toujours!"*

The man grinned.

Will shook his head. "You'll have him on our doorstep every morning."

"I had to be polite, didn't I?"

"Uh-huh. You picked up the French flirting thing really well. But onward…here's the plan for the day. I don't *have* to go to work, because work, after all, is irrelevant to life. But I do have a couple things I should do there. So you could either come with me— shouldn't take me more than an hour—or you can stay here for that hour. After that, well, you can't be in Paris and not do certain things."

"Like…?"

"You're a girl, so you have to do a *parfumerie* or two. Then there's the old Halles marketplace near the Centre Pompidou. That's like hell on earth. You know. Shopping. Little shops, zillions of them. If you like cooking stuff, Le Creuset is there. Or Sabatier knives. Or copper cookware…"

"Please don't look at me when I'm drooling. It's embarrassing." She made a vague gesture. "You'd actually shop with me?"

"With you, yes. With anyone else, no. Then after that…well, you have to see the Marmottan Museum.

God knows, there are a hundred museums around here. But that's the one with the Monets. Then there's the Musée Rodin, which I swear is seriously cool. Then there's Sacré-Coeur. I don't know if it's a mortal sin to be a Catholic and miss Sacré-Coeur, but it's gotta be close. And we have to hit a garden or two. Boulogne or Tuileries or Monceau. It's spring. The gardens here are an absolute."

She looked at him and kept on looking. He was beyond good-looking. His eyes alone were mesmerizing. Not dark blue, not light blue, but kind of a clear, lake-blue. He had such a strong, sharp jaw—a measure that he was more stubborn than a bulldog, she realized now. And she figured he wore that rumple of blond hair a little on the long side to illustrate that he didn't care, was a lazy wastrel type.

He wasn't a lazy wastrel type.

When she didn't immediately respond to his plan, he hesitated. "I know, Kel. You didn't really come here to sightsee. And I don't even *do* sightseeing. But the thing is, you've had a major stress load. So you've got to balance it. You're stuck waiting until some things happen, like getting your passport back—"

"After which, I have to go home."

"I know you do. So we have to schedule your time, find a way to make the most of it."

Truthfully, Kelly didn't need to do another thing to know she'd never forget a second of Paris…or a second she'd spent with him.

"But," he said, as if that single word were a sentence in itself.

"But?"

"But maybe you have something else you want to do? Or something you want to add to that agenda?"

She nodded. "I'd like to do everything you said, Will. But I'm afraid I can't think, can't do much of anything, without doing something more about my father. What to do, I don't have a clue. But right now, I'm just feeling…"

When she couldn't come up with a word, Will said, "The French have a word. *Dérailler.* Feeling derailed. Thrown off track."

"Exactly."

"Okay." He thought. "So we'll start out the day at my work. Leave there, hit a library, research some background information about your father. After that, you can decide if you want to try to make another face-to-face connection. If you do, I'll go with you."

Very casual, her Will, she mused. He never made anything sound serious. Certainly there was no protective tone in his voice, but that quality was there. From the instant he'd met her, he'd relentlessly found ways to help her with each and every mess she'd landed herself in.

"I need to do this alone, Will," she said gently.

"Why?"

"Because it's my problem."

He made a Gallic gesture. "How can my being

there make it any worse? It's already awkward and upsetting. And if I drive you, we'll be able to cut and run and go get drunk on bad wine if it turns out wrong. Why not have some company if you're going to be miserable?"

"That's like saying you should get a tetanus shot if I'm stuck getting one. There are some things you shouldn't ask someone else to share."

"Damn right. I'm not volunteering for the tetanus shot, so don't even try asking."

"I wasn't!"

But somehow it all ended up just like he said. It was a long day of discovering Will was a manipulative son of a gun. He used charm and subterfuge and tricks—like ignoring her, or agreeing to something she'd said and then just bulldozing in the same direction he'd planned from the beginning, or kissing her every once in a while. Out of the blue. In a way that bamboozled her thought train so completely that she forgot whatever she'd been staunchly arguing about.

Even before noon, Kelly had his newfound character flaws inked in her brain. Her mother loved quoting the old saying, make a fool of me once, shame on you…make a fool of me twice, shame on me. So Kelly planned to have her guard up tight before Will was ever successful with those underhanded methods again.

But she changed her mind in the afternoon. Some of his underhanded, manipulative methods seemed to unexpectedly work out.

By then, of course, they'd been to his work. She'd met Yves, his boss, a little guy with a fuzzy head of hair who treated Will like a god. And then there was the receptionist, Marie, who clearly ruled the office with gum-popping efficiency and a snappy tongue. There were only a handful of others—it wasn't that big a facility—but whenever or however Yves had hired Will, Will was clearly the one making the business decisions. All of them.

"You realize you're running the place?" she asked when they left there.

"Not really. Yves has outstanding products. And he's a good guy. He just never had Business One-O-One."

"Will. You're doing a lot more than Business One-O-One for him."

That was one of the times he kissed her. Right in the middle of the street—and God knows, the traffic was homicidal on a Paris street during a workday. At the time, she forgot that she'd been trying to get him to talk more about his job, to explain the complete lie he'd told her. He had so clearly said that he couldn't stand going into his father's business, that he wanted nothing to do with business ever in his life—when she saw for herself that business was as natural for Will as milk for a baby.

After that, though, he rushed her off into an elegant old library, where they hung out in the research section, diving into old Paris newspapers. Normally research was her bread-and-butter, her love, and being nosy had always been a boon in her job, but she'd never tried researching anything in French. Or had a reason to experience research directly in another country.

After the research binge, Will insisted on feeding her. He picked a bistro in the Latin Quarter, where they had something called Bresse chicken, washed down with a liter of wine.

"I don't drink during the day," she objected.

"You haven't had anything to feel guilty about so far. You know you won't survive a whole day unless there's something you're wringing your hands about. So guzzle it, baby."

She didn't want to guzzle it. She needed a clear head to process all they'd learned about her father and the Rochard family. Her head was already reeling and dizzy, long before she'd had the first sip of wine.

"Will," she said, "he's rich."

"I'd call that a pretty good understatement," Will said. "The French would use the word *rupin*. As in, filthy rich."

"You knew."

"Not *knew*. The Rochard name is too common here to be sure your family was one of the badass rich ones. But the address made it pretty impossible for your father to be basic middle class. No one can afford that community who isn't pretty much rolling in it." He refilled her wine, and when he saw a pastry tray circulating, motioned for the waitress. "You ready to call him?"

"In a minute."

"Kel, there's no point in postponing this if you want to see him again directly. You only have a few days."

"I know, I know. And if there's any chance he might be willing to see me today, I need to call immediately. But, Will, I'm still dizzy. And it's not the wine."

In her job, Kelly had tracked enough missing persons and stolen identities to know how to get to the bottom of things.

Money was always at the bottom of things.

She could read more French than she could speak, and Will had helped interpret any material where she'd stumbled. Apparently her grandfather, Pierre Rochard, had some Jewish blood. He'd been injured in WWII, had been found and taken in by a Catholic family who'd hidden him for the duration of the war. When it was over, he discovered that he'd lost his entire family...and when he came home to the only place he'd ever lived, he found the house in shambles, his art and family treasures all stolen.

Until the war, the Rochards hadn't had big wealth, but they'd been furniture makers, successful, thriving. Her grandfather had turned his loss and anger into a cause—seeking out old art treasures.

She'd found two magazine articles highlighting different aspects of her grandfather's life. Initially, justice had been Pierre Rochard's motivation for finding things that had once belonged to his family, and then he had wanted to help others do the same. But over the next couple decades, finding stolen treasures became his life's work.

"You know what I found amazing?" Kelly mused to Will. "That's what I do, too. I mean…I don't do anything as big or fascinating as what my grandfather did. But there's still a similarity. Tracking down credit card theft and fraud—it's all about the hunt, the search and the love for that kind of thing. You have to like poking into corners, people's private lives. You think that could be an inherited trait?"

Will appeared to consider this question, then gravely shook his head. "At a guess, I'd say nosiness at your level is probably a lot more of a practiced, perfected art form."

And then, just as she was about to smack him, he leaned over and came through with another kiss. It was another one of those forget-where-she-was, who-she-was kind of kisses, and she knew he'd done it deliberately.

"I'm on to you now," Kelly said, vaguely aware that the waitress was hovering with a tray.

"On to me about what?"

"About your wicked, manipulative ways."

"Yeah?" A quiet flush seeped up his neck. He was clearly delighted by the praise.

"Anyway," she said vaguely, and then picked up a spoon, unsure how a lemon ice had appeared in front of her. Her lips still felt kiss-stung. But eventually her mind wandered back on track to her father.

Her dad, Henri, had grown up with that background—only unlike his father, he tackled the treasure-hunting bug from a different angle. His work was insurance—insuring art treasures—while he developed a major collection of his own along the way. Kelly still hadn't grasped how that amounted to tons and tons of francs, but apparently it did.

"Thirty million. Isn't that what that last article claimed he was worth?"

"Something like that," Will concurred.

Bucks, francs, euros, who could keep them all straight? And Will didn't seem particularly impressed by the figure, but then his family already had money. Kelly was used to having none.

She motioned with her spoon. "I can't fathom how that number is supposed to mean something. I don't even know how many zeroes are on the end of that. I'm used to thinking in terms of clearance sales. I'm a hard-core T.J. Maxx-er . When I was little, my mom was a rummage-sale addict."

Will frowned. "What's a T.J. Ma—?"

"Never mind. Trust me, you wouldn't understand. The point is, *I* don't understand how my mom fit into this. I mean…some of what she told me *had* to be true. How else could she have met a Frenchman if she hadn't been over here studying at the Sorbonne? But from everything she said, even if she invented a bunch, I never had the impression she thought he had any money."

"Maybe he wasn't the kind of guy to show off his wealth. Your grandfather certainly sounded like a quiet, reclusive type. Every article we found on him made a big deal out of how quietly he lived, not wanting to be noticed."

Another thought occurred to her. "Now it makes more sense why my brothers—my half brothers—took such an instant dislike to me. I couldn't understand why they leaped to the conclusion so fast that I was a gold digger, but that was before I realized how much money there was. Now I get their attitude. And I have to tell my father that, Will. Now! Today! That I don't care about the money, that was never why I tracked him down, that I never even knew about that—oh my God!"

"Oh my God, what?"

"I just called him my father. As if I really believe it."

Will lifted a hand across the table and took hers. Met her eyes. "Now," he said gently, "I think you're ready to try calling him."

"No."

"Yeah, you are. You're ready to see him again, too."

"No, I'm not!"

"Uh-huh. I'll be right with you." He stood up, as if expecting her to rise, too. Granted, they'd finished eating ages ago and they'd already argued about the bill and then Will had paid it, and they couldn't very well sit there all afternoon.

But her eyes narrowed. Nobody bullied Kelly Nicole Rochard. Nobody. She wasn't going to do this until she was downright good and ready.

Only then, of course, Will kissed her again.

CHAPTER SIX

"DID I MENTION before that you're a manipulative, sneaky, underhanded son of a gun?" she asked him.

"Not in the last five minutes," Will assured her, and managed to park his Citroën in a space that couldn't possibly be more than five inches by six. She didn't notice his incomparable skill. She was too busy looking belligerent and strong—and grabbing his arm in a killer vise when he came around to her side of the car.

A few clouds fluttered overhead, but mostly the sky was a pure blue, with a warm sun beating on their heads…and the view. The 7th and 16th arrondissements were traditionally the most expensive real estate in Paris. They were only a skip away from the Eiffel Tower and Musée d'Orsay, but Will didn't suspect Kel would be up for sightseeing after this.

The Rochard house was classic—tall with a steep gabled roof, oriel and bay windows, leaded stained glass. Sculpted shrubbery framed the long steps to the front door, and a wrought-iron fence protected the Rochards' privacy.

The place wasn't remotely ostentatious. It just looked like serious old money—well kept, well cherished. Somebody loved that house.

"Will," Kelly said firmly, "it's not fair that I dragged you into this."

"Sure it is. The man is nothing to me. If he's mean to you or makes you uncomfortable, I can deck him. No qualms. And if you two get on fine, then I'll go sit on the front step and smell the aristocratic air for a while. Great spring day, no sweat."

"I'm no coward."

"I know that, cookie. Cowards don't travel across the Atlantic alone."

"He can't really want to see me."

"He had a chance to say no when you called. Instead, he agreed to another meeting, so he must be willing to see you."

"But now I remember the way he looked at me the first time…believe me, he doesn't like me. Or want to believe I exist. He probably only agreed to see me this time because he was afraid I was going to be trouble."

"Honey, you *are* trouble. And if you're his daughter, you're damn well entitled to be trouble. Look at me." At the door, before knocking, he straightened her collar, pulled up her shoulders, smoothed her hair. Then he kissed her nose. "Let's do it."

He knocked. He didn't have a clue what she was barging into, but he was damn well positive no one was going to attack her. No, he didn't intend to deck anyone, but he knew exactly how rude the French could be—and how nontough Kel could be. Whether the meeting became awkward or awful or both, he wasn't about to let her face it alone.

Yet when the door opened, Will was tempted to gape. Maybe before, Kelly's story had seemed half-way like a fairy tale to him, but the man who opened the door was somewhere around his early sixties. His hair was distinctly brandy-brown. He was tall, no pansy in build, but still unusually fine-boned. And he had brown eyes so startling they made you want to stare. Like Kelly's. Exactly like Kelly's.

He had a thin mouth, sharply defined. Like Kel's. He had the same perfect skin.

His nose was bigger, but the slant of cheekbones and the shape of his chin…hell. They were all Kel's.

No one could doubt the relationship. And from the sudden change of color in Henri Rochard's face, he realized exactly who Kelly was.

"Bonjour. Et vous êtes…?" Henri looked at him.

Will introduced himself. Rochard took his mea-sure, then ushered them into a room off to the left. Double doors led to a front parlor decorated with heavy drapes, crystal, antique chairs, lots of ornate gold work. It looked to Will as if the room was done in one of those Louis periods, Louis XIV or what-ever.

He had ample time to look around, because Henri's

attention was on Kelly. He could barely take his eyes off her.

"Demitasse?" he asked, inquiring whether either of them wanted coffee.

"Non, merci," Kelly said.

She finally let go of his hand, but likely only because her palm was slicker than a slide. Henri motioned her to sit in a chair close to him. She opted for a love seat that looked harder than a rock, but at least he could sit next to her.

"Kelly..." Henri started to say, his voice so low he sounded hoarse. "This is difficult. *Ce n'est pas facile...*"

"It's not easy for me, either. Could you just tell me... Did you know my mother was pregnant? Did you know I existed? What really happened between you and my mother? What—"

Henri looked at Will for the first time, showing a hint of humor.

"Kel," Will said gently. "I think you might want to give him a chance to answer one question before you pelt him with the next thirty."

Yet Henri spoke up, with his own agenda. "You will need a DNA test."

"Why?"

Again, Henri looked at Will. "To verify if we are relative. Related."

"You look at me—I look at you—and you can doubt the relationship?" Kelly said disbelievingly.

"Non. Not exactly. But legally, there must be

verification. And I would appreciate knowing why you came to France *now*. How you found me, how you knew about me."

"I knew about you from my mother! But I thought you died before I was born. That's what I was told."

"Then how did you happen to come here? If you thought there was no one to find, no father." He steepled his hands, sank into a chair that seemed to swallow him.

"I had three letters that you wrote to my mom— I thought this was after you two were married, that you'd gone back to France for some reason and my mom had stayed in the United States. Now...well, I'm just saying that *I thought* you and my mom were married..." Kelly's voice caught. "But that was another lie, wasn't it? You were never married."

"*Non. Ce n'est pas possible.* A marriage was never possible."

"Because you were already married?"

Henri took a long, slow breath. "*Oui.* Because at the time I met your mother, I had a wife and two sons. Divorce was never even a remote option." Again, Henri glanced at Will, then quickly returned his attention to Kelly. "Where are these letters?"

Kelly stiffened up like a coiled spring. "You think I made them up?"

"*Non, non.* No sense for you to invent this. You had to have means to know this address, to know about me. So I am asking you. Where these letters are."

Henri revealed little emotion in his expression, but from his language, Will could readily discern he was upset. Henri was fluent enough, but when Kelly said something that troubled him, his English seemed to deteriorate. And his eyes never left Kelly's face, as if he couldn't stop looking at her.

Will kept trying to read the man. There seemed more suspicion than any fatherly love in his behavior, but that didn't seem totally odd under the circumstances. More than anything, Henri simply acted as if he'd been thrown by a wallop of a shock from his past, and he was doing his damnedest to determine what it meant, what to do about it.

Kelly, on the other hand, had turned into one hundred percent estrogen. She was absolutely clear about where she was coming from. She suddenly had a live father in her life. All the lies she'd been told were being painted with bold strokes, the color of anger. And loss. And feelings of abandonment. And plain old temper.

She rose like a tight spring when he brought up the letters again. "Do you think I'd use them? To blackmail you or get money out of you? Henri… Dad…for God's sake, I don't even know what I should call you! Whatever. Try and get it through your thick head that I don't want anything material from you. I just wanted to know something about who my father was. That's the only reason I came here. To get a sense of family, the part of my blood

I never had a chance to know. I'm not here to cause you any kind of trouble—"

When Kelly stood up, so did Henri. And just as fast, Will lurched to his feet. Kelly had tears spitting from her eyes.

"Kelly," her father said calmly. "I want you to have a DNA test."

"You want a DNA test? Fine. I'll have your test and then you can shove the results where the sun doesn't shine." More tears. She whirled around, bumped into Will, whirled back again. "If you don't want a daughter, believe me, you don't have one—"

"Kelly, I didn't say that. *Ma chère*—"

"You haven't asked me one thing. About my life, who I am, what I do. You don't want me in your life. I get it. It was mighty inconvenient for me to show up—"

"Mighty—" Henri looked at Will.

"Maybe not the easiest thing to translate," Will murmured.

"You think this is inconvenient for *you?*" Kelly ranted on. "I didn't know you were alive. I'm just finding out that my mother apparently had an affair with a married man. That she fabricated a whole life about you that wasn't true. You think that's convenient for *me?* I've got *brothers.* My God, I have *family.* Only apparently, thanks to you and my mother both, I'll never have a chance to know you. Or my brothers, who seemed to hate me on sight."

Henri shot Will a frantic glance now. Kelly was clearly talking too fast for him to completely follow, but like any man—and certainly a Frenchman—he recognized a woman's meltdown when he saw one.

"Kelly. *Ma chère*. I have perhaps not handled this well—"

"Damn right, you haven't. You've handled this totally badly. And that's just fine. But I'm not going to stay here and get beat up for something that was none of my fault, none of my doing. And damn it! Those letters were the only thing I ever had from you!"

This time she spun around and headed for the door, clearly intent on leaving immediately.

As it happened, she aimed for the wrong door— some door that led deeper into the house.

But Will cut her off at that pass, did a defensive play he'd learned in football, scooped her under his arm in a shielding position and redirected her toward the front door. "I think it's probably best that we cut this visit short," he said to Henri.

"This is very, very difficult—"

"Yeah. But it's not going to get better right now."

"I can talk to him. Don't you talk to him. I can handle this myself," Kelly said.

He knew she could. But there was so much anguish on her face, and her voice was so thick with tears, that he figured she needed out of there. Now. Any way he could get her out.

And that worked. Sort of. Except that once he had

her stashed in the car and immersed in the fury of rush-hour Paris traffic, she put her spring jacket over her head. That was goofy enough, but underneath she was crying. Not making a lot of noise, but her body was shaking with it, and he could hear the massive gulps.

At one point a hand reached out from under the jacket.

He handed her a tissue.

She took it back into the jacket cave, honked her nose and started again.

He wanted to pull over. Wanted to disappear into Austria or Australia. Wanted to pretend she wasn't crying as if someone had broken her heart. Wanted to go back and kill her damn father.

But midafternoon traffic in Paris was a lot like NASCAR back home. You just didn't have a choice about paying attention. It was that or die. The other drivers were a lot more homicidal than suicidal.

"He didn't want me. At all," Kelly said from the muffled, dark depths of her jacket.

"Now, Kel. That's not necessarily true. Finding out about you was obviously a shock."

"Well, it's a shock for me, too! Everything's been a shock for me since I got here. He didn't even say once that he was glad I was his daughter, or glad he had a daughter."

Oh, yeah. He liked these kinds of conversations. Not that he'd ever had one exactly like this before, but a guy didn't need to be shot to know a bullet wasn't fun. "Now, cookie," he said gently, "those were complicated waters you two were trying to wade into. Even if he'd felt that way, there might not have been a chance for him to say it."

"Horse spit. He found plenty of chances to bring up DNA. That's all he wanted to talk about. Proof. When all I had to do was look at him to know we were related. He had to know the same thing, looking at me! But he was so...cold."

"Now, Kel." Other drivers were shooting him fingers right and left. And sweat was clustering at the nape of his neck, not from the drivers, but the stress of this whole type of emotional conversation. "I don't know that he was cold. I really think he was just stunned, that he wasn't sure what to do, what to say, how to react."

"And I had magic answers for those things? How would you like it if you found out your mom had slept with a married man? And I don't even know if she knew. But *he* sure as hell knew he had a wife and kids when he seduced my mom. And then to just drop out of the picture before even wondering if she could be pregnant—although, of course, maybe he did know. Maybe he thought she'd get an abortion. Or maybe he didn't care. Or maybe she didn't tell him. I mean, how does he get credit for suffering more shocks than me?"

Her hand reached out from under the jacket again. He handed her another tissue, and hoped that'd be enough, because there were no more. Ten more minutes and they'd be home. Ten more. She just had to hold it together for ten more.

Finally they got there, but he'd barely squeezed into the parking place before she'd flown out of the car. When she yanked off the jacket, he saw her face.

She'd stopped crying by then.

She'd stopped talking.

Usually that made him feel grateful, but now he wished she'd chatter up a storm. The look on her face killed him. The gorgeous eyes and nose were all red. No color in her cheeks at all. She looked so damned…sad. Sad and lost. From the inside out.

"It's okay," she said. "Don't look so scared. I know I was having an emotional fit, but I'm through now, honest."

Maybe she was, but that didn't really help him. He started to say something, then realized, for the dozenth time in the past hour, that he didn't have a clue what to say. What she needed. What would help.

He'd been rescuing his sisters—and other damsels—since he was in diapers. Granted, he was fed up with that. But for the first time in a blue moon, he actually wanted to rescue a female, and he didn't know how.

He turned the key, pushed open the door. She ran inside first, and said, "I'm going to call my mother."

He'd barely hung up the keys and scooped up the mail before she returned from the living room.

"Well, that's not going to work. I dialed. But then I hung up. Darn it, I can't talk to her. Not until I'm a lot less upset and can be a whole lot clearer about how I want to bring all this up."

When she scrubbed her face with a tired hand, something snapped in him. That was it. He'd had enough. He crossed the room in four long strides.

She saw him. In fact, she cocked her head when she saw him slamming across the room, but she still looked surprised when he suddenly grabbed her. When he lifted her up, she just naturally wrapped her legs around his waist for balance, which enabled him to take off with her down the hall at a hell-bent pace.

"Will—"

Yeah, yeah. He could guess all the crap she wanted to say. She was miserable. Not the right time. Not in the mood. And he didn't pull caveman stuff, because he wasn't a caveman type. That Rhett Butler scene in *Gone with the Wind* where Gable carts Scarlett up the stairs—not for him. He liked to know he was wanted ahead of time. He liked an engraved invitation. He hated sticky stuff, never dove in until he'd thoroughly tested the waters, got queasy when he thought of pushing a woman to do anything.

But this wasn't like that.

That was more like…a guy had to do what a guy had to do.

She wasn't crying anymore today. He couldn't fix her complicated life. In the long run, probably it'd all work out, anyway. It was just now, this week, this day, these past hours, that had her so twisted up and confused. It would have helped if Henri Rochard had at least given her a hug. Or said a simple hello to his daughter. Or said something, anything, the son of a bitch, that indicated he noticed that she was a beautiful woman. Beautiful, interesting, wonderful, independent and courageous.

Okay, so she wasn't so courageous at just this second.

But that was the point.

That was precisely the reason why, right then, he dropped her on the bed. Dove in. Dove on.

Strips of hot afternoon sunlight striped her face, so bright she had to close her eyes, which made it all the easier to kiss her long and hard.

She didn't reject the kiss. Didn't scream or rant at the behavior or anything, but she didn't do much of anything until he took her tongue.

Then, suddenly, she unraveled. All that miserableness seemed to gather up inside her, transform into another kind of energy altogether. That long kiss he was coaxing from her turned into a bite—a bite coming from her—and then she was pulling, yanking on his clothes.

He twisted around to help her, only his movements enabled her to climb on top of him instead of the other way around. She'd played the inciter before, but not the aggressor. It wasn't so easy for her, being vulnerable that way, admitting what she needed, going after it. She was raw-new at it, elbows appearing where no one wanted them, her knee threatening his groin, her hair tangling in his fingers…amazing, how all the awkwardness inspired them both.

At least it inspired him. And for sure she was responding.

Her skin needed cherishing, he thought. And once he had her naked, he obliged. The curve of her shoulder. The tender crease under her breast. The inside of her thigh—oh, mama. She all but sprang off the bed for a tongue there, and hell, he hadn't even started.

THE SHARP, HARSH ribbons of sunlight seemed to soften. Outside, traffic started to quiet down. The air stilled…. They must have napped after the first time, because when he opened his eyes next, the ambient light was the fuzzy violet of dusk.

She was draped over his body like a blanket, her cheek carved into his shoulder. He turned his head, kissed her forehead.

It was enough to wake her. "You hungry?" she murmured sleepily.

"Beyond belief. I could eat a pair of steaks."

"Me, too."

Big talk, he noted, for a woman who stretched like a lazy cat and then curled right back on top of him and closed her eyes again.

"Will?" she murmured.

"Hmm?"

"You make it all go away."

"Make all what go away?"

The piker was only pretending to be sleeping. She eased up, her eyes open and alert and aware, her mouth still swollen red from all that endless kissing. "I have a lot to face. A lot I have to figure out. But the way you love, Will…at least the way you love me…makes me feel whole. In every way."

Well, hell. Dinner would have to wait.

He was already hard. From the sound of her voice, from the lazy winsomeness in her eyes, from her fingertips curled around his neck. Her body was already warm, for him, with him, from him.

He told himself it was so good because he knew her body now. Knew that a certain stroke ignited her sensual core. Knew that the undersides of her breasts were exquisitely tender. Knew that she liked to ride as much as she loved to be ridden. Knew that she was wary of being hurt, because she had this way of tensing right before he entered her, as if any lover or lovers she'd had in the past hadn't taken care to insure she was ready.

Knew that sometimes she liked speed and a fast pump.

That sometimes she liked slow and long and whispered words.

He knew so much about her now. But he had a bad feeling, after they finally crashed from the last rocketing orgasm, that none of those factors explained why it was so impossibly good between them.

It was starlight.

And spring moonbeams.

And Paris.

He closed his eyes, thinking he was so wiped he was going to sleep forever. Yet he didn't sleep for ages, just held her, inhaled her, long after she'd zonked out completely.

It was the magic of *her* that made it so different. So right.

He knew it. And so did his heart.

KELLY WOKE UP to the sound of a ringing phone. Eyes still closed, she patted the bed next to her, thinking she'd better make sure Will knew he had a call. But the smooth sheet was already cool, and when she opened one sleepy eye, she found boundless bright daylight. Below, the lusty roar of traffic was near deafening, even if she hadn't realized it a second before. The day had galloped into full gear while they were still snoozing.

At least while *she* was still snoozing.

She pushed away the covers, aware that every private part of her body was tender. Embarrassingly so. So embarrassing that she seemed to have a smile on her mouth that wouldn't quit. Even before coffee.

"Will?" she called, and then chuckled when she saw him standing in the doorway.

Her hero, her lover, her darling, was holding a fresh mug of coffee. He was also wearing only jeans, and the bare feet and bare chest aroused fresh desire in her when, Lord knows, she should be satiated times ten.

"Hey, y…" A teasing greeting was on the tip of her lips, but it died. And so did her smile.

He was just standing there, but something in his expression alerted her to a problem.

"What's wrong?" she asked immediately.

"Nothing. Nothing at all." He brought the mug over, handed it to her and said in a hearty voice, "The call was from the consulate. Your passport's ready. I gave them heaps of praise. They did everything but stand on their heads to get the paperwork moving this fast. They even booked you a first-class ticket home, for the same price as the flight you had to cancel. Tomorrow morning, at the crack of dawn. As close to your original departure date as they could get."

"Oh." Her cheerful smile suddenly felt as frozen as his. "That's wonderful." She felt as if her chest had caved in from the blow of a five-ton lead ball. Or a heart attack. Or maybe it was just that her heart suddenly felt broken. "I thought everybody complained about the bureaucracy in France. And here they came through like troupers. Arranging the ticket home was unbelievably nice."

"I think they felt bad about the mugging. And they didn't want an American going home, whining about the French."

"I wouldn't have done that."

"I know, but they didn't. Anyway, it's really great," he said.

"Really great," she echoed, and then couldn't seem to speak at all.

She didn't have any more vacation time. Piles of new crises were up in the air—like the knowledge that she had a father and brothers. She also had a life impatiently waiting for her back home. A job, the need to make money. Her mom.

And oh, yeah. Jason. Her fiancé.

She *had* to go home.

It didn't matter how she felt about Will. All she'd shared with him, all she felt for him.

Didn't matter how deeply and insanely and crazily she'd fallen in love with him.

She had to fix her real life. Her American life.

"Well," she said, and then couldn't seem to remember how to breathe.

"Quit looking like that," Will said suddenly, swiftly. "We've got one more day. And there are some places you have to see, things you have to do."

"What?"

"You'll see," he said.

She'd barely showered and dressed before he hustled her out the door. He bought beignets from a vendor for breakfast, then took her down to an old part of Paris. The sign over the door read Chemist, but she discovered it was really a *parfu-*

merie, where the chemist created an individual perfume for each customer.

"This is going to be too expensive." She didn't actually know the cost, because no one had mentioned anything specific. But she'd seen two clients amble in, one wearing an Hermès scarf and the other a Chanel bag, which was clear enough proof the scents weren't cheap.

But nothing could talk Will out of this. Heaven knows, he looked like an antsy tiger in the cage, but he kept talking to the chemist, a wizened little man with a beak nose. Apparently the process began with the chemist asking questions about the woman's natural likes and dislikes.

"I can understand him well enough to answer those questions," Kelly said.

"No. You don't know about you. Not like I know about you," Will said, and turned back to his conversation. The chemist did some patches on her skin, testing for pH, but the questions were all about her. What scents were more natural to her—flowers, musk; did she tend to be sexy, sweet, exotic, Oriental, what was her nature?

Will told the chemist that she was elegant. Fresh. No musk, maybe something with flowers, but not heavy flowers-in-your-face. Sexy, but not the kind of scent someone would pick up unless close to her. More a scent just for a lover. Not gaudy, not look-at-me. But something in the scent needed to have a hint of a surprise, something you'd never expect.

"That's how you see me?" Kelly asked.

By then Will had rejected the first scent, insisted the chemist try harder. And then they had it. The exquisite little vial was sapphire-blue, her favorite color, and when the chemist put a drop of the scent on her wrist, she looked up in both surprise and delight. She loved perfumes, but she'd never smelled anything like this.

An hour later, Will teased her, "People are going to think you're weird if you keep smelling your wrist."

"It's just so wonderful!"

"That's the thing. It's your scent alone. That's the whole point…." He'd managed to put together a mini picnic with bread, cheese, wine, a blanket. There were so many fantastic gardens in Paris, but Will had claimed this was a favorite of his—a spot he'd discovered the first month he moved here. It was a place in the lee of some giant old trees, where yellow and blue flowers peeked through the soft grasses, catching the warm sun beams.

They lay head to head, after eating. "Just a twenty-minute nap, no longer," he warned her. "We still have miles to go today."

Midafternoon, they caught a mime show in a park. Then Will insisted they needed to take one last run through Notre Dame, and since she knew how allergic Will was to churches, she was touched he was willing to do that for her. After that came a winding walk on the rue Monge, with all its Latin Quarter flavor.

From the old Halles market, he bought her a scarf—blue and white, silky and long—and then a silly, touristy Eiffel Tower key ring, and then, it was on to dinner. The restaurant had neither a sign nor a name. The place was perched high, where the windows overlooked the night lights of Paris. Inside was candlelight, a rich merlot and the chef who informed them what they were going to eat—and that they were going to love it beyond anything they'd ever tasted before.

Dinner was delicacy after delicacy. Then they drove back to Will's place and walked around. He got suckered into buying a bouquet of flowers from a vendor who was closing down, so she carried those in one hand, sniffing them every few moments, clasping Will's hand with her free one. Dusk faded into night, night into long past midnight. Yet still they walked, block after block, until their feet were tired.

She knew they had to go back, knew she had to pack, but she knew they'd make love one last time in his apartment, and she didn't want there to be a *one last time*.

Around three in the morning, a mist settled, making the streets glow and the night lights shine like diamonds. They looked at each other, and finally turned around and started the return to his place. Neither said anything…until Will was turning the key in the lock, and she had the hopeless, helpless thought that this was the last time she'd ever see him do that.

So she charged in, as if she had energy, determined to turn this mood around. He offered to pour her a glass of wine while she headed straight in to pack her belongings, which were scattered all over his apartment.

"We've only got two hours before we have to leave for the airport," he warned her.

"Eek." There, she'd made him smile. She put him to work folding, a job he was amazingly awful at, while she flew around gathering her things.

At least, that was her intent. And it worked, her busyness, until she dove in her bag for her tickets...and came across the blue vial of perfume. The scent of it, the sentiment of it, the uniqueness of it, reminded her of everything she'd found in Paris.

Especially Will.

When she looked up, he was motionless in the doorway.

"Look," she said, "I have to go."

"I know you do."

"My entire life is in chaos at home. I have to get it straightened out. It can't be done from here."

"Like dumping the fiancé," Will said. He'd been folding a sweater. It looked somewhat like an accordion with arms.

She tried a watery laugh, took over the folding job. She didn't comment about dumping Jason, any more than she ever did when he brought up her fiancé. Jason was her problem, her business. She tried for a more cheerful note.

"And you, Mr. White Knight, are going to be glad to get your place back to yourself, aren't you? No more girly shampoos in your shower, no more earrings on the table, no more hogging your covers. When you saved me from the mugger crisis, it's not as if you planned on taking in a boarder indefinitely, huh?"

She thought he might laugh. Instead he hooked her hand, the one that held a handful of thongs and bras. She dropped them at the look in his eyes. "Not a boarder," he said huskily. "A lover."

"Yeah...a lover," she whispered back. And then out it came, the aching pain in her heart. "How am I supposed to leave you, Will?"

The suitcase got shooshed to the floor. With the overhead light on, her clothing draped on the spread and chairs and everywhere else, he reached for her as fast, as hopelessly, as fiercely as she reached for him.

It wasn't like the other times. She wanted to beguile him with kisses, enchant him with touch, cajole his heart. She wanted to be inseparably part of him. She wanted this to be the best sex he'd ever had. She wanted him never to forget her. She wanted to be loved, by him, only by him, forever and ever.

The first part of that was easy enough.

It was the last part she couldn't have. When it was over, when they were both lying there, damp and out of breath, she wrapped her arms around him and refused to let go.

Except, of course, the clock was ticking.

Will seemed to realize the time at the same moment. "Hell," he grumbled. "We might just make your flight if we start moving at a dead run."

CHAPTER SEVEN

THERE WAS NO GETTING around fast anywhere in Orly. It was one of those discombobulated, crazy airports where you walked miles to get nowhere, stood in lines that never ended, had your nerves and temper frayed before you even started.

On the other hand, Will thought, he'd gotten her here. His plan for the whole last day had been just this. To keep both of them running a hundred miles an hour so she wouldn't have a chance to cry, to get upset and emotional, before they had to split up.

Both of them looked like wrecks. No sleep at all. But she looked like a cute wreck, with her flyaway hair and whisker-burned cheeks and lopsided sweater. He was standing with her through the initial check-in procedure, which was going—naturally—slower than molasses.

And that was when—instead of doing the emotional thing he'd been trying to avoid—she did the nosy, prying thing.

He almost wished she'd have cried instead.

There were still six passengers ahead when she

started. "Will…you know, if I'm stuck straightening out this impossible relationship or nonrelationship with my father, I think you should feel stuck working out something with your father, too."

When he'd fallen insanely in love with her, he'd forgotten that part—the part where she opened emotional doors without knocking and talked in completely feminine sentences. "One plus one does not equal Q, Kelly. Your issues with your father are a universe different than the issues I've got with mine."

She moved up a spot, but her gaze was on him, not on the line. "Actually, they're really similar. They're both impossible situations. They're both our fathers. And our unresolved issues with them have defined who we are. And…"

"And what?" He was getting miffed.

"And if you decide to mend fences with your dad, then you'd have to come home to South Bend."

But he couldn't go home.

Suddenly it was her turn in the line, and then she had to go through security, past the gates where he couldn't go.

He kissed her, long and hard and hopelessly. She walked backward, as if she wanted every last second of looking at his face that she could have. And when she was hustled through the last gates, out of sight, he searched for a waiting area with windows where he could watch her plane take off.

The spring morning was still misty and damp. Rude travelers jostled for spots at the window and he just jostled back, watching until the plane turned into a bird, then disappeared in the sky altogether.

He couldn't go home, he repeated to himself. But the sudden hole in his gut felt like nothing in the known universe could fill it.

There was nothing really new about that hole. He already knew he'd fallen in love with her. In love, like he'd never been in love. Love, like he'd never known love. A woman...like no other woman.

Bleary-eyed, zombie tired, he battled his way through the crowd toward the exit.

People think they fall in love in Paris every spring, he told himself firmly. It was a fantasy. It didn't mean it was real.

It was just...Paris.

And spring.

And her unforgettable brown eyes.

He put his hands in his pockets and stalked outside, trying to remember where he'd parked the car. The late-night mist had turned into a steady morning drizzle that soaked his head and blurred his vision. His thoughts were just as dark.

He couldn't go back to South Bend. Kelly didn't know, couldn't know, how bad it was for him there. It wasn't an option.

And there was nothing he could do about it.

WHEN KELLY CLIMBED off the plane in South Bend, the clock claimed it was two in the afternoon, but Paris time would be nine at night…and since she hadn't slept on either of the flights home, her body didn't know what time of day or night it was.

While she waited for her luggage, her stomach kept lurching and her head refused to stop pounding—possibly because her body was so mixed up, but more probably because being home felt like landing on an alien planet.

She was supposed to be Kelly Nicole Rochard. Or she assumed she'd feel like herself when she got home again. The impossible, crazy, wonderful love affair with Will should have felt like a distant dream, a fantasy.

This was supposed to be her real life. Right?

A young woman with spiked red hair hurled through the doors near baggage claim and shrieked when she saw her. "Kelly! I'm so glad you asked me to come! You look *wonderful!*"

Kelly figured she actually looked what she was, tired and crumbling from the inside out. But Brenna, the girl Friday in the office, was an ideal chauffeur for this venture.

Originally Kelly had thought to have her mother to pick her up, but she'd changed that plan. She needed to talk to her mom, soon and seriously, but not yet. Her first crisis had to be a confrontational talk with Jason, come hell or high water, sick or not sick, tired or not tired. And Brenna was perfect company, first because she was thrilled to have the excuse to get out of the office, and second, because she was impossibly easy to be with.

Skinny as a rail, tottering on four-inch heels, Brenna yanked all Kelly's luggage away from her, wrapped her hands around a fresh chai and chattered the whole drive. How was Paris? Were the men hot? Did Kelly hate not being able to eat American food? How scary it must have been, to get mugged and lose her passport. She'd been missed; her desk was heaped to the ceiling, and no one could calm down Myrna in a snit the way she could. Myrna could be getting a divorce. Everyone knew her husband was fooling around. Sam had got a new dog. He'd brought it in to the office one day and it had peed all over the place.

"Do you want me to come in and help you unpack?" she asked at the apartment, looking hopeful.

"Thanks, Brenna, but I can take it from here. I can't thank you enough for picking me up. I owe you a dinner. And I'll see you at the office tomorrow."

Brenna looked crestfallen at not being able to cop more time out of the office, but her expression brightened almost immediately. "You're probably hot for the reunion with Jason, huh? You two lovebirds haven't seen each other in two weeks now! I'll bet you can hardly stand it!"

"Hmm," Kelly said.

And then there she was. Alone, standing in front of the apartment. The place was just a few miles from the Notre Dame campus, and a mile from the infamous shopping on Grape Road. It was one of those typical complexes for young professionals. Most of the occupants were single, a few married, but nobody had kids yet. The place could get pretty rowdy on a Friday night, but midafternoon, like now, there was barely a car in sight except for her white Saturn, sitting, dusty, in the spot next to Jason's.

She lugged her gear up the walk, turned the key and pushed open the door. Her heart sank lower than sludge when she let herself inside.

The only sound in the place was a ticking clock, a clock she'd bought herself two months ago, on sale. It had been Jason's apartment before hers. She'd moved in because there came a point where it seemed ridiculous not to. He'd given her the ring. They'd been sleeping together. Their families and friends had been expecting the marriage announcement for years—probably close to a decade. It just didn't make sense to pay two separate rents when they were consolidating what they had together.

She swallowed hard, looking at everything that should have been familiar, but it was as if she were wearing glasses with a tint. Nothing looked the same.

The red couch was hers, the leather recliner his. The plasma TV and terrific sound system, his. The two museum prints on the far wall, the vacuum cleaner, the massive pot of shamrocks—dead, she noted, from lack of watering—hers.

The place was small, just a living room with an el for a dining table, a kitchen, two small bedrooms. A pretty patio led out to a long, glossy lawn area, though. And the living room got a ton of light. They'd bought the bookshelves together. The splashy rug under the TV.

She wandered into the kitchen, the one room that was almost entirely her doing. She'd chosen the dishes and decor in a flurry of nesting, picked out blue-and-white china, a French-looking pattern, which struck her as ironic now. The blue goblets still wore their price tags. She'd been planning on putting blue-and-white tile behind the porcelain sink herself, planned on throwing out Jason's decrepit college silverware and choosing her own pattern, something they could register for as a wedding gift. And she desperately wanted copper pots, knew perfectly well how insanely expensive they were, but she loved them so much, and thought…

All her musings suddenly seemed light-years past. Kelly sank against the counter in the kitchen, remembering the plans she'd had only a short few weeks ago, and felt a sharp, raw pain in her throat.

It was almost two hours later when she heard the front door open. The sound made her jump. By that time she was back in the main bedroom, mainlining her third mug of coffee, filling a suitcase full of shoes. There were already two suitcases and various bags stuffed in her car. Clothes, not furniture. Toiletries, nothing that was mutually bought or used. She'd emptied the bathroom and the bedroom, but only of her own personal things.

"Hey, Kelly—"

Jason's familiar voice jolted her a second time, but then there was a sudden silence. She squeezed her eyes closed. Jason, being Jason, had likely figured things out a millisecond after walking in.

She found him in the kitchen. He'd put two glasses—mismatched—on the table, was fumbling in the cupboard over the fridge. When he turned around, he had a dusty bottle of whisky in his hand, left over from at least the Christmas before. When he saw her, his shoulders were already slumped, his eyes flat as dull coins.

"Somehow I figured your homecoming would work out a little differently," he said.

"So did I." A thousand memories stood between them. She'd known him from first grade, gone trick-or-treating with him at Halloween, hurled on him in fifth grade, gone to proms and movies and football games with him. His parents loved her. She adored them. He looked like a younger version of his dad, soft dark hair, bright dark eyes, good-looking in a quiet way. What killed her, though, was knowing that she loved him. Had always loved him. Probably always would love him.

The way she'd love a brother.

How come it had taken her so long to figure it out? And man, it *hurt* to hurt him.

He watched the play of emotion on her face, in her posture, and said, "Whatever it is, we can fix it, Kelly."

She said softly, "No. We can't. I only wish. I wish from my heart."

"That's bullshit. You haven't even told me what the trouble is."

Jason never had much of a temper, but she saw it now, the control of it, in a flash of his dark eyes.

He splashed the liquor in both glasses, drank his, and then refilled his glass. "You met some guy in Paris, is that it? You screwed around?"

"That's not it."

"Come on, I've known you forever—that *has* to be it. You left here two weeks ago ready to marry me. We set up the apartment to live together, be together. Our families were part of it. It's what we've been working for, waiting for, since we were riding our two-wheelers around the block, for God's sake. You never said anything before this, so don't waste your time lying to me. It has to be another guy."

"No. Not in the sense you mean," she said quietly, and saw another flash of anger in his eyes, so sharp it made her flinch.

She suddenly saw their history together as one-

sided. Jason had always pursued her. Always made
sure he was in the same room, same corner, same
place—always there, before another guy could walk
into the picture. He'd been patient and kind and
loving. But relentless. He'd always been that sure he
wanted her, sure they belonged together.

He threw back the second shot of Jim Beam. "It'd
be *insane* to throw it all away. We've been part of
each other's lives forever."

"I know."

"I know every flaw you've got, inside and out. I'm
still here. I know what you look like with the flu. I
know your moods."

"I know, Jason," she said quietly.

"Your mother loves my mother. My family all
love you. Everyone in the old neighborhood, the
schools we went to, everything—they're all part of
this. Part of us. You wouldn't just be hurting me by
breaking up. You'd be hurting a ton of people, all the
people who are part of our lives. And for what? I hope
to God you've got a damned good reason." He
snapped, "You couldn't *have* a good enough reason."

She took a breath, and tried to speak. Couldn't
find her voice. He had every right to yell, to be angry.
To try to reason with her. To be hurt.

She had every reason to feel guilt and anguish
over hurting someone who'd been nothing but
good to her.

Worse yet, she looked at him and still loved him. The

way she'd always loved him. She wasn't just losing a fiancé out of this mess. She was losing her oldest friend.

"You know what?" He tipped back his glass again, his gaze boring into hers. "I'll go out right now. Go hit some bars. Find a woman, screw her. Then we'd be even. So if it's just about that, some short-term cheating, I think it sucks, but we can get past it. I *know* we can get past it."

Tears welled in her eyes, but she refused to let them fall.

She was the one at fault for this, so she wasn't about to let herself play the tears card. And she ignored his suggestion about the mutual cheating—it was so like him to want a nice, tidy way to fix things. Only what was wrong with her and Jason wasn't about Will, and it wasn't about anything that could be fixed. "Jason," she said gently. "I'll love you until the day I die. But not the way you want to be loved. In the long run, there's no way in the universe it could have worked for us, because I'm just not the woman you think I am. The woman you want me to be."

"That's *my* call. You think I never realized your feelings aren't as strong as mine?"

"They never were," she agreed softly. "That's exactly the problem. I never realized it before. We were always pushed to be a pair. Our families always wanted us together. We had aunts planning our wedding when we were in middle school. You never looked at anyone else."

"Because I knew it was you from the time we were kids!"

"And I tried to be—I wanted to be—your other half. I wanted to be as in love as you were. I wanted to feel like you did…." She could see in his face how much she was hurting him. It sucked. Trying to explain was only making it worse. Every word she said made him feel more unloved.

After a while, though, he lost the crushed look and thankfully started getting mad. What did she expect to do with the apartment? All their mutual stuff? Had she told her mother? His? What was she going to say? What were they supposed to tell everyone?

"I'm moving out," she said. "It was your place first. You can have everything. I'm only packing up my clothes and personal stuff."

"Well, that's just more shit. You knew you were going to do this without even talking to me?"

The scene deteriorated further after that. He called her selfish. Stupid. She was making an impulsive decision that involved the rest of their lives, and she hadn't thought it through. She'd had a momentary change of heart, a panic attack, which was normal for everybody, but no, she had to turn it into a god-awful, hurtful, life-altering event for both of them, and for what? "Haven't I been there for you? You've got a decent guy who loves you, who's always stood by you—that'd be me—and you're throwing me away like I was nothing?"

When he left, he slammed the door so hard her ears popped. She sank onto the couch, with her hands shaking and her eyes stinging hard.

Okay, she thought, but of course, nothing was remotely okay. Her stomach lurched. She sprang to her feet and barely made it into the bathroom before hurling.

Somewhere in the packed bags was her toothbrush and toothpaste, but she had no idea where.

She leaned over the bathroom sink and splashed cold water into her mouth and squeezed her eyes closed. Her head was pounding so hard she could hardly think. She hadn't slept in more than twenty-four hours, had no idea when she'd last had a meal. She had no idea where she was going to sleep, no plan for a place to live, now had to tell her mother and everyone else about the broken engagement and had to confront her mother about her father, as well…

A sudden picture of Will popped into her mind. His smile. The way he'd taken charge after the mugging. The way he'd spun into her life, pulling her into a dance of love and life and laughter and passion. His face. His eyes. The shape and texture and heat of his mouth on hers.

She sucked in a breath.

Banished the memories, the picture.

Paris was a fantasy. She might as well steel herself to reality, because there was every chance she'd never see Will again.

Still, it mattered. What he'd taught her about emotion and love—and herself. Without Will, she'd never have figured out what really mattered to her. She'd have settled for something that didn't.

In the meantime, though, she had a whole life to tear up. So far, it seemed to be going as pleasantly as a train wreck.

TWO MORNINGS LATER, Kelly was pacing inside the door at the Olive Garden when her mom walked in.

She quit chewing on a nail and breathed in. She'd called her mother before this, obviously, to let her know she was home safe and sound. But this was their first face-to-face meeting. Kelly had chosen her mom's favorite lunch haunt, given herself a couple days to gear up for this major powwow and told herself that a public place was the ideal spot for this meeting. It was the only way they'd both have a shot at keeping the discussion quiet and relatively unemotional. They'd have to stay rational in public.

But Kelly wasn't positive she could approach this rationally, no matter what. She felt roughed up and ruffled before she even got here.

Char flew in the door, eyes zooming across the lobby until she spotted her. In an instant, Kelly was smothered in a boisterously warm hug and kiss.

"God, I've missed you. Maybe you were only gone for a couple weeks, but I worried so much about how that mugging affected you. And I just missed talking to you. And my heavens, you look so different. A little shorter hairstyle? Very French. But you've lost weight, sweetheart, and you really could use a few pounds. Gaynelle and I went shopping again and found our dresses, did I tell you? We both picked out peach. Hers is fussier, naturally, you know how she likes her ruffles and frills. But that's the thing, the dresses are so different that I don't think it matters if they're a similar color—"

"Mom, I need to get this said right off. There isn't going to be any wed—"

"Oh, *honey*. That blue top looks fantastic on you. Did you get it in Paris?" Her mother was dressed for a typical high-powered real-estate day, a spring-lavender suit with matching heels, her blond hair worn simple and sleek, in a long, smooth comma that framed her face.

All Kelly's life, she had thought her mother was outstandingly beautiful. Still did. Actually, she'd always felt like an ugly duckling next to her mom, which was pretty stupid, considering her mom didn't have a vain bone in her body and had never done anything but praise her only daughter to the high hills and back.

"Mom." Kelly tried to interrupt the soliloquy again, but even when the waitress led them to a table in the back rooms, even when Char swiftly ordered for both of them—it was easier that way, always prevented a world war and a two-hour discussion—Kelly had a hard time breaking in.

"You don't look any the worse for wear. A little tired and a little thinner. But otherwise...well, I can see that *something's* different. Besides the blue top. I talked to Jason's dad when I dropped off Gaynelle. He said he hadn't talked to Jason in a couple of days, but I think everybody was trying to give you two a little space, knowing you were fresh back and hadn't seen each other in a while." Her mom smiled mischievously, then zoomed on. "It's killing me. Thinking of what I want to give you for the wedding. I know, money is all kids want today. But I'd really like to give you two something seriously—"

"Mom, the wedding's off."

"—unique. It's not about expense. It's about something seriously personal—" Abruptly, Char snapped her fingers. "Darn it, I forgot to tell you! Your aunts want to have a shower. We know, we know, you haven't set a date for sure beyond sometime close to next Christmas, but that's just the point. It takes time to find the right place and get it reserved, and especially around the holidays, things get booked fast. We're thinking about a couples' shower, because it's so much more fun. So in the evening. And—"

"Mom—"

"What, dear?"

"Jason and I broke up. There won't be a wedding. I'm not living in the apartment anymore."

"What?" Her mom had just dipped into the bread basket by then, had a knife with a pat of butter all

ready. Her smile and vivacity suspended as if suddenly frozen.

"I called it off," Kelly said quietly.

"You can't mean it." The bread dropped back to the plate. So did the butter. "You can't. Everyone knows. People have already started buying gifts. You've already moved in with him, bought all that stuff for the apartment yourself, were setting everything up so beautifully…"

"Mom—"

Her mom leaped to a conclusion. "Did he do something?" In a flurry she changed gears, turned into mother lioness. "I would have thought better of Jason, but you were gone for a couple weeks, honey. If he went out drinking, or ran up some bills or—"

"No. He didn't do anything like that. He didn't do anything wrong at all. I'm the one who moved out." Kelly took a breath. "And there's another thing I have to tell you that's going to be just as hard, so let's get it all done at once. When I was in Paris, I met someone."

Her mother swallowed hard. "Well, I have to admit, that's about the last thing in the universe I thought you were going to say. It's so totally unlike you, but, honey—"

"I met my father. The father you always claimed was dead."

Her mom started to respond, then went silent as stone.

A baby started crying from a nearby child seat. A couple teenagers took the far table by the window, were whispering to each other with gooey eyes. A trio of businessmen in a close booth kept glancing at her mother—they were eating, doing their business, but they obviously appreciated a good-looking woman. As always, Char didn't notice.

"You met your father," she echoed, in a fainter voice.

"Yeah. I did."

Her mom shut her eyes for a moment, then seemed to gather herself, find some starch to put in her shoulders. "Well…damn. That subject is going to take a very long, very private conversation."

"Yes, it is," Kelly agreed, in the same painful, soft tone.

Char hesitated. Both of them seemed aware how special their relationship had always been…and how suddenly precarious. But her mom didn't have a long history of loving her for nothing. Given two bulls, she took the one by the horns that she thought was more important. "We'll talk about your father. But not now, Kelly, please. I can see you're upset, but that *is* the past. And right now, the really immediate crisis is you and Jason. It's about whatever happened in Paris that made you come back so…different. You and Jason were completely happy before you left on that crazy fool trip."

"Mom, could you try and listen?"

"Of course I will."

Kelly doubted she would or could. Her mom's

face was flushing from the neck up, a sure sign she was upset. And when Char was seriously upset, all she wanted to do was act and order and fix, not listen.

Since Kelly had the same flaw, she understood it perfectly. "I don't know how to explain this well. But Jason always...surrounded me. The closer we came to setting a formal date, the more I felt as if I were facing a sentence in a cage."

"Don't you think that's a little drastic metaphor?"

"No. I think it's exactly how it was. Jas was always great to me. Always seemed to love me. Always chose me. But, Mom, he always hovered so tightly that I never had a chance to look at anyone else. Test anyone else. Even to test *me*. And everyone we knew was always so happy about us. Always labeled us a couple..."

"And this is terrible how?"

"Not terrible. But it was what Jason wanted. Not what I wanted. And I went along, because there wasn't anything specific that I wanted differently. But I started to feel more and more trapped. That's why I went to Paris to begin with. To be alone. To get a better feel for who I was—"

"Kelly Nicole Rochard, that sounds like the kind of crap coming all too much out of your generation. Psychobabble. An excuse for being irresponsible and selfish."

"That's not fair," Kelly said unhappily. "Come on. When have I ever been irresponsible?"

"You'll disappoint everyone. Your aunts, your cousins. All his family, who are *crazy* about you, for heaven's sake. The priest—have you at least counseled with Father Donovan before you make such a wildly impulsive decision? You're ruining everything without thinking it all through."

"I believe I have thought it through."

"Good men aren't easy to find, Kelly Nicole. You should know that from my life. You don't just throw one away because you get a whim about 'finding yourself.' Oh." Her mother tossed down the white napkin. "Frankly, I'm too upset to eat. Or talk. You know perfectly well I'm on your side no matter what you do, anytime or anywhere, but I would like to believe you'll come to your senses about this. I want to think before talking together again. And I want *you* to think. So we can both have a conversation without shouting at each other."

The baby across the way quit crying. The child's mother, the gooey-eyed couple, the businessmen, all looked at her when Char stood up and hustled for the door, a flash of emotional tears glistening in her eyes. The strangers stared at Kelly as if she must have done something hurtful and awful, as if she were an ogre who should be shot.

Well, Kelly thought desperately, I seem to be batting a thousand.

Everyone was furious with her.

CHAPTER EIGHT

THE GLOOMY SKIES WERE just starting to clear when Kelly walked out of church on Sunday. Maybe some sunshine would lift her mood, she thought, but parking in front of her new apartment, she had to shake her head.

This was so *not* how she'd planned to live at her age.

Unfortunately, beggars couldn't be choosers, and right now, she was sure as Sam Hill in the near-beggar class.

She tiptoed in the door, wary of waking her new roommate. Skip was a Notre Dame graduate student, an absolutely wonderful nerd who'd offered to float her the first month's rent until she got her life back together. Hopefully she wouldn't have to stay much longer than a couple months, but she'd left Jason's with little more than her clothes and a few personal things. Her life was requiring a total start-over.

In the meantime, she discovered that the new apartment hadn't changed since before she left. Even though the clock claimed noon, Skip was still asleep. The place was decorated like typical college digs—

early-computer. Crates. Formica slabs for desks. Three computers, blinking lights at all times. Cords, thousands of them, writhing like dusty snakes.

The place was unappealing, but Kelly figured it didn't matter; she'd go into work this afternoon. No one would be there on a weekend, so she could get ahead, catch up on some projects. Her office might only be a cubicle, but at least it was hers, with her colors and some light and some privacy.

And she'd leave her cell phone here, so no one could track her down for a few hours. God knew, her phone had been hot since she'd split up with Jason. Via the grapevine, she'd learned that Jason had disappeared to somewhere unknown. That was her fault, too, like everything else.

Jason's mother, and his whole extended family—which was considerable since he was mixed Irish and Polish—had called to lament her behavior, the change in plans, to pray she would "see reason." Even Father Donovan had gotten into the scolding act this morning before church, hustling over to offer her advice, thanks to her mother's tattling.

Three weeks ago, Kelly thought morosely, she'd taken her "darling" status for granted. Now she was under *S* for "shit list" in everyone's book. Her popularity was on par with a python's.

At least her new roommate was pretty tolerant of the incessant calls. In fact, the little squirt had a protective streak. Skip was about five-three, with wiry hair, no whiskers and little glasses that kept sliding down because he didn't have much of a nose. He ambled out of his bedroom in his boxer shorts, which made Kelly want to sigh. Skip just didn't have a strong sense of boundaries.

"G'morning," he said groggily.

"Morning. I just made fresh coffee. I'm headed into the office for a few hours."

"Kkk," he mumbled, which was likely his version of language for "okay." Skip didn't usually try to speak until he'd had three cups of caffeine.

She changed clothes, filled her travel mug and headed back out. The watery morning was fast disappearing, and suddenly there was a winsome, sassy-fresh smell in the air that reminded her of…well, it reminded her of Paris, but then everything reminded her of Will and Paris, and that made her heart feel like one huge aching bruise. She shut herself up in the car, put on some dark alternative music, and zoomed downtown.

For once, she had her choice of parking spots. She was relieved that there was no one to see her scrabby jeans and old tee. She'd scooped her hair back in a clip and rubbed on lip gloss only because her lips were dry; certainly there was no reason to fret her appearance.

The offices for Find Anyone, Inc. were on the fourth floor of one of South Bend's old buildings, which meant the elevator creaked and the air-conditioning worked sporadically. When Kelly searched her bag for her office key, she thought the creaks and gloomy corners would suit her mood, but inside, instead of silence, she heard the sound of laughter. The front desks were all empty, and there was no reason why Brenna or Myrna or Sam would be anywhere around.

The voice turned out to be Samantha, talking into the phone, and moments later, her boss showed up in the doorway of Kelly's cubicle. Sam, as always, looked ready for a party in Vegas. Her jeans had rhinestones down the sides, her hair was bleached within an inch of its life and her mascara was troweled on in more layers than an archaeological dig.

Kelly had never met a more brilliant human being, so she figured Samantha's look was about some kind of unresolved rebellion. The staff were hard-core number-lovers—alias the geeks of the universe—a tag that had never bothered Kelly. But Samantha's blatantly flashy style seemed to shout that no one should assume she was a dull-accountant type.

Samantha tapped a high-heeled boot from the doorway. "I just want to say one thing," she began.

"Yeah?"

"Please, please, don't solve this life mess you're in. If I can do anything to make it worse for you, let me know."

"Thanks so much," Kelly said wryly.

"This has been like a dream. My best employee, putting in spare hours on Saturday, Sunday, after-work hours, never complaining, just happy to be here, pouring on the coals." Samantha sighed lustily. "I'm so happy you're miserable, I can't tell you." She added, "If I could call your mother, roil things up even more for you—"

"That's okay. Thanks for the offer, but no."

"Shoot," Samantha said with feigned disappointment in her voice, and then disappeared before Kelly could even laugh.

Well, there was plenty of work, primarily because she'd taken on a double workload since coming home from Paris. It was the only thing keeping her sane. Her office was smaller than a closet, but the window looked out over the river. She'd put a bright print on the wall, an artistic splash of purples and blues. A dish of shiny purple stones sat next to her computer, and she had a foot-warming alpaca rug under the desk, because she always kicked off her shoes and worked in bare feet. Across from the desk was a monster-size picture of a cat, a ragamuffin, peeking over the side of a table.

That was her, Kelly had always figured. The kind of person who peeked out before she risked showing herself. Curious, nosy, but ever worried about unknown dangers out there. The field of forensic accounting was such a natural for her, because she loved diving into other people's business—both the people whose identities were stolen, and the people who'd choose to steal someone else's name and identity.

In the past two weeks, the issue was naturally especially ironic for her, because her own identity might as well have been stolen.

She sure as hell didn't have one of her own, anyway.

She scrabbled through the files on her desk, booted up the computer, got a good, messy, confusing monitor full of open screens going...and then the office phone rang.

"Find Anyone," she answered impatiently, and immediately recognized her mother's voice.

"Good grief, I've been trying to track you down all over the place. I need you to come over," her mother said. "Right now. As quickly as you can get here."

They hadn't had a civil conversation since Kelly had come from Paris, and her mother had refused to say anything about Kelly's father, yet she barreled straight into the *mess* Kelly was making with her life every time she called. From Kelly's viewpoint, her mom had temporarily turned into an incessant pain in the keester.

All of that would matter again, but not now, not if her mom actually needed her. Kelly's pulse went into immediate take-charge protective mode. "What's wrong? Are you ill? An accident? What happened?"

She was already shoving her feet back into shoes, scrounging around for her bag and keys.

"I'm not ill. No accident. But you *need* to get here as soon as you possibly can."

"I'll be there. Eleven minutes." It wasn't as if she didn't know how long it took to get to her mom's place from the office. Football weekends in the fall were different; then the drive could take hours. Of course, football weekends, she wouldn't have been at the office—she'd have part of the throngs at Notre Dame.

Now she passed the familiar golden dome of ND, and thought of nothing but Paris. Passed the familiar billboard for Maguire Industries, and thought of nothing but Will.

That, of course, wouldn't do. She put her foot to the pedal, and headed for the treelined street where her mom lived. She braked in front of the house, and then paused for a few seconds. Long enough to reapply her lipstick, whip off the clip in her hair and run a brush through it.

Vanity wasn't the issue. But her mother could tell at ten paces, blindfolded, if Kelly was tired or stressed. And if her mom was upset, Kelly wasn't about to add to it.

She grabbed her bag, charged out of the car and up the front-porch steps. The brick bungalow was snugged between two larger brick homes, but her mom had snazzed up the place with artsy landscaping and cool window treatments and carriage lights. Kelly was just reaching for the door when her mother answered it.

On a weekend, Kelly was rarely out of jeans. Her mother, by contrast, looked ready to host a dinner party, wearing so-called casual black slacks and a black-and-white this-old-thing cute sweater.

Expecting trouble, Kelly startled at the shrewd look in her mom's eyes.

"There's a crisis?" Kelly asked.

"Oh, yeah, there's a crisis. *Finally* I get it, Kelly Nicole."

Kelly heard the use of her double name, and smelled major trouble. "Get what?"

"What it's all about. What everything's all about. This whole mess you've got yourself into. There's a visitor in the kitchen."

"What is this? Are you speaking in code for some reason? Who's here? What are you talking about—"

"Just go into the kitchen," her mother said, in her marching voice.

Still frowning at her mother, Kelly tossed her bag and then moved.

She'd had a stepdad for about six years—George Matthews—and still saw him now and then. He'd been a good guy, the kind of stepfather a teenage girl dreamed of—willing to forget curfews, okay teenage sleepovers and endless noise, always up for a talk without ever preaching or fretting rules. When George split, Char had redone the entire house in peach and cream, as if to announce loudly, in her most feminine voice, that she was done with marriage.

Kelly loved the house. It was like walking into a

peach parfait. Past the peach tufty couches and peach
velvet draperies, the cream bookcases and alabaster
tables, was the turn into the kitchen. And nothing
could look more incongruous than the leather-
jacketed blond, with the linebacker shoulders and
whiskered chin, hunched on one of her mother's
fluffy peach cushioned kitchen chairs, staring outside
at her mother's peonies.

She whispered, "Will?"

Apparently her voice didn't initially register,
because he didn't look around. And then suddenly,
as if sensing her presence, he turned his head.

There it was. Just like that. Paris. The whole fantasy that couldn't be real…that sharp, strong glint in
his eyes. That you're-mine glint. The kind of glint no
independent woman could possibly find acceptable,
yet Kelly melted like ice cream in the tropics. No
man had ever looked at her the way Will did. No man
had ever invoked the heat between her thighs, the
yearning in her pulse, the way he did. No man ever
made her feel as if they were two people alone on
their own planet, didn't need anyone else but each
other. No man had made her feel…

Magic.

"I'm dreaming you, right?" she murmured.

"If so, we're having the same dream." His slow
grin notched up the sizzle another ten degrees.

"But how can you possibly be here?"

"I didn't know how else to find you, Kel. The cell-phone number you gave me was for the phone you lost in Paris. I tracked down your address. You didn't seem to be there anymore. I knocked next door, but the neighbor didn't know where you were living, and probably wouldn't have told me if he did know. So the only other lead I could follow was your mom, because you'd mentioned—"

"*Will.* I didn't mean how you found me literally. I meant…I thought you were never going to leave Paris. And now you're here."

She moved toward him at the same instant he moved toward her. Lightning couldn't have stopped their surge toward each other. Nothing could have stopped her from flying into his arms.

Except for her mother.

Char stepped between them as effectively as a slap. "Well now," she said briskly, "how about if I brew a fresh pot of coffee and we all sit down and have a little chat together?"

TALK ABOUT WALKING into a hornet's nest. Will couldn't remember a trickier, touchier situation— and in his family, there'd been a hundred.

It had only been an hour ago that he'd knocked on Kelly's mother's door. When the woman opened it, he'd had a strong, positive first impression. It was easy to see where Kelly got her natural good looks. Her mother didn't look old enough to have a fully adult daughter.

A single glimpse was enough to give a guy estrogen overload, but that was okay. He had three sisters. He knew how to handle females.

But five seconds later, the meeting had started skating downhill. She'd looked at him, and before he'd even introduced himself, her eyes narrowed and her back stiffened.

"You're the one, aren't you?"

"Pardon me?" he'd said.

"You have to be the reason. I knew it! I *knew* something had happened in Paris! So it was you."

Nothing like shooting a guy before he'd even had a trial. That initial warm, welcoming, very pretty smile turned colder than a witch's tit in a brass bra, as his grandfather used to say. Char had pulled him inside the house, all right, but only because she didn't want him to leave. She'd tracked down Kelly on speed dial, figuratively and literally.

Once Kelly had been located, she got here fast, but not fast enough to save him from a grilling.

He hadn't actually given anything away. It helped to be blood kin to his own relentlessly manipulative family—he knew all those tricks. The thing was, he was wary of telling Char anything until he knew for certain what Kelly had told her mother about him, about them, about Paris.

He didn't have to say much to realize that Kelly was in one heap of a mess.

He forgot all that when she showed up. He forgot

everything. Even her mother, who wasn't an easy person to forget. But it was all suddenly there.... The thick brown hair swishing around her cheeks. Her eyes, not just brown, but that brown with life and sensuality. The silky, soft mouth.

The way she looked at him. As if he really mattered. Him. Not just a guy or any guy. She looked at him as if he tipped her world in a different direction.

Maybe that reaction was silly and unrealistic and nothing a grown man should be believing, but that wasn't the point. The point was that she looked at him that way.

Rational or irrational, her gaze sent his masculine ego soaring into the stratosphere. Made him feel bigger than he was. Better than he was.

"Mom," Kelly said vaguely, looking at him, not her mother. "We're leaving."

"The coffee'll be done in two shakes," Char said.

"And thanks so much for making it. I'll call you later." She grabbed his hand in a way that made him want to grin.

Kelly was no Viking. But she was getting him out of there like a legendary Valkyrie of old. He wasn't afraid of her mom and coped just fine with the grilling, other than worrying that he could slip and somehow make Kelly's situation worse than it already was. But Kelly apparently thought he'd been enduring a real battering and was whisking him away.

She didn't speak until she got him outside on her mother's front porch with the door firmly closed.

"I don't exactly know how we're going to work the logistics of this, but I have a car. And obviously you had to get here by car, too," she began.

"Yeah."

"So I don't care which one we take, but we've got to move fast. I'm dying to know why you're here. What's happened with you. But Mom will drag us back inside if we're still here two seconds from now."

"Easy enough. We'll take both cars, so neither's left here. What's the address where you're living?"

A frown set in as he followed her. Maybe he hadn't been back to South Bend in a few years, but he still knew the area. Initially he was positive he must have misunderstood the address she gave him.

He hadn't.

The house she walked up to had a saggy roof, an unkempt community yard and trash whipping around the window.

She seemed to guess what he was thinking from his expression. "I only moved here temporarily. Very, very temporarily, I hope."

"Like that's an explanation? What's going on?"

"Oh, no. You don't get to ask questions until I do. You're the one who showed up out of the blue." She motioned. "Come on in, meet my roommate, Skip."

"Skip?" He bristled up when he heard a guy's name.

She unlocked the door and pushed it open. Faster

than a laser, Will's gaze snapped to the guy on the couch. A boy, yeah. Sitting in his shorts in front of a computer, hair unbrushed, feet bare. The general living room looked like a fallout zone—glasses and papers and silverware and shoes heaped all over the place.

"Skip, this is Will. Will, Skip."

"Hey," Skip said, and swung around to wave a hand.

Will got it. The bright eyes, the falling glasses, the three whiskers on his chin. The kid really was just a boy. But that still didn't explain why Kelly was living in such a dump, or why her mother had treated him like a hostile witness to an unknown crime.

Kelly detoured into the kitchen, emerged with two mugs of coffee and cocked her head for him to follow her down the hall.

The room where she led him revealed more information. It was shaped like an el. Boxes were tidily piled to the ceiling along one wall, all marked to identify the contents. The two tall windows were so clean the sun glared through. Her bed, a lumpy daybed, was too small but it was mounded with pillows and a deep red comforter that matched the rug on the floor.

The sitting area was just as beaten up as the rest of the house, but she had a couch, a chair; her computer equipment nested on a minidesk. A fake Tiffany lamp offered some soft light. And three unopened cans of paint stood at the door, receipt still taped on a lid.

In a glance, Will took it in, easily concluded she'd done a good job of making the ghastly place livable, at least for the short term. More than that, he saw the scarf. It was draped over the top of the bureau mirror. The blue-and-white silk scarf he'd gotten her that last day in Paris.

And on the scratched bureau top was a minitray, with the perfume.

When she saw him glancing there, she plunked down on the edge of the couch.

"Okay. I can tell you're not too impressed with my fancy digs. What can I say? This is what happens when you take off in the middle of the night with the clothes on your back and have to start over." She made a humorous motion. "Don't be feeling sorry for me. I'm not suffering. Nothing's long-term cata-strophic. I'd just bought a lot for the other apartment, and I didn't take any of it with me, so I'm just having a wee little temporary financial problem. I'm solvent. It's a no-sweat. It's just…I need to have some time to build up again."

"Why?" Not that he'd been waiting to pounce with that question, but he suddenly had too much energy to sit down. Jet lag had turned his brain to mush, but finally the obvious answer filtered through. "You left the fiancé, didn't you? That's why you're here. That's why your mom—"

She shook her head swiftly, wouldn't give him a chance to finish. "I'm not coming through with more story until you spill yours. The last I knew, you weren't coming home again. Especially not home to South Bend."

"Yeah, well, it's your fault I did."

"My fault?"

He loved the look on her face. Of course, growing up with sisters, he knew how to get a rise out of a female, but Kelly bit so easily.

At least for him. "I got a call from my father. My mom's sixtieth birthday is coming up. Family wants to do a big shindig, wants me to be part of it. It was his latest excuse to get me to come home."

"And?"

"And…you annoyed the hell out of me. Making out like I was hiding in Paris. Making out like I didn't have the character to solve my differences with him…instead of believing me, that there *is* no way in hell to solve our differences with each other."

"And?"

"And so I'm going to solve the damned problem, come hell or high water. I'll try one more confrontation. One more hash-out with the old man. It won't work. I figure the odds are somewhere around five million to one. But being part of my mom's sixtieth-birthday celebration is a good thing."

Hell. She gave him a look of such sympathy that he wanted to kick something. He'd wanted her to think it was no big deal, just something he was doing, not a life-altering problem. It had bugged him that she'd criticized him, as if he had total power over a solution, as if it didn't take two to make a mess. Damn, she'd made him feel like a weakling and a coward, both of which had hit big-time.

But now her look of compassion bugged him, too. Go figure.

"I know you won't believe this," she said gently, "but I really do know how you feel."

"About my dad?" She couldn't possibly. And somehow he couldn't sit still, had to move, stretch his legs, prowl around. He touched the Tiffany lamp, the edge of a sweater, checked out the window views.

"No, not about your dad. But...your life is just as much of a train wreck as mine is. Nothing's right. Nothing's easy right now." She sighed. "Everybody's mad at me. I swear I can't seem to do anything right, and I'm afraid it's going to be a big blue moon before I can see any light at the end of this particular tunnel."

He said slowly, carefully, "It was rough on you. Breaking up with him. You want to tell me about it?"

"Maybe. Not now. But I do want to tell you that he's a nice guy, Will, so don't be thinking otherwise. The screwup and breakup is on me, not him." She added quickly, hoping to change the subject, "How long will you stay?"

"Here, this minute? Or here, in South Bend?"

"Both."

He was willing to answer her, but his head was still back on the ex-fiancé. He couldn't help feeling high as a kite that she'd split up with the guy. But he also felt terrible because their making love in Paris had been the catalyst for all the difficult life changes she'd been making. Maybe he wasn't responsible for her being stuck living in this college-type dump, but it felt like his fault.

"Will?"

Yeah. She wanted him to answer the question. "Well, this is what's playing out so far. My parents know I'm home, but I haven't seen them yet. First, I had to get off the plane, see you, sleep off some jet leg and get my own place to stay so there can't be any argument about my staying with my folks. I've got three sisters. I know I told you that before. The oldest is Martha. We've always fought like cats and dogs, but she's got a studio apartment above her garage, so that's where I shoved my suitcase."

"That doesn't totally answer my question, handsome."

"Yeah, well. I don't know how long I'm staying. I can do some work for Yves while I'm here."

"Will."

"What?"

"Answer the question."

"God, you're a pain. I forgot how much. And how nosy." His teasing made her chuckle, but he couldn't seem to keep his mind on humor. All he could think about was her. How she looked under her jeans, under a bulky sweater. Under his hands.

He also couldn't stop being acutely aware that he hadn't kissed her yet. Or touched her. She had a hint of wariness in her eyes, which he could understand. His coming back created even more complications in her life, and right now, Kel had no way of knowing whether they were going to end up together.

Hell, neither did he.

He cleared his throat. "The truth is, Kel, I can't give you an absolute about how long I'll be staying. One way or another, I'm determined to come to some kind of terms with my father. I'm staying for however long it takes to do that right."

He wanted to add, *More than anything else, I'm staying for you.* He hadn't slept since she'd left Paris. He hadn't been able to stop thinking about her, stop remembering their time together.

But being with her now, those words weren't so easy to say even if they were part of the real truth. Because now he realized she'd come home and torn her whole life apart. The jerk wasn't right for her. Will didn't have to meet the fiancé to know he wasn't worth Kelly's little finger. This Jason guy hadn't been there for her when she'd been in trouble in Paris, hadn't been the one she'd called, hadn't been the one she'd asked for money until the paperwork all went through. She was well rid of him.

That's what Will told himself. What he'd believed before seducing her. What he still believed.

But there was a blot on his conscience. Just

maybe, if he hadn't entered her life, Kelly wouldn't be in this mess right now.

"Good grief," Kelly said suddenly, and started to laugh.

"What?" he demanded.

"I don't know…. It's just that your life sounds as complicated and awful as mine is right now. And I don't mean that's laughable! But it keeps striking me as ironic that we're in such a similar boat. And…well…this is just so *not* like Paris."

"You said it." He swiped a hand over his face. "Paris was…a dream."

"A fantasy," she murmured. "A few moments in time when the rest of the world seemed to disappear, and there was just the two of us."

"It was good," he said.

"Beyond good."

"But we both knew it wasn't real."

She nodded vigorously. "Absolutely. Neither of us had any crazy expectations."

"We both knew it couldn't last. That it was just a dream."

"Totally," she agreed.

And then he jumped her.

He hadn't intended to. He hadn't known he was going to do it ahead of time, even seconds ahead of time.

It just seemed as if he couldn't survive another

second without touching her. Being with her. Getting lost in her.

Her mouth melted under his, heated for his. Her arms roped around his waist, pressing closer to him, a soft, helpless sound vibrating in her throat at his touch.

How was he supposed to resist that?

"Will," she murmured. "Close the door."

He'd forgotten, that fast, that she had a roommate. That they were in this crazy rented room of hers. That there were other people in the universe.

He booted the door closed.

"Will," she murmured. "Don't let me go."

He hadn't forgotten, even for a millisecond, how those sexy orders from her did him in. "I won't."

"I mean it. Don't let me go. Even for a second. Or you're in big trouble."

More orders. Could it get any better than this?

But of course it could. Pulling the sweater over her head. Drawing the bra straps down her arms. Getting to bare skin, soft skin, real skin. Not a lot of swell over the bra cups, but more than enough to incite him to madness. It was his favorite part of her, that soft swell.

Or maybe her throat was his favorite part.

Or her navel. Once he had her pants shucked down—at least as far as her ankles, where she could shake the rest off—he remembered all those other body parts. Upper thighs. The thatch of springy hair—on the red side, redder than her head hair, anyway, which made him remember that that was a favorite part of her, too.

Aw, hell. He was in love with all of it. All of her.

Laughing, she bounced on the bed, encouraging him to dive in after her. Her low, throaty chuckle enticed him to more acrobatic feats. She practically forced him to kiss her deeper, harder, longer. Her long, slim legs scissored around his waist, her thigh muscles stronger than he would have believed, but hey, when she was in the mood, she wanted him inside her now. Now and deep.

The way he was raised, a gentleman took care of a lady. He did his best.

In fact, he did his zealously devoted, conscientious, meticulous, Boy Scout best to give her all the trouble she was asking for and more.

Aeons later, when he finally peeled off of her— dragging her on top of him, because he hadn't forgotten his orders to not allow any separation between them—he seemed to be panting like a worn-out hound…and smiling so hard he couldn't even wipe it off.

She felt…impossibly good.

He never wanted to let her go.

CHAPTER NINE

WILL FIGURED this moment had to register as the most perfect of all time. Kel felt like treasure in his arms. His stomach had started rumbling a while back. So had hers. He was hungry and jet-lagged and had a mountain of things he had to do yet today, but he still didn't want to move. Not while he had her right where he wanted her, cheek and arms and boobs and legs sprawled or snugged so she fit just right against him.

Of course, eventually the obvious came out of her mouth. "Will, this was wrong."

He didn't open his eyes. "Talk about déjà vu. I could have sworn we had this same conversation in Paris."

"No, we didn't. Well, I guess we did, but it wasn't exactly the same. In Paris, I already knew I wasn't going to marry Jason, that I couldn't. So it was wrong that I hadn't severed that relationship before sleeping with you. But it wasn't wrong to fall for you."

Thankfully he'd learned a lot since meeting her. He didn't try suggesting that was convoluted reasoning, for example. He simply said, "Damn right, it

wasn't," and then peeked under the sheet, because…
well, because looking at her naked body was stress
reducing.

When it came down to it, he could think of forty
reasons why looking at her naked body was a good
thing. And that was without even applying his mind
to the task.

Kelly seemed on a slightly different mental
street. "Generally, I really believe that a couple can
solve problems together. That they should solve
problems together."

"Damn right," he agreed.

"But right now I have problems you can't possibly solve. And you have problems that I can't
solve. They're not *our* problems. They're individual problems."

"Hey, that doesn't mean we can't still help each
other."

"And I'm for that," she agreed. "But I'm not for
adding more complications to the mix."

"Which means what?" Will already knew this
conversation was going in the wrong direction. He
just didn't know how bad it was going to be. And she
was stroking her fingertips on his chest, making it
impossible to concentrate.

"Which means," she said gently, "that if my
family realizes I'm sleeping with you, they're going
to think I broke up with Jason because of you. I don't
want them prejudiced against you, especially because

you'd be blamed for something that wasn't your fault. I need to face my own music there. I also have to figure out this housing thing, because I'll never survive living like a college kid for long. So I have to get this whole broken-engagement business off my table completely. And as for you…"

"Me? What?"

"You're in a parallel situation. I can listen to you, about your dad and your family. I can be with you, whenever you want me to. But you have to decide what you want to do about the situation. I don't even want to try to influence you. I want you to do whatever your heart tells you is right."

He heard all that. But he still hadn't heard the bottom line. "All of which means what? Somehow I sense this has to do with sex."

She leaned back so she could face him eye to eye. "That's just because you associate everything with sex. You're male."

"Yeah, so?"

"So, in this rare, rare case…you're right. About the nature of the problem. I think we should, um, refrain from sleeping together. Until we get our lives a little more under control."

"I think that's a lousy idea," he stated firmly.

"You want to get even more involved with me— if you end up deciding not to stay in the U.S.?"

He opened his mouth, closed it.

"See? We're just not in a good place to put hopes

or plans on the table. At least not yet. All sex could do is make our situations messier."

"Sex is good in all circumstances," he began.

She slugged him. "Look. I'm not for abstinence—"

"Neither am I. Ever." He wanted his vote on that to be crystal clear.

"—but I think a little stretch of it is necessary. Look, how long could it take for you to work through the problems with your family? For me to get my family to accept that my engagement to Jason is undeniably over? I mean…one way or another, these things are going to happen. They're just not problems that are fixable in a blink. But this couldn't take more than a few weeks to get straightened out, right?"

He frowned at her. "I don't know when you started doing all this thinking, but I want you to quit it, right now."

"Will, we can do things together. Talk together. Even go to things involving our families together. But I think we should be able to say, to anyone who asks, that the decisions we're making right now are not connected to each other. Otherwise you're going to get blamed for my mess with Jason."

"You think I'd care if anyone blamed me?"

"I'd care."

He wanted to offer an argument but couldn't. Because reality was exactly what she'd said. "I don't want to make anything worse for you," he said honestly.

"I made it what it is. You didn't. But the fact is, we've only known each other for a very short amount of time."

"Three weeks." Even when he said it, he couldn't believe it. How could he only have known her for three weeks?

"Exactly. Three weeks. Hardly a lifetime. Yet we fell right back in bed together as if we were…well, as if we were a couple. When there are still dozens and dozens of unsettled things between us. My life is here. Yours has been in Europe. I'm a practicing Catholic. You've got an allergy to religion. You come from money and you have money. I'm beyond broke. I'm into guilt, and that's not a small thing. I could wear you down over the long run. You could find me exhausting. Tedious. I'm trying to say…honest to Pete, Will, we really don't know enough about each other to be sure we've got anything long-term going on. We don't have to be in a rush."

"Kel…" He wanted to wash a hand over his face. And he would have if his palm hadn't been occupied keeping her right breast warm. "I'm afraid you're all mixed-up. It's the guy who's supposed to say, why be in a rush. I'm supposed to be the one who talks you out of using sucky words like 'commitment' and 'long-term' and all that."

"Will?"

"What?"

"You're in sex with me. And I'm definitely in sex

with you, too. But I'm not positive we've got the scary four-letter word going for the long run."

She didn't have to spell out the *love* word. But it miffed him that she didn't. "Maybe it isn't. But I think sex is damned important."

She grinned at him. A roguish, impish, archly feminine grin. "So do I. With you. And actually, that means that a little stretch of abstinence could be a lot of fun."

"No, it couldn't," he argued immediately. "Abstinence is never fun. And it could never be fun with you. Assuming it's even possible."

"Will."

"What now?"

"Get serious. You know I'm only saying what you're thinking."

He opened his mouth, but that was such a confounding thing for her to say that he couldn't think of a single response.

And then she bounced out of bed—out of his reach.

OKAY. He accepted it. Kelly was more trouble than a pack of puppies.

Will parked his rental car in the driveway, and mentally braced before climbing out. His parents' house was an architectural wonder—lots of glass, lots of redwood, a shake-shingle roof with a variety of pitches and angles. The layers of landscaping added to the impression of a home that had endless twists and surprises, no two rooms alike, no two views alike. The place was spectacular. Aaron liked to say, with pride, that he'd managed to build it for under three mil.

Will remembered a picture that used to be in his bedroom when he was growing up—a framed photograph of a wolf in sunlight. You couldn't see the barbed-wire fence, but the shadows of the wires showed on the wolf's face. The animal was trapped. It was in his eyes. And that was exactly how Will had always felt when he was around his old man.

He climbed the steps, thinking that was exactly why he couldn't get his mind off the discussion with Kelly. The woman was damned annoying—worse, when she was right.

The truth was, he *did* have five miles of trouble without adding more to his plate. Another annoying truth was that he couldn't very well offer Kelly a life together until he had a clue what his half of that life was going to be. So she was absolutely right. It was nuts to think about their future as a couple when neither of them even knew what country they were going to live in.

Damn woman.

At the top of the front steps, he rapped a couple times on the Chinese lacquered door, then turned the knob. "It's me!" he called out.

"Will!"

His three sisters all charged him at once, with their

mom letting the girls reach him first. He never could come home without being smothered in estrogen. Martha had already seen him, of course, since he was staying at her place, but not Laurie and Liz.

Liz, the youngest, had a new short haircut, very spiky, and was duded up with a bunch of gaudy baubles. Liz never saw a new style she didn't like. Laurie, the middle sister, was just the opposite—she'd worn her hair in the same sleek, smooth style since high school, had the same sapphire ring that was her only regular jewelry.

All three of them kissed and grabbed him the same way, though, jabbering at the same time, giving him more ardent smooches and hugs…until his mom's voice intervened.

"Oh, Will…you look so, so wonderful!"

Damn it. His mother crossed the room with tear-filled eyes. He swooped her up and spun her around—she never had weighed more than a half-pint. That made even more tears glisten in her eyes, but at least she started laughing, too.

"Oh, honey, you look so good," she whispered. "I've missed you so, so much."

Hell, he'd missed her, too. He'd forgotten her slight frame, the scent of Shalimar and the gold heart she always wore and that gentle, quiet voice of hers. She'd been there for him a hundred million times. It wasn't his mom's fault he'd taken off for France.

At the time, he'd thought an ocean wasn't enough

distance to put between him and Aaron, but that wasn't to say he'd ever wanted to desert his mom.

"Hey. Did you get a face-lift?" he asked her.

"Oh, you. Of course not."

"Are you sure? You look so young and gorgeous."

His mom's face flushed with pleasure. "I've missed your blarney, Will. Come on, though. I made all the things you like for dinner, but there's chilled shrimp first. And lemon-meringue pie for dessert. And ribs that have been simmering all day."

His sisters separated him from his mom and promptly grabbed both arms. "She thinks she's gonna spoil you, but I've got news, brother," Liz warned. "You're getting nothing—no food, no water, nothing—until we hear what's going on in your life. Is there a woman? What are you working at? Did you bring pictures? If you're going to stay over there, can I come visit you for a while?"

As the exuberant chatter continued—they didn't give him a chance to answer a single question before plying another—Will kept thinking that Kelly would have been okay with every part of this. If she'd been here, she'd not only do the estrogen fest, she'd have a blast with it. If she just saw his family like this, it'd be okay.

Then the far door slammed, and his father walked in.

Aaron Maguire had always been larger-than-life to Will.

The look was tall and strong, stern-faced and handsome. The posture reflected an iron will and the character to back it up. Aaron never gave up, never gave in and, on top of stubbornness, was smart and ambitious and would kill for his family. His employees always jumped when he walked into a room, but no one could claim they outworked him, because he never asked anyone to do something he wasn't willing to do himself. But then, he wasn't human, Will had always thought.

Aaron was beyond human.

That hadn't exactly changed, only Will suddenly shifted uneasily. When had his dad gotten those wrinkles? Lost the ruddiness in his face?

Aaron strode forward, clapped a hand on his shoulder, then yanked him close for a heavy hug. "Good," he said heartily. "Good, you came home for your mother."

He felt his mother and sisters fall quieter than midnight. He knew the women were worried there would be friction.

"Yeah, I did," Will agreed. "And it's really great to see everyone. I missed you all."

And that's how it went for a while—light and easy. He kept thinking how Kelly would see it all. She'd think he'd been stupid to hide out in Paris. Stupid to miss out on the family laughter, and the big dinner spread his mom put out, and his sisters driving him crazy with all their teasing and prying questions.

There was no household help on the weekends, never had been, so when the meal was over, he got up with his mom. It wasn't as if he liked dishes—who the hell liked dishes? But his sisters were happy to escape KP, so nobody interrupted them. He piled dishes into the dishwasher and watched as his mother wrapped up leftovers.

"You know that was the best dinner I had in four years, don't you?"

"In Paris? With all those French chefs?" She wiped down the counter. He started turning off lights. He knew how she liked her kitchen left, just the light over the stove as a night illumination. "Will...is there a girl?"

When it was just him and his mother, different things got said. "Yes. No guarantees it'll work out. But...yes."

"I can see it in your face. That there was someone serious. Someone you really care about."

Will nodded. "I do care."

"She lives here? Or in France?"

"Here, Mom."

He could see the relief in her smile. "Am I going to meet her?"

"Yes. Soon. I hope, anyway."

Happy with that answer, she didn't push, just sneaked right into the subject she wanted to talk about. "He's tired, Will. Tired of the ninety-hour workweeks. You can see he's having trouble, from the way he walks, the way he moves. He wants to act like the thirty-five-year-old bull he once was. But he can't run everything at his age."

"Has he been to a doctor?"

"Yes. But he won't tell me. I don't know the whole story. I know he's got the obvious—cholesterol, some arthritis. But the thing is, I want you to be gentle with him." It was the only thing his mother really lifted her chin about. She wanted him to be good to his father. "It's past time you two got along."

"That's the point, Mom. It takes two."

"No. It's going to take you to be the better man. I'm asking you to try—for his sake. It's not as if he doesn't love you, Will. You're half his soul. And it's not as if he was ever a bad father. Be a bigger man than he is," she whispered. "I know you're capable of it."

Okay, Will thought. The first pressure gun had been fired. It wasn't as if he hadn't expected it, and as long as his mom didn't cry again, he could handle it.

It was one example, though, of what Kelly didn't understand when she blithely told him to get his butt in gear and fix it all. She seemed to think he had miraculous powers. That he was some kind of hero who could change anything with enough character and strength and all that crap.

Then, of course, came the second round of pressure. He had only disappeared for two seconds to take a leak, but Laurie and Liz were waiting for him when he emerged from the upstairs bathroom. He sensed a trap.

"We both have to head home, but just wanted to catch a few minutes alone with you," Laurie said.

Laurie was always the ringleader, at least when Martha wasn't around. They herded him into his old room, which, naturally, his mom had long redone. But still there was the desk where he'd sat doing calc and physics…where Whiskey, their old Irish setter, had hung out at his feet…where a pile of football and sports and academic letters and trophies had hung on the far wall.

Liz caught him up on her life story. She'd graduated, finally, after six grisly years of trying to pin down a major and a potential career. "But now I know how much I love interior design. I want to move to Chicago, set up there. I mean, how much can I do in South Bend? I need a real city, a place where there's some serious action in my field."

Will mentally translated. She needed money for a car, for an apartment, a stake in a business or in a partnership. A high-end stake.

Laurie had a different tune. She was just a year younger than he was, and the two of them had been thick as thieves as kids. If Laurie got in trouble, Will had always been at her back. When he warred with their dad, she was always there to listen.

"I've got a guy," she said.

"A good one?"

"You'd like him. He's very nerdy. Smart. All A's all the way through high school and college."

Will could have smelled the "but" from five miles away with his nostrils clamped shut. "So what does he do?"

"He's an artist. But don't be thinking he's the lazy, starving-artist kind..."

Five minutes later, Will knew the guy was a loser. His sister would be supporting the jerk, if they got married, which was what Laurie wanted to do. "I haven't told Dad and Mom yet," she confided.

Naturally. Their dad would raise the roof over her marrying a lazy loafer, but after a bunch of protests, Aaron would come through with a big wedding, a house for a wedding present, and yeah, he'd set the guy up with his own studio or whatever. Because that's what his dad did. He coddled the girls.

On the surface, Aaron Maguire came across as the most generous man alive.

That's how Kelly would probably see him, too, Will thought morosely, as he made his way downstairs a few minutes later. Everybody thought Aaron was a god and a half—a generous, fabulous father, devoted to his family, hard worker, blah-blah-blah.

He found both of his parents in front of the theater screen, the volume on low, heated brandy snifters in front of them—and an extra poured for him.

His mom looked at him with hopeful eyes, then

excused herself to go to the bathroom. She didn't come back.

That's when he knew the big-pressure gun was already cocked in his direction. Aaron flicked off the TiVo and motioned for him to sit down.

Aw, hell, Will thought.

"I can't tell you how happy I am that you're home, son, how much we've missed you. Tell me what you've been doing. I want to hear everything."

It all sounded so good, Will thought. So nice. So fatherly. So loving. That's how Kelly would see it, too, he was positive. She'd take one look at Aaron and think he was a darling. Aaron would take to her like another daughter added to the fold.

Will hadn't been in the room with his dad three minutes before feeling strangled.

They made it five before voices were raised.

Seven before they were shouting at each other.

SUNDAY MORNING Kelly pulled into her driveway and spotted the lone figure sitting on her front porch step. She recognized Will in a second flat.

Her mood hopelessly, helplessly, lifted sky-high. But that didn't prevent her from immediately intuiting that something was wrong. Her first clue had been his failing to call for several days—not that that was a crime—but his showing up on a Sunday morning before ten without a check-in call first definitely indicated trouble.

The instant he heard her Saturn's engine, Will's head shot up and he was on his feet and striding toward her, giving a low, wicked whistle when he saw the legs, the swish of skirt and apricot top.

"You been out on an early date?" he demanded, with just enough jealousy in his tone to sound as if he meant it.

"You bet. By ten on Sunday, I've usually seduced a couple of guys and am ready for a break."

He knew she'd been at church.

"Did you see your dad?"

"Sure did."

"How'd it go?" She opened the door and immediately lowered her voice, knowing her roommate would still be sleeping. Will did the same.

"Went fine. No sweat." He averted his eyes. "So what's your agenda for the day?"

Apparently she was going to have company today. "My original plan was to paint my room. Even if I'm only very temporarily living here, I can't stand that dirty gray color even a day longer."

"You're not exactly dressed for painting," he noticed.

"By the time you pour me a mug of coffee in the kitchen, I will be."

Okay, so maybe it took a little longer to find her old paint shorts and Notre Dame tee, yank them on and clip up her hair. Still, she was a skilled hustler when she needed to be. Within twenty minutes they were hanging at the paint counter at Lowe's. At least, she was hanging. He was fidgeting, male style. That roll of his eyes communicated the intrepid male *are we going to be here all day?* look.

"I'm not being fussy," she insisted. "I'm trying to pick a color that'll work for the tenant after me. The landlord'll subtract the cost of the paint from my rent. So I don't want to screw it up by picking something really off."

"Hey. I don't object to painting. Good thing to do on a Sunday afternoon. But how about white?"

She laughed.

"What's so funny?"

"Men and white paint." She murmured, "I'm thinking cinnamon. With vanilla trim."

"That isn't paint. That's food. What's with the ex? Any more problems with Geronimo?"

"His name is Jason. And apparently he has left town. Decided to take a week's vacation without telling anyone."

"Then how'd *you* know?"

She sighed as she handed him the three gallons of paint to juggle on the way back to the car. "Because his mother called me. Then his sister. Then his brother. Then my mother. First, because they had no idea where he was, and then, after someone contacted his boss and found out about the vacation, they all had to call me again. They seemed to feel I'd want to know that I was responsible for Jason's being so depressed that he had to leave town."

"Hell. That doesn't sound like a depressed guy to me. It sounds like a coward, getting out of Dodge so you'd be stuck handling everything."

"Well, I can't fault him for that. Since I'm the one who broke it off, I don't see why he should have to deal with the aftermath. I just have to admit, this hasn't been a real fun week." She studied him when they climbed back in the car. Looked close and hard. Didn't kiss him, didn't touch him, just...looked.

"What? I have a bug on my nose?"

"No bug. It went that badly with your dad?" she asked gently.

"Hey, I told you. It went okay."

Yeah, right. Back at her place, they went back to whispering. Will hadn't come dressed to paint, obviously, but he kept saying his T-shirt and old jeans didn't matter. Within minutes, they'd pushed furniture and boxes to the middle of the floor and had laid down tarps.

She did the trim; he did the rolling—a division of labor that she considered sexist and unfair. His response to that was a major "duh," as if it would have been obvious to any man in the universe that guys didn't do trim. Still, clearly in an extreme effort to be accommodating, he offered to wrestle her for rights to the roller.

"You're going to be *such* hard work for any woman who thinks you're marriage material," she said disgustedly.

"Hey. You like me. Warts and all."

"I am able to tolerate you," she corrected him. Of course, that was a complete lie. Even worried about whatever he was hiding from her, her mood was singing high just from being with him. Even if they both were taking ridiculous care not to accidentally touch. And teasing helped. "Part of the reason I'm able to tolerate you is because you're capable of being a hero when a girl gets mugged. It makes up for your being a royal pain in the keester the rest of the time."

"Welllll…I'm not sure you should be giving me credit for being a hero. I mean, I don't do much unless there's a whole lot of incentive. Such as, say, outstanding sex."

He was dreaming if he thought she'd let him get away with that one. "We weren't talking about sex. We were talking about how things went with your dad."

"No, we weren't. But if you're determined to bring up fathers, what's the story with yours? Has there been any contact between you two since Paris? And have you confronted your mom?"

"Ouch. Neither of those are easy issues. I brought up the subject of my dad once to my mom. At the time, she was focused on the broken engagement, couldn't let that go. But now, she hasn't mentioned my dad again, and I can't seem to." Just trying to talk about this made her feel flustered inside. "Darn it, Will. I need to understand. I'm hurt that she lied to me—not just that she wasn't married but about never telling me I had a father who was alive. I want to know why she lied. I want to understand…"

"Hey. You're clear enough about what you want to say. Why is it so hard to get it out on the table?"

"I don't know." A drop of vanilla paint plopped onto her cheek. "I just can't start the conversation. I get too upset."

Somehow he'd moved across the room and found a wet rag to swipe the paint off her cheek. She tensed up in strong sexual awareness with Will that close, but he didn't pounce. He just rubbed at the paint spot. And forced her to endure a combustible amount of chemistry that she was determined to ignore.

And then, of course, he took his rag and his rascal smile and moved back to rolling paint.

After the job was finally done they moved outside, to wash out their brushes and the roller pan with the hose. It took forever to get the stuff clean, and the hose water was freezing cold. Once most of the paint was cleaned off, they moved back inside to do a major hand and face wash in the bathroom— together. Kelly couldn't help noting that both of them were still carefully not touching.

After the cleanup, they took five minutes to just stand in the doorway of the room and admire their handiwork.

"Well, it's not like anyone could turn this place into a spread for *House Beautiful,* but we do good work, don't we?" She really was in awe. It hadn't taken *that* long to paint the sucker—four hours or so? And it looked so much better. She'd been telling herself that she hadn't minded going from a nice apartment, filled with decent furniture and matching towels and her own colors, to living like a college student, but that was a lie. She'd been depressed up the wazoo.

Will said, "We still need to get rid of the tarps, get the bed moved back and all that. But I'm voting for a break first."

His theory was a predinner ice-cream cone. Kelly thought she was in no shape to be seen in public, but he looked adorable, with the streak of cinnamon-colored paint on his neck and another spot in his hair. Kissably adorable. Not that kissing him was on her mind.

Cotton-candy ice cream was. Her favorite flavor. And once he handed her a double-decker cone, he asked if she'd been in contact with her father since she'd left Paris.

"When he asked for that DNA test, he royally ticked me. But I went to a doctor, did a swab at a lab and had the results sent directly to my father's Paris address. Then I stewed." Her tongue swiped at the ice-cream cone. Man, it was good. "We had exchanged e-mail addresses the first time I met him. I thought that was interesting. I mean, obviously he didn't want mail or phone calls to come to the house from me. By giving me an e-mail address, I didn't know if he was trying to prevent direct contact or trying to keep a door open. Anyway…"

"You've been writing him?"

She nodded. "I don't know if I want a relationship with him—or vice versa. But I'll be damned if he gets to pretend that I don't exist, now that we both know about each other. And it still bugs me, that my half brothers believed I was after his money. So I started sending him a post every couple of days. Telling him things about my life, who I am. Not asking for a response."

"Has he responded?"

She shook her head. "The e-mails haven't come back, so I assume he got them. I mean, I realize he could have blocked me, or just deleted the e-mails without reading them, but there's nothing I can do about that. The only thing I have power over is keeping the door open. Even if he doesn't want to believe I exist, I still feel this…need. To know more about him, about that side of my family. Like, what were my grandparents like? Are there any family-related health issues? That's part of who I am. Who my kids will be, too." She almost got an ice-cream headache, she had devoured the cone so fast. But then she sighed. "The whole thing has had me in a muddle. Cripes. *I've* been a muddle since this all started—"

"All right, all right. We'll go shopping."

"Huh?" She blinked in surprise.

It was his turn to sigh, one of those heavy, testosterone-laden sighs. "You think I don't know when I'm being set up? It's okay. I get it. You've had a rotten time for weeks. And now you've ended up working like a dog on a Sunday, a day you should have spent relaxing. Obviously you need some kind of female pick-me-up. So where are we stuck going? The mall?"

His face said it all, that he considered shopping to be the ultimate sacrifice. "How about a movie instead?" she asked.

"A movie?"

The look of relief on his face almost made her burst out laughing. "When I'm stressed, I love to see a movie, any movie. Of course, we've still got paint on our clothes."

"Dried paint. And not that much."

It was hysterical, she thought, how willingly he'd do anything to get out of shopping. And even more interesting, how he'd just shown up and fit into her life all day as if he belonged there.

Her heart started aching. And the ache had intensified by the time she was sitting next to him in the dark theater, stealing his popcorn, shoulder-touching, knee-brushing, smile-sharing.

Desire, suppressed all day, appeared, ugly, annoying and refusing to disappear. She didn't want this yearning, this need to be with him. She told herself that she wouldn't mind so much if the whole thing were just about sex.

Sex was just sex, after all. Even when it was fantastic, fantabulous, fantilicious sex. Sex was only dangerous. It wasn't petrifying, like when doing ordinary things like painting a room and going to a movie felt impossibly right.

A bunch of blood and guts showed up on the movie screen. Kelly chewed on a nail. She wasn't going to start believing that the fantasy was real. This wasn't Paris. They were home now. Reality was reality. He was from a very, very rich background and had family problems beyond her ken. She was having identity issues of her own, not even counting how fractious her family relationships currently were.

So she ate his popcorn and she forced her mind off sex and she told herself, several zillion times, that the fantasy was over. When that didn't work—as they were walking out of the theater—she tried the one subject that should have been guaranteed to jam him up.

"So it went so bad with your dad that you can't even talk about it?"

She must have worn him down, because this time he didn't even try to duck. "It probably could have been worse, but I don't know how."

When he didn't come through with any details, she said, "Okay. I have an idea."

"What?"

"Ask me to dinner. With your parents. Pick a nice place, but more ordinary than ultrafancy. You know. Comfortable, with nothing about the atmosphere to add stress. They'll come because they'll be worried about what kind of girl you're seeing, so the heat will be on me instead of you. And it'll give me a chance to get a take on your dad. Maybe I could be of more help if I knew the players face-to-face."

"That's really a dumb idea," he said.

"Uh-huh." She thought again. "I can't tomorrow or Thursday. I'm clocking a ton of extra hours, trying to make some extra money. But Wednesday night would work well. Say six-thirty?"

They'd just stepped off the curb, crossing with the light, aiming for the parking lot across the street. People were milling all over the place, some exiting the theater, others going to dinner.

When Will grabbed her arm, her first assumption was that there was a problem—like she hadn't been paying attention and there was a car headed toward them.

She glanced around, yet there didn't seem to be any sudden cars in their way. And when she looked back at Will, his expression had turned sober…as if that first touch between them was all it had taken to create a conflagration within him. As it had for her, too.

His arms swooped around her.

Her arms wrapped around him.

His mouth claimed hers in a hot kiss that went on and on and on. She claimed his mouth right back, asking for more, needing more, demanding more.

Tension and tenderness swirled between them. She couldn't smell anything but him. Couldn't see anything but him. Couldn't feel anything but him. "Will," she said softly, full of longing. He answered with another wild, slow kiss.

A car honked.

Then another.

Then a semitruck—loud enough to wake the dead.

She pulled back from him, startled at the sudden appearance of other people, cars, trucks. They were in the middle of the road, for Pete's sake.

And this wasn't Paris.

CHAPTER TEN

WILL FIGURED this dinner with Kelly and his parents was going to be as much fun as, say, cuddling up to a hornet's nest. Suffering a flat tire in Alaska in the dead of winter. Having your wisdom teeth pulled.

He pulled into Kelly's driveway, then positioned the rearview mirror so he could fix his tie.

He hadn't worn a tie in years. He hadn't done *stress* in years. He'd been doing just fine in Paris, leading a devil-may-care life, strolling through each day, getting his Ph.D. in irresponsibility. Nothing had been wrong with his life. Nothing!

He scowled in the rearview mirror, found a cowlick in the back of his head, scowled at that, and was just slamming out of the car when Kelly showed up at the front door.

He stopped in midstride.

She looked damned adorable. Not remotely like her, but damned adorable. She was the textbook model for a Woman Meeting the Parents. She'd tamed the curls, pulled them all back somehow. The white top was sleeveless, natural for the balmy night, but the high neck was suitable for a nun. A navy skirt danced around her knees, not too short, nothing wild. The sandaled heels showed off bare legs, but weren't too high. Her toes and nails both had a soft pink polish that matched her lip gloss.

She was using the blue-and-white scarf he'd given her in Paris as a shawl.

Her face, apart from looking breathtakingly beautiful, had a scared expression on it.

As she headed for him and the car, she took in his own scared expression and laughed. "We're one heck of a pair."

"You have nothing to worry about. They'll love you."

"Yeah, right." She moved close and shook her head as she reached for his tie. She fumbled with it for several minutes, while he stood there, liking her hands on him, liking her near, recognizing her perfume as the scent he'd had made for her. He noticed that he was harder than a rock…and before dinner with his parents.

Finally she laughed and looped the tie from around his neck. "This is dumb. Why do you need a tie? It isn't you." She threw the tie into the backseat, tilted up long enough to brush his lips with a completely unsatisfactory kiss, then darted around the car to climb in the passenger side. "What'd you do to your hair?"

She reached over, pushed down the cowlick,

and when that didn't work, licked her hands and used the spit.

"I can't believe you did that," he said.

"I can't believe I did, either. Would you quit looking so nervous? This is going to go just fine."

Oh, yeah. *Just fine*, like her living in that dive because of him. Just fine, like her tearing up her whole life because he'd promised himself that sleeping with her wouldn't hurt anybody. And yeah, she had needed to shake the turkey, aka Jason, but that wasn't the point.

"You don't have to do this," he said for the dozenth time.

"A free meal? At Joseph's?" She named the ritzy restaurant that his mother had chosen. He smelled her scent again. It hovered around her neck, like a peek of cleavage or a flirting smile. She wasn't giving him flirting smiles or cleavage. It was just the perfume. "If you think I'd turn down a great dinner like this, you've got another think coming. But you have to relax, Will. You look like you're ready to climb the walls."

"I'm perfectly calm," he snapped. Guys weren't nervous. Guys were calm in a crisis. Guys took charge. Guys were tough.

When they walked into the restaurant, the tuxedoed maître d' hustled forward to take care of them. Will tensed all over again. He and Kel were early, but he should have guessed his father would arrive even earlier. Aaron, being a classic control freak, liked to study the stage, maneuver where everyone would sit, get all the details set up the way he wanted them.

His father stood when he saw them approaching. Kelly's face lit up as if she recognized her new best friends. "I couldn't wait to meet you two," she said warmly.

She reached out and hugged Aaron, as if she'd been hugging him all his life, then bent down to hug his mom, who was dressed—how did women *do* that?—in navy and white just like Kel.

She turned back to Will and said, "I'm in love. You told me I'd like them, so I should have guessed I would on sight."

He'd never heard such bullshit. He'd never said anything of the kind. But Aaron was beaming—of course. His father had always been putty in the hands of a female.

Whatever seating Aaron had planned, Kelly chose the chair between Will and his father. Drink orders were taken. Kelly said she was having whatever his mom was having but, on discovering that was a martini, blushed like a bride and said maybe she'd better stick with wine.

"So how did you two meet?" Barbara asked.

Will braced. The grilling had begun. But Kelly seemed primed for it.

"Will saved me. I'd just gotten into Paris, hadn't even recovered from jet lag, when this mugger grabbed me. He took my purse, every valuable thing I had, scared the wits out of me. Will could have walked on by, but thank heavens he stepped in. I had no passport, no money, no way to even call home, and I was scared...."

Aaron shot him the first look of approval that Will had seen in, well, somewhere in the vicinity of twenty-five years.

"Where do you work, dear? Do you live with your family?"

Kelly named her firm. "I'm a forensic accountant. I love it. Some days I think somebody created the job just for me. And no, I don't live with my mom, although we're really close—and I never knew my dad. For a while, I had a stepdad, a really super guy, but most of the time when I was growing up, there was just my mom and me. I moved out on my own after school. It seemed time for my mom to have her own life, without feeling she had to take care of someone else all the time."

Will caught his father and mother sharing a half dozen glances. They approved. In fact, by the time their meals were served, Will wondered if he could just put his chin in a palm and nap. He'd known Kelly was sneaky before this, of course, but he'd never dreamed her skill level was this high. Somehow everything she said made his parents believe she was God's gift to their son's life.

Actually, she *was* God's gift to his life. He'd just

never seen that sneaky streak of hers show up in his favor before.

Somewhere between the after-dinner brandy and the French pastry choice of desserts, his mom laughed softly, and charmingly went straight for the throat. "So…are you and Will serious?"

"Now, honey, you've been hounding the girl with questions all through dinner. Let her be," Aaron said, shooting Kelly an I'll-help-you-out-here-darling expression.

"It's all right. I don't mind answering anything," Kelly said disarmingly. "The truth is, Will and I have only known each other for a short time. Neither of us wants to rush into anything impulsively. He flew home especially for your birthday, Mrs. Maguire, not for me. But yes, we've been seeing each other. And even though that's going great, there's nothing to guess at yet."

"I love how you handle yourself, dear," Barbara said warmly.

"I'm a big believer in honesty," Kelly said as she slid her bare toe up his pant leg under the table. It was an acrobatically challenging thing to do when she was sitting next to him. Normally he wouldn't have thought her toes could bend at that angle. "Really, though, I'd much rather hear more about *your* family. And your business, Mr. Maguire. Everyone knows about Maguire's in South Bend, but I have no idea how your family got into it, how it all happened, if you are from here generations back and all…."

That was it. His dad was happily occupied for dessert, coffee and two brandies, while Kelly sat, looking rapt and enthralled.

His mom didn't want to leave. His dad didn't want to leave. Kelly didn't seem to want to leave.

"Well," Will said heartily, "I'm afraid it's past ten, and an early workday tomorrow for Kelly—"

"Oh, that's all right, Will. I'm having a great time." But Kelly suddenly shot a charmingly stricken look at his parents. "Although I know how long we've been sitting here. If I'm monopolizing your evening—"

"You have to be kidding, honey," Aaron said warmly.

Past eleven, the three of them were still merrily chatting and laughing and sharing stories in the parking lot. Will had had his keys out for ten minutes, Aaron for about the same time. Starlight sparkled in Kelly's hair, on her animated smile when she hugged his mom, his dad.

Everybody had a hugfest.

Aaron hugged him, as well, and vice versa. Will knew damn well the other night's harsh words had not been forgotten, but he'd been raised a certain way. No personal problems showed up in public. The Maguires were a united family.

By the time he climbed into the car and turned the key, he was more wiped out than if he'd climbed Everest *and* K2. Five straight hours of racquetball couldn't be this tiring.

Kelly nestled in, and although she pulled on her

seat belt, she managed to curl in the seat with her legs drawn up like a tired puppy's. The brilliantly happy smile she'd had all evening suddenly disappeared in a long, lazy sigh.

"Okay," she said, "I've got a better picture of the whole situation now."

"Huh?" She went from the dazzling, sweet, shy, guileless charmer of a new girlfriend to businesslike in two seconds flat. Except for the curled-up legs. That was pure Kel. "They loved you. Not that that's a surprise."

"They didn't love *me*. They'd have adored any woman you brought home. They'd have groveled at my feet, even if I showed up in a rhinestone cowboy hat and hooker heels and had kin in jail."

"Say what?" He couldn't imagine where she was getting this.

"Will. If you fall in love with someone from *here,* they think you'll be motivated to stay in South Bend. They'd do cartwheels and handsprings, anything, everything, to get you to stay."

Okay. He got that. "They still loved you."

"I liked them, too."

"You didn't see my dad's manipulative side, though. Don't be thinking all the arguing is my fault." When she didn't immediately respond, he glanced at her. "What?"

"I was just thinking…"

"Why does your 'just thinking' strike terror in my heart?"

She grinned, but the humor faded quickly. "Do you know why it's tough for you to communicate with your dad?" She answered her own question before he could have a chance. "You're so much alike."

"Not in this universe."

"You're both ambitious, driven. Both very bright. Both the kind of man who has to work for himself, because neither of you could take orders from anyone else. You both take terrific care of those around you but don't let others take care of you. You've both got a charming, public side. You both treat women and men differently. You're Galahads with women, but with men in business, I'm guessing you're both cutthroat."

"This is all fascinating. You got all that from one filet mignon and two brandies?" He added, "I'm not remotely driven. I could sit around and do nothing forever and be perfectly happy. Quit it," he said sharply.

But she didn't. She started laughing and wouldn't stop. Worse, it was damn clear that she was laughing at him. "Will," she gasped, "you're a born business tiger. I'm sorry you don't realize it, but c'mon. Get a grip. Anything you do, you put out five hundred percent."

"I do not!" Where did she get this crap?

"It's really no wonder your dad wants to turn over the business to you. And yes, of course, I can see why that's a problem for you. Hard to imagine how you could work for your dad. It'd be like putting two tigers in the same cage. A major uh-uh. But the thing is...he knows how good you are. He knows that you could run a business, any business, and be fabulous at it. So it's totally natural that he wants you to follow in his footsteps. You're a natural—"

"The one thing in the entire universe I don't want to do—the *only* thing—is run his business. Much less be manipulated or tricked into doing it. I won't," he said.

She didn't hear a word he said. In fact, she was still laughing when they got to her place. And yeah, of course he walked her to the door and stood there until she was safely inside, but for the first time since knowing her, he didn't kiss her. Or even want to.

When she closed the door, he sighed and told himself it was a relief—to be so damned mad he didn't want to jump her.

She'd gotten everything wrong, misunderstood everything. For some stupid reason—even though he'd never wanted or allowed sympathy from anyone in his life—he'd just wanted a little taste of it from her. Some compassion. Some empathy. He'd really believed she'd listened to what he tried to tell her.

Instead she'd waltzed right in, schmoozed his parents, and now seemed to think she had answers to everything. One dinner. Hell. He not only didn't want to jump her, he didn't even *like* her at that moment.

Her front door flew open again before he'd even reached the car. She charged toward him in bare feet though the sidewalk was midnight-cold.

"I forgot to thank you for the great dinner," she said.

He wanted to roll his eyes—you'd think they were still kids in high school who had to dot those *i*'s. He wasn't about to let loose that she'd hurt him. Or made him madder than a kicked porcupine. She lifted up on her bare toes and smooshed her lips against his.

It was less than a kiss. It was more a two-second lip-smash. The contact was barely enough to feel her breasts crush against his chest, her blue-and-white scarf flutter around his neck in the midnight breeze. Barely enough to feel the brush of her fingertips on his neck, see the tea-brown shine in her eyes, feel the satin of her mouth.

And then she severed the connection and went back down on her heels. "Don't be mad," she whispered.

"I am not mad."

"They're good family, Will. You don't throw good family away. I mean, it's not as if they're drug addicts or abusers or alcoholics or terrible people—"

"Kelly. Maybe we could talk about this five years from now on a Tuesday when we're on different continents. But right now—"

"I know. You're mad as hell at me." She patted his cheek, had the bloody nerve to smile at him, and then turned on her heel. "I'm freezing! I have to go in!"

"So go in!" And don't come back out this time, he thought darkly. Yet he stood there, long after she'd gone in the second time, long after he heard the door lock.

He didn't want to go home. He just wanted to

stand outside her damned door in that damned decrepit neighborhood and pine for her.

He was turning into a lovesick goose. A complete
fool. A mindless idiot who was so stupid he wanted
to be around a woman who made him crazy and didn't
even stand by him. She'd taken the enemy's side
instead of his. She'd backed them up instead of him.

He was not only going to stop loving her.

He was going to leave a good long space before
he saw her again.

SINCE WILL COULDN'T sleep, he quit trying around
three in the morning, made some black-as-mud instant
coffee and installed himself at his sister's prissy provincial desk with a phone. Maybe the U.S. was asleep,
but it was working hours in France. He called Yves,
who expressed surprise at hearing from him.

"I thought you were on holiday," Yves said. "Busy
with family."

"I am, I am. But I had a few minutes with nothing
to do." And Yves was helpless at certain things, Will
knew. Like marketing. Costing out a new project
and tax implications. International freight proce-
dures and laws.

Nothing complicated, but Will knew details like
that gave Yves anxiety attacks, and that was the point.
He could talk Yves through those issues, sipping
coffee with his feet up, playing Spider Solitaire on
his laptop at the same time.

"How will I do all this if you don't come back?" Yves fretted.

"I told you I was coming back."

"I know what you said. But I always knew you wouldn't stay with me forever."

That was so French thinking. Yves was always the pessimist, not exactly a handwringer but always braced for bad news. After that hour-long phone call, Will finally managed to close his eyes and crash… but it seemed like only minutes later that he heard noisy pounding on the door.

The pounding stopped, but only because Martha barreled inside as if she owned the place. Which, come to think of it, she did. And being the disgusting, exasperating sister she was, she seemed to feel she had every right to pull the covers off him and tickle his feet.

"I wouldn't have to go to these lengths, you cretin, if you'd just answer your phone."

"I didn't hear the phone."

"That's the point. You were sleeping like the dead. I made a big breakfast, but it's not going to be hot if you don't come over this minute. Besides which, I can't leave Ralphie. So get your butt up!"

She slammed the door closed before he could answer. In fact, before he could take the pillow off his head and face the daylight. The apartment over the garage looked the same as it had yesterday, displaying Martha's latest decorating scheme—which happened to be purple and yellow and French provincial furniture. Every time he looked at the mustard yellow, he thought he had to get out of there. Soon.

But then he'd woken up grumbly, partly because he'd only had a few minutes' sleep. Mostly because he'd argued with Kelly in every damn dream.

He took his pitchy mood across the flagstone walk to his sister's kitchen. Martha, typically, looked ready to run the universe. Her hair, fresh out of the shower, had the artful messy look that probably cost her three hundred a month at a hairdresser. Her makeup was perfect, her white shirt had a collar turned up just so and her kitchen was blindingly clean—from the Sub-Zero freezer to the range big enough to feed forty-seven for lunch.

Martha's counters had never seen dirt. Will wasn't sure how she did it, but nothing ever stuck to her pans. Nothing ever spilled in her oven. Even his youngest nephew, Ralph, sitting in his booster chair with his cheeks stuffed with breakfast, had tidily tied shoes and an unstained junior-sized Ralph Lauren polo.

Martha's scene boggled Will's mind. More to the point, it scared him. She was a very scary sister, even when she charged over and gave him a loving peck before pointing the royal finger at where he was supposed to sit.

"All right, I admit I'm sorry I woke you up, but I just couldn't wait another minute. How'd the dinner go? Who's the girl? How serious is it? Were you decent to Dad? Did Mom like her? What'd she wear? What does she do? What did you all talk about?"

"Man, the price of breakfast is sure high these days."

"Shut up and talk," Martha said as she served him coffee, and then a plateful of...well, hell, he didn't know what it was.

Avocados? Papaya? Some kind of gourmet muffin that looked like a mix of tofu and grass? A few weeds? He looked at the weeds with some interest, but they definitely weren't *that* kind of weed. Not with his sister. "Ralphie gets Cheerios. How come I can't have some of those?"

"Because you're my brother and I'm the boss of you."

"Does that mean you're not the boss of your own son?"

Martha plopped next to her toddler and folded her arms. "You start talking or I'll make you sorry you were ever born. You just remember—I beat you up when we were kids, and I could still take you on."

"The only reason you ever beat me was because of the rules that I couldn't hit a girl."

"I won. That's the point. Not what the rules were. Now talk."

He'd have done anything for the coffee. To find out the real reason she'd yanked him over here, though, he realized he had to make a dent in the petrifying meal and come through with some gossip. The latter wasn't hard. He'd been handling his oldest sister from the day he came out of the womb. "Went to Mom's favorite restaurant. Had the filets. Just as good as always. Dad and Mom were great to her. Her name is Kelly. Dad was fine. No, we didn't fight. No, no one fought. They loved her. And no, sorry, nothing embarrassing happened."

Martha recovered from this utterly boring account and moved on, thankfully, to her real agenda. Ralphie let out a squawk when he'd stuffed in enough Cheerios. She wiped his face, let him loose, then sighed when he hit the floor running. "He'll be filthy in five minutes flat. And he's got a playdate at nine."

"A playdate? Does that mean he's authorized to play doctor with someone of the opposite sex already?"

But she couldn't be diverted from the next sneaky line item on her agenda. "You know I've got the Sabre in Lake Michigan. A really nice slip in St. Joe, on Harbor Isle. It's not that far a drive, if you'd like to take her out for a sail while you're here."

His eyes narrowed. "Why are you being nice to me?"

"Because you're my favorite brother."

"I'm your only brother."

"I love you."

Will swiped a hand over his face. "Okay, I can't take much more of this sweet talk. Just spill it out. What do you want?"

"Nothing." She poured him a fresh mug of coffee—French vanilla, one of his favorites, which was the kind of thing Martha specialized in knowing. "But…Will…I was thinking…"

"Uh-huh." The way only an idiot walked into a dark alley at night, Will knew anything his sister said from here on out was dangerous. Afraid to take his eyes off her, when he felt the tug on his leg, he automatically pulled Ralphie onto his lap.

"If you happened to take the boat out, I was thinking you might not mind looking at a little cottage for me. It's right on the lake. There's a dock there, so you could pull up and see it. The cottage isn't fancy or anything, but while Ralph and Daphne are still young, I was thinking how great it'd be to have a place on the lake. Where the kids could swim and learn to sail in the summer, and the family could all come for picnics."

Both his other sisters could do it. Add two and two and end up with fifteen. More interesting, they never thought anyone would notice. Hypocrite that he was, Will kept sipping her coffee because, damn, it was good coffee. But he was wondering what Kelly would think of his sister, what she'd say, how she'd handle the whole conversation.

Will could have known where this was going in his sleep.

Martha's husband made a decent living as a mid-level manager. Nothing wrong with Bob—he was a good guy all the way—but he didn't make enough to pay for the castle on the ravine, the garage with the apartment overhead, the beauty of a Sabre sailboat, the vacation overseas every year. Martha had never worked. She was a good mom, devoted to a bunch of seriously good causes, as well.

If she wanted a cottage, it wasn't going to come out of her husband's salary. It was going to come out of their dad.

"So," he said, "you want me to see this cottage and then talk Dad into buying it for you."

"Of course not. I can talk to Dad on my own. I'd never ask you to do that. You two are oil and water, besides. But it'd help if you thought it was a good idea. Because even when you and Dad are fighting, he listens to you."

That was so ridiculous that Will almost burst out laughing. Only he suddenly couldn't seem to hear his sister. Suddenly couldn't seem to feel Ralphie yanking on his ear with sticky fingers. Suddenly couldn't focus on anything in Martha's pristine kitchen.

Nothing had gone well since he'd come back, and making lemonade out of all these lemons was going to be nonstop challenging if not downright impossible. His father wasn't going to bend. His sisters were already playing him, his mom applying emotional thumbscrews, the whole shebang thorny and unfixable, just like always.

Yet it suddenly filled his head that he didn't want to return to Paris. Because even if he had no faith that anything at home could get better, Paris hadn't been the same once Kelly left. Paris was no good alone anymore.

He wanted Kelly in Paris.

Kelly in *his* Paris.

"Earth to Will, earth to Will," Martha scolded.

"I heard you." He took his empty mug to the sink. "Okay."

"Okay what?"

"Okay, I'll take the sailboat out."

"And you'll look at the property?"

"Martha, Martha, Martha…" Swinging Ralphie high in his arms, he rose from the chair and gave his sister a smooch. "You know I'm putty in your hands. I'd do anything you asked me to do."

Martha gave him a suspicious look. They had, after all, been related all their lives. He'd been the one to squish shaving cream in her training bra and freeze it. His sister knew that he wasn't altogether trustable.

But that was about sisters.

Not about Kelly. Kelly could trust him with anything, including her life. His mind was already spinning possibilities. All of them about Paris and Kelly, and choices that had never occurred to him before.

CHAPTER ELEVEN

KELLY DECIDED that her office was starting to resemble a cave. The door was still visible, but the windows were now blocked with case boxes and texts; her desk was heaped high, and files had started wandering around, to the floor, to the chairs, to the windowsills.

The chaos was unavoidable. It happened every time she neared the end of a case. Like now.

Peripherally she was aware that Samantha had shown up in the doorway, but some things mattered more than bosses. Will, for example. One reason she was working herself into a frenzy was because it put relationship worries on the emotional back burner, at least for a few hours.

The current case was about a woman named Penelope. From the instant Kelly uncovered the name, she had a mental picture of highlighted hair and upper-crust bones. Somehow Penelope had copped a dozen or more credit cards. From the stolen cards, she'd ferreted out social security numbers, birthdays and all the other personal ID info that enabled Ms. Penelope to rob a half dozen innocent people.

Kelly's love of snooping had practically reached orgasmic proportions on this one. The credit card companies had all been contacted by the various people whose identity Ms. Penelope had stolen. So had the police. But everyone else had been stymied in the quest to identify the culprit…except for Kelly. Who hadn't yet found her, but man, she was sure on the cusp.

Ms. Penelope only purchased certain items with the cards. She didn't pay rent or make car payments. She bought Coach handbags, Versace clothes, Mackie tops, Wacoal underwear. She made a lot of long-distance calls to Los Angeles. She'd paid for a visit to a plastic surgeon in Minnesota.

Ergo, Kelly figured she was a hotshot wannabe, probably an unemployed actress with some youth and looks, willing to do anything to get what she wanted. Kelly had pinned down the first name for sure. The woman moved around, so finding her wasn't going to be a matter of pinning down a base address, but where she was trying to function, en route to Hollywood.…

"Kelly." Samantha let out such an exasperated shout that Kelly finally looked up.

"I'm sorry, what?"

"I've been trying to get your attention for at least four minutes!"

"I'm sorry, I'm sorry." Well, she wasn't. Not only was she close to solving this particular identity-theft problem, but coming back to earth meant coming back to reality. Family messes. Life messes. Will, who hadn't called since the dinner with his parents, and who she knew darn well was mighty ticked at her.

She also knew why. Will wanted her to take his side. Instead, she'd felt compelled to tell him that he was being bullheaded. Of course, she shouldn't have been that honest with him. What man ever wanted to hear the truth?

Samantha stepped in, giving her another exasperated look, as if her boss was well aware she'd mentally wandered off again. "Two things. This—" she put an envelope on Kelly's desk "—is a bonus. I can't give you a raise right now, not until your review in August. But you've poured on the coals so thoroughly that I had to express my gratitude."

"Thanks." Kelly didn't mean to rip open the envelope like a kid with a candy bar, but her fondness for living in student rental housing—even after the paint job—was paper-thin. She was saving money now, but she wasn't about to start looking for new digs until she'd scared up a seriously heavy down payment. Anything extra was more than welcomed.

Her jaw dropped, though, when she saw the amount printed on the check. Yeah, she'd done an outstanding job in the past few weeks. But after all, it was her job. And maybe she'd saved credit card companies considerable money. But that was her job, as well. "Wow," she said honestly. "Thanks so much. What a surprise—and I really appreciate it."

"I just want you happy, Kelly. I don't want you looking for another job."

"You know I love the work."

"Yes, I do. But I also know you're working too many hours. I don't want you burning out."

"I won't. I won't."

Her boss lingered one more minute. "The second thing I wanted to tell you—just as I was going through the lobby, a man was walking in to see you. I told Brenna I'd let you know so she wouldn't have to page you."

"Thanks!" Kelly popped out of her chair thinking it was Will. No, she wasn't expecting him. And no, she couldn't imagine a reason on the planet why he'd stop by her place of work in the middle of the afternoon, but it wasn't as if clients normally showed up out of the blue, either, so it *could* be him.

Even if her thinking was illogical, her heart was still soaring before she'd reached the door, then she ran back to the desk, opened the middle drawer, brushed her hair and smacked on coral lip cream. Her tan slacks and salmon shirt were hardly femme fatale attire, but en route to the lobby, she undid an extra button at the throat and put some sauce in her step.

Her enthusiasm was squashed when she saw the man in the lobby—the guy facing the windows, jingling change in his pocket. The one with the dusty-brown hair and skinny shoulders and handsome features. Familiar, handsome features.

Jason spun around as if sensing her presence. His expression was hungry and raw even if his posture was protectively stiff. "I've been out of town. Just got back."

"I heard you were gone."

He nodded. "I went on the honeymoon we were supposed to take together." He barely paused. "All I could think of was speeding from the airport, getting here, seeing you. I've got something I have to say."

Kelly thought she knew every flavor of guilt, but this taste was acid all the way down. She herded him into her office, aware of faces and eyes drawn to doorways. They all knew Jason, all knew of her wedding plans, her broken engagement. And seeing him again made her heart clutch. His dear face was as familiar as peanut butter.

She did still love him, the way she loved cocoa in winter and peppermint ice cream and snuggly slippers. It was a real enough love, even an important love. But there was none of the excitement she felt with Will, none of the fierce loneliness when she wasn't with Will, none of the singing joy of life or the lusty pizzazz.

She couldn't treat Jason as an enemy, because he wasn't. But she wanted this conversation with him like a hole in the head, and he started in the instant she closed her office door.

"Kelly…on this vacation, I drank. Swam. Took a lot of time to think. I think you're making a mistake. I think we both are. I want you to give us another try."

She started shaking her head, but he wasn't about to let her answer. Not yet. He jammed his hands in his pockets and slowly stalked around her bitsy office like a wounded cat. "I don't care what you said. I know there was a guy. There just *had* to be a guy, because nothing else makes sense. So let's get that out in the open. I don't care. I mean, of course I care. But I still love you. I still think we can make a damn good marriage. Lots of people have flings before the wedding. Weddings make people panic. When people panic, they do crazy things. So maybe that's wrong and not smart, but it's still one of the mistakes people make."

She tried to interrupt him again, but he'd obviously prepared this whole speech, and he was already gulping for air between sentences. Her work phone rang. Then the song on her cell phone started playing. Her coworker two offices down—Myrna, the one getting the testy divorce—pushed open her door and started to ask a question, saw her with Jason, backed right out again.

And Jason kept talking. "We've known each other our whole lives. I *know* you love me. I love you. Maybe we forgot some of the romance because we knew each other so well. But both of us could take a fresh shot. We're invested in each other, Kelly. We have shared family, shared friends, a shared history. It's just plain crazy to throw that all away."

He'd been talking so steadily that she wasn't expecting him to suddenly move toward her, clearly intending to pull her into an embrace. She froze like a scared rabbit. "Jason," she said, "I'll care about you forever. I'll always love you. But not the way—"

She smelled the familiar scent of him, the familiar feel of his hands on her shoulders, the familiar way he approached a kiss and her stomach rolled. His lips came down, yet thankfully within seconds, he stopped, jolted upright.

He met her eyes. He looked sick. She felt sick, too, but there was no way to pretend a feeling that didn't exist.

"You can't even try?" he asked thickly.

"It doesn't take *trying* to care about you, Jason. But it's not there—the kind of love you want. My heart can't make it happen."

"That doesn't make sense. What the hell is the right kind of love, the wrong kind of love? Love is love. It changes over the years, anyway. So we hit a lull. So what? It doesn't mean we won't care for each other ten years from now. Or twenty."

Her office phone started ringing again. Another coworker, George, poked his head in and backed out faster than a fire.

Kelly sucked in air, thinking this was about as much fun as a case of leprosy. Slowly, carefully, she said, "We're not getting married, Jason. I hate hurting you. I'm terribly sorry. But I am one hundred percent positive that it isn't going to happen."

He put up his hands in an exasperated gesture of giving in, and finally started shuffling toward the door. "It's your mother's birthday party next week. I assume the neighborhood will put on a big block party, same as always. So if you think we won't be talking again, trust me, we will. But I can see there's no point in trying to get through to you anymore today."

Talk about a way to put a girl in a funk. Kelly couldn't reclaim her workaholic mood after that, couldn't get anything done. She grouched around her office until she finally gave up. Outside, it had turned hot and humid; South Bend traffic was as snarled and grouchy as she was, and once she deposited the bonus in the bank, she holed up at home.

Her room had no air-conditioning, so she stripped down to shorts and a tee, slapped together a peanut-butter sandwich and then sat at her laptop to pound out an e-mail to her father.

It was a waste of time, she knew. Her father didn't care, and pretending otherwise was getting a little ridiculous. But sometimes, Kelly figured, a woman was entitled to beat her head against a wall if she wanted to, and right then, she was definitely in that type of mood, which possibly affected the tone of her e-mail.

Hi, Dad. You haven't responded to any of my other e-mails and I suspect you won't to this one. But I'm still writing to you.

I'm really sorry you were a low-down cheater who never considered there might be consequences from your having a good time. But you affected my mother's whole life. And mine.

I always, always tried to be a good daughter, a good person. I never took chances, never did anything wrong if I could help it. I know, I know, you don't care, or you'd have written me back by now. But I'm trying to tell you that's who I've always been—a girl who was afraid of taking risks—and I think it's partly because I had no dad. No sense of someone who could pick me up if I fell really hard.

My mom has always been there for me. As I hope I've been for her. But there's always been a hole...a wondering how different my life might have been if I'd had a dad, known a dad.

And I do get it, of course. Why you haven't responded. My existence is just a nuisance for you. But I'm angry, do you understand? Angry at you. Angry at you for not knowing about me, for not caring enough to even find out if your actions created a baby. I'm angrier yet that you never even considered whether having a daughter might have added something good to your life.

I guess I've never been real to you.

I'm starting to understand that I was never all that real to me, either. But now there's a man I've fallen in love with. Real love. The kind of man I think I could spend a life with...except that I'm not sure of anything right now. I thought I was a "good girl." Now I'm doing some pretty wild things. I thought I was the daughter of a single mom. Now I know that's not true, either. I thought I knew myself— what I wanted, what I needed, what I was capable of. And all that seems in question now, too…

I know you don't care, so I don't know why I kept venting to you, why I…

Kelly startled when her cell rang. She didn't want to answer. Her mood had evolved from low to sub-terranean. Bleak, dark. Cry-close gloomy. PMS with thorns. She had absolutely no motivation to push that on anyone else.

But the phone kept ringing, too distracting to concentrate further on the silly e-mail that her father was just going to ignore anyway. Finally she jerked out of the computer chair and tracked down the phone in her purse.

"What?" she answered crossly.

"Kel?"

Damn. Just like that, a single syllable in Will's lazy tenor, and the nasty mood she'd been clinging to disappeared like dust in the wind.

"Yeah, it's me, Will, but—"

"Are you free this Saturday morning?"

"Yes. But—"

"Pick you up at ten. No questions."

"But—"

"Bring sunscreen. Sunglasses. A hat, if you have one. Otherwise, just think ultracasual. No-worry clothes."

"But—"

"Plan on the whole day, all right? Because I can't give you an exact time when we'll be back. Ten," he repeated, and then clicked off.

THE INSTANT Will pulled into the driveway on Saturday morning, Kelly flew out the door. She was dressed as instructed—a blue-and-white shirt and capris, a white hoodie for the cool of the morning. Her hair was freshly washed and held back with sunglasses and her tote carried the required sunscreen.

She had no idea where they were going and didn't care. When she climbed into the unfamiliar BMW convertible—which was satin-red and cuter than sin—she immediately pounced on Will about what mattered. "How come we're doing this?"

He looked her over with lecherous eyes. "Because I thought of a splendiferous way to spend a Saturday. Specifically with you."

"But you're mad at me. Remember?" She swallowed him up in a look. She hadn't seen him in a whole week, a stretch of time that seemed longer than months. Heaven knew what he'd been doing. His nose was sunburned; his right knee was skinned; his chin had a brush of blond whiskers and he looked edible—edible, jumpable and lovable—in frayed cutoffs and a Cambridge tee.

"I was never mad at you," he corrected. Two turns later, they were on the freeway headed north. "I was slightly aggravated at having dinner with my father. Being with my father, anytime, under any circumstance, is a guaranteed way of yanking my chain."

"But it was me you were aggravated with, not your dad. Because you thought I wasn't taking your side." At last she had a chance to get that out in the open. "But I *am* on your side, Will. Totally. Completely. It's just that being in your corner doesn't mean I always have to agree with you, does it?"

He shot her a quick look, then reached over faster than quicksilver and traced a fingertip down her ribs.

She convulsed. "Is that your way of avoiding a serious discussion, you varmint? Tickling me?"

"Yeah. My sisters taught me that trick. Besides—there are rules for today. It's a playday. We've both had too much family stress. No serious discussion allowed. This is a day for forgetting all the heavy stuff and refilling the energy wells."

"You think that's possible, huh?" she murmured. She wished it were but didn't believe it. Hiding from problems never got them solved. Taking a break made her feel she was running away and that a lightning bolt of guilt was going to slash out of the sky any second and catch up with her.

Still. The wind tugged at her hair; the warm sun

beat down, and Will flipped to a radio station playing such god-awful, twangy, corny country songs that she had to either groan or hum along. He kept sending her lazy grins. She kept trying to hold on to a careful, wary, worried mood, but as the miles sped by, serious thoughts ebbed away.

It didn't take her long to figure out their destination, since 31 North led straight into Michigan, and in less than an hour, Will turned off at St. Joseph— an old-fashioned town built on top of a bluff overlooking Lake Michigan.

Kelly knew the town, had known the area for years, because the beach was fabulous and the shopping was fun. The long street was packed with little shops, lots of art, interesting jewelry, cafés, a blend of things to do and see.

Will bypassed the shopping section—no surprise. That left pretty much nothing to do but the beach.

"I know the temperature's warm out," she said tactfully, "but in case you've forgotten what the lake is like at this time of year, it's colder than ice. Maybe you could handle swimming, but I really—"

"We're not going to swim. We're going to sail."

"Sail," she repeated warmly, trying to treat the demented man with kindness. "The way I heard it, it's awfully tricky to sail without a boat."

He grinned at her teasing. "Luckily we happen to have a boat. A thirty-foot Sabre, in fact. Waiting for us."

She stared at him in confusion, until he turned

into a marina called Harbor Isle. The place was more crowded than a zoo, with massive yachts and sailboats everywhere, a fancy crane operation going on where big boats were being hoisted into the water, and people wearing everything from painting clothes to jewels to anything in between. Will parked in front of a long, sleek white baby with a blue sail cover. The side of the boat read *Soul Asset*.

"It's not mine. It's my sister's. Or to be more accurate my dad's—he's the one who paid the bill—but, regardless, it's ours for the day. Tell me now if you tend to get seasick. I've got some—"

"No, not a problem."

"Good. And I've been sailing all my life, so don't start worrying I'm going to tip us over or strand us…that is, unless you want to be stranded. I stocked her up yesterday, so there's nothing you have to do but slip off your shoes and climb aboard. There are extra jackets below if it gets cold. And if you want to be busy, I'll give you things to do, but the boat's set up for single handing so you can sit back and put your feet up and relax."

She wanted to say something—when had she ever been speechless? This was such a surprise. She'd expected an extra-nice lunch or dinner, maybe. A picnic. She never dreamed about spending a day doing anything like this.

Will zipped around the boat like an acrobat, untying lines, unbuttoning the sail cover, starting the engine. He unlocked the companionway to the cabin below, brought up thick white cushions and ice water, and then they were off.

"We're actually on the river here, and we have to go through two old-fashioned drawbridges before we reach the lake—and they're a pain." As they neared the first one, Will picked up an air horn, let out an earsplitting long toot and then a short one. "That's the signal, asking the gatekeeper to open the bridge for us. As soon as we're out of the river channel, we can cut the motor and put up the sails."

It was Greek to her. She'd been on boats before, even a few sailboats—South Bend was so close to the lake that kids just naturally had a chance to enjoy it, growing up. But she'd never been on a beauty of a boat like this.

They passed a red-and-white lighthouse, piers and a white beach dotted with sun worshippers. Then civilization faded away, leaving nothing but an open lake with silver-hemmed waves. Will flipped a cleat and suddenly, a huge white sail zoomed up the mast. He turned the winch, cranking her all the way until the sail touched sky, then repeated the same procedure with a second billowing sail.

Last, he cut the engine, and suddenly there was silence.

Magic.

She didn't know what else to call it.

People and city sights and sounds disappeared. The wind cupped the sails and they flew across the water, the sun blessing her cheeks, the air brushing her hair like sensuous fingers.

"You want to take the helm?" Will asked her.

"Are you nuts? Do you want me to sink this gorgeous boat?"

He laughed. "You can't sink her. Promise. I'll be right behind you."

He was. Right behind her. Perched on the fanny of the boat while she stood at the wheel. There were dials—for water depth and wind and speed and Lord knew what else. But Kelly was conscious only of him, of his sun-warmed body just behind her, shirtless, his brown chest nestling against her back. The boat skimmed the water in a silent dance and unbidden, unexpectedly, she felt a burst of emotion. A feeling like freedom. Joyful. Easy.

"Did you know," she asked, "that I couldn't have needed a day like this more?"

"We both did," he said, and then snapped his fingers. "I forgot something. Just a second."

He peeled down the steps to the cabin, emerged seconds later with two Notre Dame sun visors. He perched one on her head, one on his. Then readjusted hers, to fit her smaller head, making her laugh— which made her accidentally turn the wheel too hard, which made the boat suddenly dip and the sails wildly flutter.

"Whoa there, lady."

But her heart didn't want to whoa. Her pulse was racing, chasing, as exuberantly as the wind. He smoothed sunscreen down her arms and neck when she had the helm, and she did the same for him when he took his turn at the wheel.

It was foreplay, that touching, the smell of Coppertone and water, the ripple of his skin under her hands, the responsiveness and heat of her skin under his. He knew. The way he looked at her. With invitation. With wanting.

With waiting.

They sailed the shoreline until around lunch. Will didn't stop the boat or throw out an anchor, but he did something with the sails he called "heaving to." Once the boat stopped, he gave orders. She was to close her eyes. Sit there. Not move. "And for damn sure, don't think."

"Hey." She put plenty of "insulted" into her voice, but he just laughed.

She closed her eyes, as ordered, heard him rummaging around, up and down the steps, humming an old rock song under his breath. She was aware when he finally stopped moving, because there was suddenly complete quiet—except for the sound of a distant gull crying in the sky and Will's shadow cooling her hot cheeks. And then something else. A sensation of something fluttery-light and soft and fragrant raining on her head.

Her eyes popped open. Everywhere, on her shoulders, her arms, the deck, were rose petals. Bowls of them, buckets of them. She wanted to laugh, and did, but something squeezed her heart—the gesture was so frivolous, so romantic. So Paris.

Suddenly he was watching her in a way she couldn't back away from. The way the wind ruffled his hair, the rush of heat in his eyes, the electric tension between them—every detail invoked a flush of memories of Paris. It was as if they were there again, in his bed, waking up to warm rumpled sheets and a patch of lazy sunlight and street vendors below, hawking flowers to lovers.

Lovers like they'd been.

Lovers...the way she still felt with him, for him.

"Lunch," he murmured. "French style. Baguettes. Cheese. Fruit. Wine. There's ice water, as well, because I figured we'd be thirsty."

She tried to eat. She was certainly hungry enough. Will wolfed down lunch easily, but then he stopped, poured the wine, hunkered down next to her on the long white cushion.

That was the last time she could put a bite in her mouth.

"You know what occurred to me?" he asked lazily.

Everything before really had been foreplay, she thought. The looks. The smile. The sun and sea and sexy white sails. The hopelessly corny rose petals and French picnic and wine.

All that was nothing, though, compared with the next seductive trick he pulled.

He lifted the forefinger of his right hand, hooked it with the forefinger of her left hand.

Was that the act of a low-down sneaky creep, or what?

That was all. Absolutely no body parts touched except for their two fingers. And then his lazy, quiet voice asked, "You know what I was thinking about?"

Torturing women? "What?" she asked in a reasonably normal voice.

"I was thinking that this was how it was in Paris with you. As if there were just the two of us. The rest of the world didn't mean a damn." He added carefully, "Have you noticed that I haven't made a pass?"

What could she say? *No? Why haven't you jumped me?*

"It's because you asked me not to, Kel. Because I've tried to honor what you asked of me." He lifted their hooked fingers, waggled them together playfully. "You felt there was too much confusion and trouble in your life, that you needed to work some things out before tangling your life up with sex."

"Yes." Why had she said that? When had she been that sane? That stupid? The tip of his forefinger circled hers, such an innocuous, lightweight caress that there was no explaining the thrumming low in her belly.

"And I wanted you separated from that guy before I made any more moves. But you did that. And now

I think we're both ready for a new plan. I want you to come back to Paris with me."

"Paris," she repeated.

"Just listen." Still he caressed her finger, slowly, gently, as if there were nothing in the universe hurrying either of them, stressing either of them, worrying either of them. "There's nothing holding you here. You've come home to nothing but trouble. You love your mom, I know that, but she could visit us in Paris anytime she wanted. I'll pay. I've got money, Kel. My grandfather left me a good inheritance. Anytime you wanted family to visit—or you wanted to come back to South Bend—we could swing it, absolutely no sweat."

She was getting dizzy from his eloquent finger caress. From his soft, slow, tender voice.

"You could work there. Do whatever you love to do there, no different than here. We could find a place of our own, if you don't like mine. Are you hearing me? We could do this. Go back to Paris. Be in Paris together. Forever, if that's what you wanted. There's nothing we can't do together, Kel. Nothing we can't try."

She turned to face him directly. She didn't interrupt him, but as if he feared she was about to lodge a handful of protests, his voice sped up. "Nothing was right for me after you left. Nothing's right here, either, until I'm with you, and then everything works. It's not the boat. It's not the day. It's being with you. Everything gets right again when I'm with you. Kel, come to Paris with me. You know how it was. You know how it can be again."

She didn't know she was going to kiss him. She'd been wary of Will seducing her, not the other way around. She'd wanted Will to seduce her, not the other way around. And vaguely she recalled having at least a dozen reasons why making love with Will again was temporarily a terrible idea, but just then, she couldn't think of a single one.

He needed love, right now.

And it was easy to give him.

The only thing hard, all this time, had been holding back. And maybe she should try to hold back for her own emotional protection, before she fell any deeper, but Kelly suspected it was already too late for that.

She was already so deeply in love with Will that she couldn't imagine surviving without him. Couldn't imagine another man in her life, ever, not intimately. Couldn't imagine wanting to take risks...like the risks she wanted to take with Will. Couldn't imagine feeling lust or fear or frustration or tantalizing dreams with any other man. Not the way she did with him.

His lips were warm, his body absolutely motionless when she turned her head and took his mouth. But that first one was a gentle kiss—a tease, like the wicked, wild foreplay of their entwined fingers.

When she climbed on his lap—making the boat suddenly buck and rock—she really kissed him. Just bent her head and took it, like a brazen hussy or a woman with a mission or the boss of the universe. All of which she felt like at that precise moment, but it was his fault. The damned man responded as if she were everything—as if the touch of her, the kiss of her, was all he had ever wanted.

He let out a strong sigh, as if he'd been holding in temper and tension for years. Then he roped his arms around her and pulled her into the warm circle of his skin, his heartbeat, his strength. "Hey," he murmured thickly. "I thought we were supposed to behave."

"Behaving is so overrated. I've been behaving all my life." She kissed his earlobe, the spot right underneath it. "Until you." She felt his hands sneaking under her tank, his hand on the strap of her bra. "You're the only one I want to behave badly with, Will. What do you think that means?"

She couldn't continue talking for a second, because the tank was swirled over her head. Her bra seemed to come off it with it. In fact, her bra seemed to miss the seat and instead take a dive into Lake Michigan, a bobbing bit of red-and-white polka dots that matched her thong—which he was likely to discover soon.

Very soon.

"I think it means…" he said, and then lost his breath. She was already on top of him, so it was easy enough for him to angle kisses down her throat, down to her breasts, the nipples, the swelling round, the underside crease, her ribs. He seemed to forget what he'd been about to say.

She forgot whatever had ever been in her head, anyway. She'd never been bare naked outside before, in open sunlight. It didn't matter if there wasn't a boat near enough to see; it felt brazen and wicked and delicious.

He suckled her breast, tight, pulling her into his mouth, nuzzling, tasting. Her back arched like the sway of a reed. Desire elevated her awareness. Need magnified her senses. Or maybe it was just Will's touch, his scent, his eyes, his mouth that could do these things to her. All she knew…was wanting him more. Intensely, fiercely, greedily wanting more… and wanting to give him more. To make him feel sky-high as a man, the way he'd made her feel sky-high as a woman from the very start.

Out of nowhere, she heard a discordant sound. A distinctly civilized sound.

"Will?"

"I know," he muttered immediately, as if answering the question he assumed was on her mind. "Too damned narrow and hard and open out here. Not comfortable. The cabin. We'll go down to the cabin."

Talk was cheap. He'd barely made the incoherent announcement before he'd lowered her back to his lap. Her legs naturally wound around his waist, enabling more of those potent, dangerous kisses. They'd danced before, she knew, but this music had a beat, a power, that seemed to own her from the inside out.

They swayed into each other, a courting dance of chest to breast, lip to lip, her lap nestled against his erection. With each kiss, the dance seemed to intensify the beat of hearts, the drum of wind, the lyrics of longing and passion and fire.

The discordant sound intruded on her consciousness again.

It was a phone, she recognized with frustration. The sound emanated from down beneath the seat cushions. It was Will's cell phone—it must have fallen.

"Will," she said, and maybe she whispered it against his neck, but her tone meant to communicate seriousness.

"Forget it. I don't care. Whoever it is can leave a message."

But it wasn't that simple. The phone eventually stopped ringing and then started up again. Stopped and started...again. After the fifth time they couldn't help but notice and slowly Will pulled away from her to answer the phone.

Kelly could hear, all too clearly, the sound of a woman's frantic voice on the other end.

"Will. It's your Mom, dear. Your dad's been in an accident. He'll be fine, we're almost sure...." A catch in his mom's voice, raw and soft. "But could you come? Lakeland Hospital."

CHAPTER TWELVE

KELLY MOVED as fast as Will, had her clothes back on and was cleaning up even before Will started the motor. They headed back to the marina, taking advantage of both the sail and the ship's motor to achieve maximum speed.

She found a plastic bag below, where she swooped up the rose petals and secured them in her purse before bounding back on deck. "What can I do to help?"

"Nothing until we get there. Then you can help me tie up."

She nodded, thinking it strange how, considering all that had just happened, she hadn't forgotten Will asking her to go to Paris with him. That subject was obviously completely tabled for now. Still, her heart kept reeling from the possibility. All this time, she'd been so sure Paris had only been a fantasy she could never return to.

Well, maybe Paris had been a fantasy. But Will wasn't. Maybe they could go back.

By the time they pulled into the marina, Will's face was harsh. There were no smiles in his eyes.

"Do you want me to drop you off home?" he asked her.

They tied lines, covered the sail and locked up, then charged for his car at the same breakneck pace. "My apartment is so close to the hospital that it'll work either way," she said. "If you want to be with your family alone, then drop me off. But if you want me to be there with you…I want to. I know your family. Maybe I can help, Will. Choose whatever way works best for you."

"I want you with me." There was no hesitation in his voice. When they climbed in his car, he brushed a brief, hard kiss on her lips, a kiss of connection.

In less than an hour, they were striding into the hospital. Will stopped at the information desk, discovered that his dad had been moved from the E.R. to a private room. Halfway down the corridor, Kelly recognized Will's mom. She didn't know his sisters but the three women were readily identifiable from their blond hair to the Maguire bones, even if they hadn't instantly descended on Will like hummingbirds.

Kelly doubted Will even realized how naturally he took charge, how naturally they all knew they could let down their guard once he was there. His mom spotted her, and separated from the rest to reach out with both arms.

Kelly immediately folded the woman into a hug, saw tears start to well in Will's mother's eyes. Apparently Barbara had been determined to hold it together for her family, but given a sympathetic outsider, all the fear for her husband had sneaked to the surface. Kelly had been afraid she'd be in the way, but now she was glad she'd come.

"The doctors just talked to us. Aaron's going to be fine," Barbara said, although her voice quavered.

"That's great news."

"It was just so frightening. The car was completely totaled. And he was covered in blood and knocked out for a few minutes, so initially we had no idea how badly he was hurt. And all we could do was wait. It took ages to do all the X-rays and tests and finally hear what was wrong."

Will came up behind the two of them, heard the rest.

"He's got some terrible-looking bruises. A broken ankle. They want him completely off his leg for a couple weeks. It took forever in the emergency room because they had to stitch him up all over the place." Her voice caught again.

Will put his hand on Barbara's shoulder. "I'm going in there, Mom."

"Good. Go."

Will looked at Kelly, as if to say, *You'll watch over my girls for me?* As if he had to ask. Down the hall, there was the usual ubiquitous waiting room, where they could plunk down—or pace—until Will returned. Kelly easily got his sisters talking. They all wanted to spell out the details of the accident, over and over, as if talking could purge the fear from their minds.

"It wasn't Dad's fault. The police said the other driver was drunk. In the middle of the *day*. Swerved right into Dad's lane, and then Dad swerved trying to avoid him, only that meant that cars were coming at him from both directions. His car looks like an accordion. There's nothing to fix. It's a complete write-off."

"But really, it's a miracle everyone walked away from it," Will's mom said firmly. "A car is just a car."

"I know, Mom. I know. But who's going to run the business while Dad's laid up?"

The question was rhetorical, Kelly figured. Unless they'd all lost their minds, the Maguire women knew perfectly well how that egg was going to fry.

Will emerged from his father's hospital room moments later. The family hung together a while longer, making plans. Aaron needed serious rest, and the nurse firmly asked that there be no more visitors, that it would be better if everyone left until the next morning. Will agreed but wanted to speak to the doctor one last time himself. He sent the Maguire women home, arranged for his sisters to get their mom dinner and promised Barbara that he'd be home—her home—before dark. His mother really wanted him to stay with her that night.

Kelly hung tight until he'd talked to the doctor. By the time Will was steering her toward the exit doors, the parking lot was only half-filled, the late-afternoon sun relentless and hot. It was the first second she'd had him alone in hours.

"Thanks for staying," Will said. "I didn't realize it was going to take this long."

"It's fine. I was glad to be there. I like your whole family."

"And they adored you on sight."

"They don't *adore* me, fella. They think I'm the key to keeping you in South Bend. That gives me so much political clout that I can probably trip over my mouth a few dozen times and still land in the plus column." She added smoothly, "So…you agreed to take over the company for your dad?"

He startled in surprise. "How did you know that?"

"Because he's hurt. And he's your father. And I'm guessing it's the first thing he asked you when you went into his room."

"You've got that right." He started the car and merged into traffic. When he didn't add anything further, Kelly pushed.

"How're you feeling about it?"

"You mean, because it's the last thing in hell I ever wanted to do?"

He sighed. "It's exactly what you said. Dad's hurt. That's a whole different thing. He'll be back on his feet in a couple of weeks—which means, knowing my dad, he'll find some way to be in the office at the end of next week, no later."

"And?" She knew there was more.

"And, I knew from his expression that he thought this accident was the best thing that could have happened. He thought it'd manipulate me into sitting in his chair. Keeping me here."

"And?"

He shot her a look. "Before you were in my life, did you know, no one ever pried? I mean, my sisters did, but I learned how to play them when I was a kid. You, though, are worse than a bloodhound."

"Thank you so much."

"You're welcome." He reached over and tracked a finger down her ribs, just to remind her that he knew her hopeless ticklish spots. And to avoid being plagued anymore, he answered her questions. "It doesn't matter whether he's trying to manipulate me or not. Doesn't matter what I want to do. He's hurt. He needs help. He's family. Even when I want to strangle him, he's still my dad. And that's that."

He pulled into her driveway a few minutes later, frowning at the look of her place, the way he always did. Tonight, though, he was obviously distracted, and when he stopped the car, she insisted he not walk her to the door. She knew he still had miles to go that night, and that his mom was waiting for him.

Before climbing out, though, she said gently, "You need to be here, but I know you must be feeling trapped. Still, since you're stuck staying longer, Will, you might as well use the time to forge something different with your dad. I know, I know. It hasn't been going well. But this is another chance, right?

Whether you asked for it or not, it's still another opportunity to try something new, some way to get along better with him."

"Kelly..." She heard the annoyance in Will's voice, knew—par for the course—that she'd gone too far.

She leaned across the gearshift, which required major acrobatics, and cupped his cheek so she could kiss him. Kissing him was easy enough, but shaping the kiss she wanted was a serious challenge, because she didn't want a plain old smack. She wanted a lip-melting, down-and-dirty, heart-squeezing pressure-cooker of a kiss. When she lifted her head, her heart was racing as if she'd run a three-minute mile, and her spine felt permanently twisted.

She said softly, swiftly, "I love you, Will." Before tumbling out of the car and heading inside.

He didn't answer. But then she hadn't given him a chance to.

Right then, neither of them had answers for anything. Much less each other, Kelly thought.

She felt unsettled even before she walked into the apartment—and more so after she saw the mess. Her roommate was out somewhere. There were no signs of life beyond a mound of soda cans, dozens of beer cans, flies buzzing around pizza left in the sink from last night and the stink of dirty socks on the floor near the door.

Normally Skip was a pretty decent roommate, but

every once in a while he remembered he was still a college kid and reverted to type. A complete slob. A condemnable-by-any-health-department-standard slob.

She wasn't about to clean up after him, Kelly told herself every time. As she filled the sink with sudsy water and shook out a fresh trash bag, she told herself she was only doing this for herself, because she couldn't stand the mess or the smells. Which was true. Or true enough.

But it was also true that her plan to get out of this dump had become newly complicated. Will was staying longer in South Bend because of his dad now. He'd also asked her to go with him to Paris. She didn't know how or when any of that was going to resolve, which meant that for her to make any sudden, big moves without being sure of all the consequences seemed foolhardy.

Which meant, of course, that she was stuck in this nightmare of a place for a while longer.

Suddenly feeling too ornery to settle on any serious project, she plunked down with her itchy mood and pounced on e-mail. Naturally, there was no response from her father, but that didn't stop her from sending him another post.

Bonsoir, mon père. I see there's still no response from you...but until I get a message that my e-mails are undeliverable or some clear indication you're blocking me, I'm determined to keep up a dialogue. Even if you think I'm a complete *chameau* and a *peau de vache*—you're stuck with my being your daughter.

And since you're stuck, you're destined to hear a piece of my mind today, because I am really upset. In fact, I've had it—*had* it—with fathers who treat their children like inanimate objects. You have no idea what I've been through with Will today. He loves his dad, but his dad only seems to love him back if Will does what he wants. And then there's you. Who never cared enough to even find out if I existed.

Well, since I can't be with Will tonight—and I'm tired of living with all this unsettledness—I'm going over to Mom's to have it out with her. It's about time I heard her story about why she told me you were dead. I'd also like to know why and how she could have fallen in love with a man— namely you—who apparently didn't give a damn about her. I'm sorry to be so cross in this e-mail. It's really been a rotten day. Love, Kelly

She hit Send, and then abruptly realized that she'd written exactly what she wanted to do with the rest of her evening.

SHE FOUND her mom on the back porch, doing business...a cell phone in one hand, her laptop open on a white wrought-iron table, her bare feet cushioned on an ottoman…the toenail paint shiny red and still wet, her toes separated by white cotton balls.

Char looked up with a quick smile when she saw Kelly. Both of them had been miserable about their relationship lately, Kelly knew. Her mom's eyebrows raised when she saw the bottle of wine, but even though she continued the business call, she motioned for Kelly to come in. Kelly motioned back that she was headed for the kitchen first.

She knew where the wine opener and glasses were, filled the two goblets near to the rim—no tame drinking for this conversation—and then carried the tray through the living room and onto the back porch again.

Her mother was still on the phone, but she blinked at the size of the poured wine—shot a curious, concerned look at Kelly—and started to seriously hustle the caller along.

The white lilacs were just fading against the far fence, and the peonies tucked on the north side of the house were beginning to grow heavy with fat, pink blooms. The lawn was fresh clipped and looked luxuriously soft and green. A neighbor's mower buzzed three doors down. Somewhere kids were yelling and whooping it up on a trampoline.

Every sight and sound was familiar. Maybe there was nothing fancy or expensive about the suburb, but so many childhood memories were etched in her mind. It was the kind of neighborhood where people watched out for one another, the kind of neighborhood where she'd go to Jason's house after school as often as he came to hers, and everybody did big block parties and knew each other's business and yelled if a child did something unsafe, even if it wasn't their own kid.

She took a first sip of the wine, thinking that she wanted this. Not her mother's life. Her own. But she did want to raise kids and have a family in a neighborhood like this. It didn't have to be in South Bend.

It could be anywhere. But she couldn't deny wanting to raise a family in a neighborhood, American style. Not French.

The wine suddenly caught in the back of her throat, but then her mother finally hung up the phone and turned to her.

"Sounded like a business deal that is really going well?" Kelly said swiftly.

"Yes, a closing. A terrific deal, but forget that. What's the wine for? Did you make up with Jason? Or have a fight and not make up? What's wrong?"

"It's not about Jason, Mom. It's about you." She handed her mom the biggest glass. "Take a sip," she urged her.

"Are you pregnant?"

"Take a sip."

"God. You're not sick, are you? You look so wonderful—"

Kelly sat across from her, on the old white frame rocker that had once belonged to her grandmother. "Come on. I told you I met my dad when I was in

Paris. You know we're overdue for this conversation. Enough's enough. Tell me the story."

Her mother opened her mouth, and then stopped, looking sick and unnerved. Her mom, who never had a hair out of place, who could probably run the UN in her sleep, stared at the wine in her glass as if she were lost in the reflection.

Kelly leaned forward. "His wife died, some time ago. But his two sons are a little older than me, so he had to have been married and had those kids when you met him. I have half brothers, Mom. *Family.* Maybe none of them want to know me—and maybe I don't want to know them—but darn it, they're blood kin."

Finally Char's eyes shot up. "I swear I was going to tell you, honey."

"When I was fifty?"

Her mother's cell sang out, but Char turned it off. She closed her laptop and faced Kelly with soft, worn eyes. "This is what it was all really about, isn't it? Your breakup with Jason. Not so much about Will, but about finding out about your father."

"Maybe partly. Cripes, I don't know." Kelly sighed, a long, miserable sound coming from her throat. "I felt totally and completely thrown when I found out he was alive, when I found out who he was. I thought my dad was a hero—not a guy who played around on his wife, much less had a wife with young children. And you, Mom, I trusted more than anyone else alive. And you lied to me. I *love* you, but I don't understand why you didn't tell me the truth. I know everything in your life isn't my business, but for heaven's sake. I could have had a father in my life. Even if he was a piker, he still might have had a role in my life. Why did you *lie?*"

"Because I thought I had to, honey."

At the look in her mother's face, Kelly leaned forward and grabbed the wine bottle. This was no time for sipping. She filled up both glasses and waited.

Her mom haltingly started to fill in the blanks. "I went to Paris to study for a year at the Sorbonne—which you know. And that's when I met him. He wasn't in school. I met him at a bistro. It was chance. I took one look and fell head over heels." She pushed at her hair. "I was the archaic good girl. A virgin. And your dad…well, he was every fantasy I ever dreamed of. Strong, yet gentle. Worldly, experienced with women. He knew what to say, what to do, to make me feel like the most desirable woman who had ever been born." She sighed. "I'm sure that sounds naive."

"No, it doesn't," Kelly said softly, thinking she understood. Too well. Too much. Too completely.

"I'm not trying to make excuses. I'm just trying to say how it was. I not only fell in love, I fell way, way over my head. I didn't have a clue he was married—he didn't lie to me, he just didn't tell me. It's different there. Or it was different then. He married for business, as did his wife. They were happy enough. He just went outside the marriage from time to time for…for romance, I guess you'd say. I don't believe your father saw it as wrong. Cheating in a marriage there wasn't looked at the same way it is here. Or maybe he thought I was smarter than I was—smarter about life, smarter about men—and that I knew the rules of the game we were playing."

Lights started coming on around the neighborhood. The sound of children's voices died, as the kids were called in for bed. The first firefly showed up in the dusky light. And still they talked.

"When I found out he was married…in fact, that his wife had recently given birth to new baby, a son…I almost died. He said his wife hadn't been well enough to have 'relations' for months, as if that explained why he'd strayed. Truthfully, Kelly, I shut down like a slammed door when I found out. I bought a ticket home in a matter of hours, was throwing things in a suitcase, taking off for home at the speed of sound."

"You didn't know you were pregnant then?"

"Didn't even cross my mind. Getting away from him, from Paris, from the whole mess, was the only thing on my mind."

"But, Mom…" That time, when Kelly tried to pour, she discovered they'd finished the bottle. Undoubtedly there was wine or liquor somewhere in the house, because her mom entertained, even if she wasn't much of a drinker. But when it came down to it, she didn't want any more. And neither, from the look of her mother's face, did she. "Why didn't you *tell* me that you never got married? Why did you keep this a secret from me? Why didn't you tell him that he'd gotten you pregnant? Or did you?"

"I didn't tell anyone. Obviously, my mother knew there was a man in France, but not all of the circumstances. She nursed me through a broken heart, helped me through the pregnancy. So did the rest of the family. But as far as telling anyone else—or you—I never told because I was just plain ashamed."

"But *why?* Tons of women choose to be single moms. You weren't living in the Dark Ages, Mom. No one has to cover stuff like that up anymore."

Her mother said quietly, "He was married, with small children."

"But still—"

"He was married. With small children," her mother repeated. "I wasn't ashamed of what other people would think. I was ashamed of *me*."

Kelly sucked in a breath. "Aw, Mom. Damn it all."

"And that's why I didn't want you to know. Because I didn't want you ashamed of both your parents. Bad enough that your father was a cheater, but if I'd told you the truth, you'd have thought I was the kind of woman who'd sleep with a married man, who'd risk breaking up a marriage—a marriage with small children. I didn't want you to know the truth. I wanted to give you a family you could be proud of. I wanted you to think you came from good people. I wanted you to think that I was a good woman, a good mother."

"Oh, for God's sake, Mom…" Kelly surged out of the chair and wrestled her mom out of hers. She folded Char up in a big hug and squeezed tight.

Cripes, she'd come here afraid she'd end up crying…not making her mother cry.

And she'd come to demand answers…only dagnabbit, her mom had *given* her answers. Exactly what she wanted. Yet instead of making her feel better, she'd not only upset her mother, but made herself feel worse.

In fact, she felt downright scared.

Will was nothing like her dad. He wasn't married. Wasn't a cheater. He was an honorable guy right down to the gut. But damn…Kelly kept thinking that it was hard *not* to be afraid of repeating her mother's mistake.

CHAPTER THIRTEEN

WILL STOOD AT his father's office window. The view was his dad's favorite—not the river, not trees or a pretty landscape, but the sea of concrete and brick manufacturing facilities stretched below. For the past hour, the telephone had been glued to his ear. When he had occasion to be off the phone, it was only to turn to the mounds of crises covering his father's sleek slate desk.

The boat ride with Kelly might as well have been months ago instead of a week. His begging her to come back to Paris with him—she'd never had a chance to say yes or no. He kept telling himself she'd been going to say yes.

That yes was still possible.

He was holding on to that hope like a lifeline in a stormy sea.

"Mr. Maguire…"

Will spun around and viewed Aaron's new comptroller with suspicious eyes. First off, John Henry persisted in calling him Mr. Maguire. Second off, the guy was so perfect he probably didn't have to spit after brushing his teeth. He didn't joke, didn't cough, didn't trip, never complained, was courteous first thing in the morning—in short, he never did one human thing.

Something was off. Will couldn't pin it down, but nobody could be this perfect every second. Stranger yet was his sense of style. John Henry—what kind of a name was that?—could have auditioned for an escort service.

"I didn't mean to interrupt you," John said, "but I have the reports you asked for, and you did ask me to bring them right away."

"I did. And I needed them right away. Thanks, John. I'll get back to you later."

South Bend was famous for Studebakers—a car that failed. The city was also famous for Notre Dame, of course. And then there were the Maguires, upstart Irish once upon a time, but Irish who weren't afraid to get their hands dirty. It wasn't a romantic business his family had gotten into, just the formula for an indestructible alloy. So far the product had been used on everything from trains to computers, from race cars to military hardware.

"Will…" Ms. Randolph showed up at his door next. She'd been his father's right-hand assistant for as long as he could remember. Her age was around 110, her gray hair wirier than a terrier's, and lions couldn't compete with her loyalty.

As far as Will could tell, she was part of the evil

conspiracy determined to keep him here. Unlike any sane employee—who would surely think the prodigal son wouldn't know shit about running the place and was just going to muck everything up—Ms. Randolph acted as if the sun rose and set with him. She adored him.

More nauseating yet, he adored her.

"Your father called from the hospital," she reported. "He'd appreciate your calling him before you leave tonight."

"For a fresh set of questions and orders, and the daily tongue-lashing, I suspect," Will said wryly.

"I think he wants to pull the great escape tonight, but he won't be able to manage it without you."

"Oh my God, is he delusional? He actually believes I'd help spring him from the hospital so he could go home?"

"He does. But he knows you won't leave here for hours yet. And sometime over the next hour or so, Blake, in the finishing department, wants you to take a look at the Ariber proposal before we send it out." She glanced at him. "Blake thinks you don't know beans, so watch yourself."

"Thanks."

"Ariber can't be familiar to you. It's a relatively new customer, but one of your dad's pet projects. Not a big profit to be had on this specific project, but serious opportunities down the road. Your father felt it was an important contract to land." After filling him on the rest, she tapped her notepad. "Did you get lunch?"

"No, Mom. But I'm a big boy and can feed myself."

"Humph. I've slapped your father upside the head, so don't think I can't do it to you. You'll either start scheduling a regular lunch or I'll start having it catered at noon."

"Hey. I can fire you, remember?"

"In a pig's eye. You gave me a new job title and a salary increase the minute you got here."

"That was only because my father's stingy."

"Actually…he is. A little." She looked uncomfortable. "I don't mean to imply that your father doesn't treat me absolutely fairly in every way. And you know how I love Maguire's. I had everything I needed—"

"This wasn't about what you needed. It was about merit and power, cookie. And you deserved more power. You've earned it."

"Well, heaven knows, that's true." Ms. Randolph stalked toward the door like the martinet she was. "But for the record, if you call me 'cookie' again, you might not live to see the next daylight." She closed his door on her way out.

When she knew he had a mountain to tackle, she always closed his door, then guarded it with the tenaciousness of a street bully. And she was right. Somehow he had to pack in eight hours of work before he could leave today—and it was already three in the afternoon. And no, he hadn't had time for lunch. In fact, he was damn near light-headed from hunger.

Hunger for food.

Hunger to be anywhere on the planet but here.

Hunger to be with Kelly. Just anywhere with Kel. Alone.

Ms. Randolph paged him right when he was knee-deep in trouble, out in the prefinishing production area, where the lighting was fierce and the temperature brain-baking. Maybe the heat contributed to old Willy Blake's attitude. The foreman had never liked hearing criticism, and liked listening to new ideas even less.

Ms. Randolph said crisply, "You've got a Kelly Rochard on line three. She knows you're busy. Said she could call back, but I figured you could use the sound of a sweet voice. Particularly if you've been listening to Blake cuss for long."

Will was too whipped to even tease back. "Thanks."

He punched in line three, one hand covering his right ear so he had a prayer of hearing Kelly clearly. Which he did. And simply the sound of her voice made him grin.

"Darn it, Will. I *hate* bothering you," she said violently.

"You never bother me."

"Yeah, I do. Of course I do. But I wanted to know how your dad was, and I couldn't call you at his place, because your mom could easily overhear anything you wanted to say. And if you were back at your sister's, I figured you'd be sacked out, so I didn't want to bother you there. So the only place left to call you was—"

Before she went on explaining forever, Will figured he'd just jump in and answer her question. "Well, my dad's ornery. Crabby. Insufferable. But I'm supposed to spring him from the hospital after dinner. The family doesn't think he's ready to come home yet, worried that he's way more than my mom can handle. So he called me to come do the jailbreak."

"My. How much fun you're having, huh?"

"I don't suppose you'd like to come with me?"

"To help take your dad home? I'd love to."

There. Just like that. A god-awful job turned into something livable.

AARON WAS IN THE MIDDLE of yelling at a nurse and two aides when they walked in. When his dad spotted Kelly, though, you'd think an angel had arrived. He calmed right down.

"We're going to make Will do all the annoying paperwork, and we'll get you out of here," Kelly said immediately.

"Finally, someone who listens to me!"

"I don't blame you for being frustrated. Hospitals are terrible places, aren't they?"

That was all she had to say for Aaron to go into his monologue. "You can't rest in here. They're always poking you or prodding you. Can't even go to the bathroom on your own without some pipsqueak yelling at you. The only food they serve that's edible is Jell-O. How is a grown man supposed to get stronger on Jell-O, I ask you."

Will hit the offices, and got two exuberant kisses from nurses on the way back up to the room. He didn't figure the smooches were because of his sex appeal, just a measure of gratitude that he was taking Aaron Maguire off their hands.

Not that Will would admit it aloud, but unlike the hospital staff, he was damned glad to see his father yelling and acting feisty again. Aaron still looked beat-up, and he clearly couldn't put any weight on his right ankle. But by the time Will caught up with Kelly, she had his dad in a wheelchair and Aaron was chuckling at something she'd said.

He looked at her, just shaking his head. It wasn't a good thing, being in love with a woman who was this skilled at malarkey and charm. Everyone in his family knew Aaron was stubborn as a goat—and completely intractable once he'd made up his mind.

"Your dad and I were talking," Kelly mentioned on the drive home, her voice very cheerful from the backseat. "He doesn't need help at home. And he's sick to death of everyone talking to him about rehab. He doesn't want strangers around."

"I sure as hell don't," Aaron agreed gruffly.

"But we were figuring that your mom is in different shoes. She's so used to your dad doing things that she might be a little thrown for a week or two."

"No more than that," Aaron qualified.

"I can't imagine she'd need more than that, either," Kelly said soothingly. "But the point, Will, is that we were thinking your mom might need some help for the next couple weeks. Not for your dad, but for her. But we're both a little worried that your mom can't be talked into the idea."

"You have no idea how stubborn my wife is," Aaron affirmed.

"But if *you* could have a private talk with your mom, Will," Kelly said gently. "You know, just suggest an extra guy servant around for a couple of weeks, someone to do lifting, the heavier things around the place. We don't want to offend her pride. We could pretend it was for your dad."

At the family house, Will only had a second to say a word privately with Kelly before getting his father out of the car. "You actually did it. Talked my dad into help in the house. Made him think it was for my mom. What do you want—diamonds? A medal? A paragraph in *Ripley's?*"

She grinned. "Hey, you saved me in Paris. Just trying to do a little rescuing of my own." But then she motioned to the Maguire house with a major change in expression. "Will?"

"What?"

"Look, I knew your family was well-off. But holy kamoly. This place is just way beyond me."

He frowned. She'd never acted impressed or

scared off by the Maguire money before—well, maybe for two seconds when they'd first met in Paris—but not once they got to know each other.

Still, he tried to see the place from Kelly's eyes. The grounds looked their best in late May, Irish-green and satin-soft. South Bend was on the flat side, but his dad had the money—and the stubbornness—to build his own hills, enabling the house to be built on levels. Each floor looked out onto its own unique landscaping: a Japanese garden from the top level; a woody, sloped area leading to a pool and tennis courts from the back; and flowering trees and open gardens at the front entrance.

None of it was new to Will, but seeing Kelly inhale the grounds, he could see it wasn't too bad from the outside. Even if, to him, it was a cage.

His dad, by then, was out of the car, and his mom was peeling out the back door. Naturally Will had pulled up to the one entrance that didn't have stairs. Even so, when he maneuvered the wheelchair to his dad, Aaron immediately started a new rant, claiming that he could walk on his own, thank you very much, he wasn't an invalid, didn't need fussing over…

"Come on, Dad, for Pete's sake—"

But Kelly stepped in, as she had at the hospital. When *she* took the wheelchair, Aaron willingly sat in it.

His mom sent Will a look, as astounded by Aaron's

changed behavior as he was. Both of them had discussed getting help, but Aaron had unequivocally and furiously denied needing it. Now, as he was wheeled in the door, he barked at Will to get extra hands in the house. Immediately. For at least two weeks.

His mother cornered him several minutes later. Aaron was settled in his favorite room, the library, where dark green fabric walls matched the green leather couches, and recessed lighting in the bookshelves provided soft, unobtrusive light. A hospital bed had been set up in here, partly because it was on the first floor with an attached bathroom, and partly because it was one of Aaron's favorite rooms.

Kelly was sitting with him when Will took off for the kitchen with his mom. Aaron wanted fresh strawberries and cream. Will was putting together a half sandwich and drink to go with it.

His mother said, "My God. She's a wonder."

"Yeah, she is."

"Your sisters will never believe it. That anyone could get your dad in a wheelchair. Or that he could be conned into getting some help." Barbara handed him the tray to take in, once she'd added a linen napkin and silverware. His mom had the softest eyes in the universe, but just occasionally, they could look quite shrewd. "So…it's clearly become more serious?"

"You want help with Dad, or you want to pry?"

"I'd rather pry."

But his mom gave him a quick hug and let it go—for then. An hour later, Aaron turned from cantankerous tyrant into sleeping baby, and Will drove Kelly home.

He caught her first smothered yawn—and the second big one she couldn't try to hide. "You're beat?"

"Yeah. Really long day at work."

"And then I added this stress package with my dad. On the other hand, this means I owe you. And it's always to your advantage for me to owe you."

"Darn right," Kelly agreed.

"I have an idea. On how I could pay you back."

"Is it expensive and decadent?"

"Hey. Would I waste your time on anything less?"

"Okay," she said. "I'm game."

"Tomorrow night…"

She made a sound. "Will, I've got my mom's birthday party coming up. Tomorrow I have to take her shopping for it."

"And that has to be tomorrow?"

"Pretty much, it really does. Because we're running out of evenings to do it—and she wants clothes—so we always go together to pick them out."

"Ah," he said, thinking he should have known that from his sisters. "So…Thursday night."

"Okay, what time?"

"What time can you get free?"

"Um…six, earliest."

"Then six it is."

BY WEDNESDAY NIGHT at eight-thirty, Kelly was comatose, sprawled outside a dressing room at Ann Taylor.

She'd already raided most of Grape Road with her mom, checking out the usual suspects—Talbots, Coldwater Creek, Chico's, the mall's specialty stores. Typically her mom claimed to be a size eight, would never be more than a six, and looked cuter than the devil no matter what she tried on.

The problem was getting Char to choose. She knew Kelly's budget, and was allergic to getting anything that wasn't on sale. They'd started after work—in a downpour—gulped down fast food for energy and then begun the siege.

Outside the dressing room, Kelly was using bags and purses for a pillow. Her eyes were closed in a mininap when her cell phone vibrated. She couldn't help but smile and feel her tummy warm when she heard Will's voice.

"How's the present shopping going?"

"We're having a blast. But thank God the stores close soon." She added, "Everything okay?" Ever since last night, she'd thought nonstop about his dad, that fabulous unique mansion and how even mighty rich people could be crabby when they didn't feel well. Her ego was still soaring about that whole business. She'd loved helping Will with his parents. She'd have loved both his dad and mom even if she hadn't loved Will.

"Everything's fine…"

Her eyes popped open and she sat up abruptly. "Is there a problem with tomorrow night?"

"Not at all. We're on. Actually, I'm calling for business."

She relaxed again. "Sure you are."

"No. Really. You do searches on people, right?"

"You know I do. Primarily credit card identity theft."

"So what do you charge for doing these people searches?"

Char emerged from the dressing room in a little black dress. Kelly shook her head. First, because her mom already had a zillion little black dresses, and she almost never wore them. And second, because it was dowdy. "Do you mean, how much would it cost you? Or a normal person?" she asked Will.

"Hey. I'm normal." His tone sounded wounded.

She chuckled. "Well, the going rate is set by the hour. But it also includes expenses. Most of the time, there really aren't any. Most of what I do is on the computer. It's just occasionally I have to travel. Anyway, I can't really give you a flat rate because it honestly depends on the job."

"Okay…" She heard background noise, then a door closing. "Whatever your rate is, I'll pay it. I need you to look into a guy who works at Maguire's. Name of John Henry. I can give you his address, birth date and social security number. I know you have other irons in the fire and might not be able to do this right away—"

She frowned. Her mom emerged from the dressing room again, this time in a cream-and-coral-print skirt with a coral top. If the outfit didn't have Char's name on it, it should have. Kelly gave her an exuberant thumbs-up, but she was still frowning into the phone. "Will, you know I'm not a private investigator, don't you? Because if this is about somebody's divorce or private life—"

"This is about someone working for my dad, where things just aren't adding up. I'd like to be sure his name is real. That he's who he says he is. That's all."

She slumped farther against the wall. "Are you inventing this mini-job just to keep your mitts on me?"

"Kelly, Kelly, Kelly. That is so unfair." He paused. "If I'd thought of that, actually, I'd probably do it. But as it happens, this is on the up-and-up."

She chuckled again, then stopped. Her mom was back in the dressing room. A gaggle of women had just left, leaving the general hallway calm for that moment. She said quietly, "I talked to her, Will. About my dad."

He understood how long it had taken her to finally get this done. "And?"

"And...I went into the conversation so, so mad. Mad that she'd lied to me. Mad that she'd invented a father who never existed and mad that I never had a chance to know my real one."

"And now?"

She didn't think her mother could hear behind the closed door, but she still moved away from the dressing rooms, keeping an eye peeled in case Char came out. "Now I realize the obvious. That my mom wouldn't have lied unless she felt she had to. At the time, she just didn't think she had a lot of choices. I think she lost her head and her heart in Paris. She believed he loved her. She thought they had something real. And all that crashed when she discovered he was married, but it was even more than that. She lost faith in herself, in her judgment." Kelly would have said more, but she saw the dressing room doorknob turn. "I have to go, Will. See you tomorrow night."

Her mother saw her shut the cell phone, but she worked her over about the outfit first. "I like it, I admit, but it costs too much. Particularly when you've got a tight budget right now."

They did the same song, different lyrics but the same refrain, every birthday. "Nonsense. The day I can't buy my mother a birthday present, I'm throwing in the towel." Kelly grabbed the top and skirt before her mother could escalate the discussion.

"I heard you on the phone—were you talking to Jason?"

"No, Mom."

"But have you? Talked with him?"

Kelly dug out her wallet before they reached the checkout line. "Yup. He showed up at work. A very uncomfortable conversation, which I wouldn't be telling you about at all, except that I'm almost sure he'll show up at the block party on Saturday. He won't raise trouble on your birthday that I can imagine. But if you can't find me at some point, it's probably because I'm hiding in your closet behind your shoe boxes."

"Hmm."

"And what does that *hmm* mean?" The checkout girl took her time, way too much time, folding the outfit with exquisite care, so there was no escaping the store too quickly.

"Are you still seeing that other man? The one from Paris?"

"His name is Will, Mom."

"Yes. Will Maguire. Of the Maguires." Her mother's voice didn't drip disapproval. Just opinion. Char might have come to believe that Will wasn't totally responsible for her breaking up with Jason, but people with the Maguire kind of money weren't remotely on their Christmas card list.

"You didn't like him?"

"The question isn't whether I like him. Or you do. The question is whether you're in love with him. And whether you're ready to risk any more heartache or trauma in your life right now."

"I don't know," Kelly admitted. "Nothing seems to come with a guarantee. I'm going with my heart, and maybe that's the most foolish thing I could be doing. But the only man who really threw a trauma into my life wasn't Will, Mom. It was my father."

Her mom suddenly looked small. "That was my fault."

Guilt pinched her heart. "The hell it was. You're a fabulous mother. And you've made an outstanding success of your life, totally on your own. That my dad didn't appreciate you is his loss. You didn't do a single thing wrong. All you did was fall in love."

Her mom laughed, and they hugged, both of them carrying packages but still managing to walk hip to hip to the car.

It was later, brushing her teeth before bed, that Kelly rethought that exchange. Her mom really hadn't done anything wrong except innocently fall in love. Maybe Kelly wouldn't have lied, but she understood why her mother felt she'd had to.

What troubled her now, though, was the resounding echo of their lives. She couldn't deny it. She'd fallen fiercely in love. In Paris. At a time when her whole sense of self had been shaken up.

So how *was* she supposed to know if what she felt for Will was real?

If it could last?

Or if loving him would cause repercussions through her whole life, the way loving the wrong man had affected her mother's?

CHAPTER FOURTEEN

WILL DIDN'T usually shop at sex-toy stores before a date. In fact, he'd never shopped at a sex-toy store, ever, but after trying two drugstores and a department store for the item he needed—an item he'd have thought would be easy to find—he gave up and went to a source he knew would carry it.

Come to think of it, he'd never gone to this much trouble for any date, ever.

Not that he minded. Not for Kelly. But he was edgily aware that the stakes were damn high—and increasing by the day.

When he pulled into Kelly's driveway, he remembered how she'd described the confrontation with her mother. All this time, she'd been too upset to bring up the subject. All this time, she'd felt so wounded that her mother had lied to her about keeping her father's existence and identity a secret.

Thunder grumbled in the west. Clouds scudded overhead like tumbling balls, one falling over the other, each darker than the last. The first fat drop of rain splashed on his head, but he was prepared for that, too, and put up an umbrella before he climbed the steps to Kelly's door.

He rapped. Waited. He was still thinking about what she'd said about her mother, that her mom had lost her head in Paris, believing Rochard had loved her, then had become disillusioned.

Somewhere in her mother's story was the reason for Kelly's fears. Though he didn't totally understand it, he sensed the bottom line—that the only thing really keeping Kelly from taking off with him to Paris was this. She needed to feel sure of herself and what she felt for him, with him.

Sure that he wasn't a guy like Rochard. Sure that he wasn't feeding her a fantasy.

He was about to rap on the door again when it abruptly swung open.

His mouth framed a hello, but no sound emerged.

It was the yellow that locked up his vocal cords.

He'd never seen her in yellow before. And this wasn't yellow-*yellow*, more like a pale butter color, and he wasn't dead sure if it was a dress or underwear. The indefinably dangerous garment had tiny shoulder straps. After that it was simply silky fabric that fell from a bodice to above her knees.

He would have bet—even in Vegas—that she wasn't wearing a bra.

Or underpants.

He opened his mouth to greet her again, and again

lost his voice. This time, though, his gaze narrowed on her face.

Smoky eyes met his. Of course, Kel had always had smoky eyes, but tonight the lashes looked long and sultry, the brows arched with a delicate curve. Her lips had this…this *red* on them. Not siren-red. Just…sex-red. Her hair was scooped up in a messy little heap on top of her head. And the expression on her face was pure…tease.

"I got a little dressed up," she murmured.

"I can see that."

"You said this was a payback dinner. That you owed me. So I figured I'd make you pay back big."

"I'm already paying," he assured her drily, making her laugh.

"Not *that* kind of paying, you nut. I meant…a seriously good dinner. Like lobster or something."

"Trust me," he said in the same dry voice, "you can have whatever you want for dinner. Lobster. Me. Steak. Ribs. Me—"

She rolled her eyes. "You are so easy…and speaking of sex objects, you look edible yourself."

He'd tried. His sisters were responsible for anything decent in his closet, since the girls had told him from birth that he had no taste and they did. So the dark blue shirt and black summer slacks were supposed to be the right thing.

As long as Kel liked them, that was all that mattered. "You're going to get a fancy dinner, I swear. But the place we're going is a surprise."

"What kind of surprise?" she asked suspiciously.

"The kind of surprise you can't guess."

As expected, she looked completely bewildered when he turned into a neighborhood near the Notre Dame campus, and even more confused when he pulled into the driveway of an unfamiliar house.

"We're eating with friends of yours?" she asked.

"Nope." The street was shaded by fat, old maples. Most of the homes were brick with landscaped yards, the tip of ND's golden dome visible in the distance. "An economics professor used to live here," he said as he opened the car door and motioned her toward the front.

"And now who lives here?" she asked.

He grinned. It wasn't a big house, just one of those English Tudor bungalows—redbrick with a high-peaked roof and dormer and a pretty oak door. When he unlocked the front door, she stepped inside.

The foyer was a semicircle of cherry paneling. The paneling was unique, but the wood floors definitely needed a refinish. A thin set of stairs led to a single giant bedroom and bath upstairs, not that Kelly could see those from here.

The immediate view showed a small living room with a bay window and white stone fireplace. Beyond was a dining room, looking over a shaded backyard, and beyond that was the kitchen. The kitchen had old appliances, but the room had been renovated fairly recently with cobalt-blue counters and white trim.

Kelly glanced around, then back at him, and when he didn't produce immediate answers, she started ambling around. The more Ms. Curious poked and prodded, the more confused she appeared. Apart from a full downstairs bathroom, done in a ghastly shade of pink, the downstairs held two more rooms— one long, narrow family room, and the other a medium- sized den, where she paused in the doorway.

The den had ceiling-to-floor bookcases and a corner fireplace. Dusty, long drapes fell to the floor.

"There's no furniture in this place," Kelly said bewilderedly.

"I know."

"Except that I smell food in the oven."

"Yup, you're right again."

When she looked back into the den, it had to be pretty obvious where they were eating. On the carpet. He'd been here ahead, of course, set up an old blue blanket, opened the merlot to let it breathe, ab- sconded with major-size pillows from his sister's place and a tray of vanilla candles. Late-afternoon sun was still filtering the west windows for now, though, making candlelight a little premature.

"Okay," she said. "Cut out the suspense. You know I can't stand it. You said an economics professor used to live here. But who does now?"

"You do. If you want."

"Huh?"

There. The look of stunned surprise was worth all the running around he'd done to put this together—and of course, this was just the first part of the evening, and not the end of the surprises. But it was a pretty good zinger for an opener, if he said so himself.

Dinner wasn't too challenging. Wine. Strawberries dipped in cream cheese and brown sugar. Fresh bread, just baked. A crab salad and some sushi and other delicacies he knew she liked, followed by a complete tray of desserts. It wasn't exactly his kind of meal, but when he'd called his favorite restaurant to cater, he was thinking of what worked for her. Chocolate. French pastries. The ease of bread and fruit and all, where they wouldn't need knives and spoons, so much, just an occasional fork.

By the time he had her shoes off—which didn't take long—she was sitting cross-legged on the blanket, the silky yellow dress bunched between her legs for modesty. She was still trying to absorb what he'd told her, but it was uphill getting her to accept this particular gift.

"Maguire's owns the house. Actually, the family owns a fair amount of real estate around the university. Anyway, the economics professor who lived here got a divorce, moved away in the middle of the semester. That left us stranded in more ways than one. You'd be doing me a favor if you lived here."

"In a pig's eye," she said. "A favor is when you

need to borrow a cup of sugar. Or a ride to the airport. It's not giving someone a place to live."

"No, no, this is for me. Not you. See…the guy had the place forever, so some things need updating before it's rentable again. Like…the wood floors need sanding and varnishing. The downstairs bathroom needs somebody to pick out a different color and do something with it. Several appliances need an upgrade. Almost all the rooms need fresh paint."

"Will. I'm not exactly sure where you're going with this, but I'm way, way smarter than I look. You're not going to sell me roses in the desert."

"Would you *listen?*" He put some petulance in his voice as he stacked the dishes on the tray and poured her more wine. Her second glass.

"I *am* listening, but I'm not a charity case, buster."

"I keep telling you, this is a favor to *me*. It's one of my dad's messes. There's more to Maguire's than just the manufacturing facilities. The company has real estate. Houses and office buildings, and other holdings beyond that. And the thing is, to get this place ready to rent—or sell—someone has to oversee the renovations. Make the choices about paint and colors and crap like that. Report if the workmen aren't up to snuff. I can't be ten places at once."

"Your sisters could do it. Or your mother."

This was a lot trickier than he thought it was going to be. "Yes. They could. But their taste is in their credit cards, if you know what I mean. They'll spend more than the house is worth. I need someone to look at the house, update where it needs updating, choose what makes sense for the place. Someone like you. And in the meantime—" he raised his voice, because he could see she was about to make another protest "—you could live in the place. It'd be disruptive, but it'd be all yours. That way, you'd get out of that wreck you're in. It's still close to your job. It's a good neighborhood. And…"

He popped the last strawberry in her mouth just to keep her quiet for a moment longer.

"And, when you come to Paris with me, when we have all our messes straightened out—which, I admit, is taking a tad longer than I expected—it'll be easy for you to get out. Besides which—"

"I didn't realize you had this whole con-artist side to your character," she said darkly.

"This isn't con-artist stuff. If you like the house, you could either rent it or buy it when all the reno's done. Say, September. So see? You're not tied to any decision whatsoever. You have all your freedom, all your choices. And I get somebody supervising the update on the place. Everybody wins."

She hesitated. Then hesitated some more, searching his face, obviously thinking hard. "There's something wrong about this deal. I just can't figure out what it is."

"God, you're suspicious. Of course, maybe you don't like the house."

"Of course I like the house! It's adorable! Two fireplaces and this great den and a blue-and-white kitchen? What's not to love!"

"You haven't seen the upstairs. Look…" He did his best to sound apologetic. "I realize it'll be a lot of trouble. A lot of dust. Workmen in and out. A bunch of crappy shopping, picking out colors and appliances and that tedious stuff—"

Possibly he'd laid it on a little thick, because she pounced. "Quit trying to be so damned nice or I'm going to smack you," she warned him. Only then she really did pounce, in a flurry of yellow silk and wine-wet lips. He'd been sitting there, with one knee up, but when she hurled herself at him, he fell back onto the picnic blanket.

All right, all right, so maybe he could have kept his balance. It wasn't as if she was remotely heavy. But she leveled him with a kiss. Her landing on top of him was ideal, after all. And in seconds, they were all tangled up, her bare legs tucked around him, the yellow dress dipping beautifully at the bodice, revealing the bare rounded breasts he'd been so close to seeing before.

It had been a long time since they'd made love.

Too long.

He needed to keep his head a little longer, and he gulped for oxygen before he was completely sucked into that taste, that texture, that look in her eyes. "You forgot underwear," he told her.

"It was a choice," she assured him.

"What happened to sin and guilt and all?"

"There's a time for that. And a time for no under-wear," she explained. "Were you objecting?"

"No." He cleared his throat. "Definitely no. But—"

Sprawled on his chest, her elbows digging into his shoulders, rubbing against him with deliberate, ma-nipulative, disgraceful invitation, she was obviously determined to destroy him. "If there's any 'but,' that's it. I'll get up and put on some good-girl underpants and a nice, thick, wired-up padded bra."

"No. Please. No." He got it, that she was enjoying torturing him. But he couldn't take much more teas-ing. "I need to do something."

"I know," she said smugly.

"Something *first.*"

She was still smiling, but it was that bad-Kelly smile. It was a smile he didn't trust, couldn't trust. An unpredictable, worrisome, adorable smile and, *damn,* but he loved Kel when she was feeling full of herself and high on being a woman.

He fumbled, fast as he could make his thick fin-gers work, and finally yanked the blindfold from his back pocket and whipped it over her eyes.

"What's this?"

He didn't answer directly, because she had to know perfectly well what it was. "I figured a silk scarf wouldn't hold for long. Or else you could peek. So I needed a real-life blackout blindfold, which was harder to find than I could believe. But just so you know—this is *not* for fun."

"Sure it's n—"

Her tone was teasing again, as if she assumed he was handing her nonsense. So he kissed her.

Only this time, he kissed her differently than before. He closed his eyes, because he wanted to be immersed in her, wanted to be blind to everything but her, aware of only the world between them, the world where only their senses alone communicated to each other.

He eased her back down to the blanket, taking her lips, skimming his tongue inside, offering a soft, dark, openmouthed kiss that silenced her. And him.

Her hair had started tumbling from its updo, loosened when he put on the blindfold, and loosened more now when he threaded a hand through those silky strands, just because it felt good. Good the way touching Kelly, any way, anyhow, always felt.

Her heartbeat quickened when he shifted, sliding a hand from her head to her bare throat, down to the loose drape of fabric at her neck. That damn dress was soft, but not as soft as her skin. Nothing was as soft as the swell of her breast. One stroke, and the tip pebbled for him. One stroke, and he was harder than stone. Hot stone.

Somehow he didn't think he'd be able to talk for long.

"Kel?"

"Hmm. I think we have an awful lot of clothes on."

"Yeah. I'm about to take care of that. In two seconds. But I need to tell you something." He tried talking again and found his vocal cords malfunctioning. A guy had priorities. Obviously before trying to complete the conversation, no matter how critically important it was, he wasn't going to be able to concentrate until he'd taken care of other pressing business first. So easily, smoothly, he shifted her to a semisitting position so he could pull that sweet wisp of yellow silk over her head.

She wasn't wearing anything underneath.

He'd guessed that from before. And she'd admitted it. But it was another thing to actually *find* her body completely naked, her breasts already swollen tight, her skin flushed with warmth. Her breath was so quick...for him. Her body hot...for him.

"Kel, the thing is, I didn't know you were going to show up with no underwear."

"Good. Surprises are good."

"Yes. But I'm just saying I thought I'd have to do the seducing."

"You do. Go to work, boy."

He smiled, kissed her again, but he wasn't suckering into that wicked mouth of hers quite yet. "I will, I will. But I want you to know that I specifically picked this house because you'd never seen it before. And I wanted you to wear the blindfold so everything else would be unfamiliar, too."

She stopped stroking him, as if finally hearing the

seriousness in his voice. Her palm touched his neck, then his chin, then his cheek, reading him like Braille, studying his expression through texture. "Why?" she murmured. "Why did you want everything to be unfamiliar to me?"

"Because you've been so worried. About all the unfamiliar things in your life. Discovering you had a father. Discovering the beliefs you grew up with were partly lies. Discovering that you felt different—about yourself—since Paris."

"Yes," she whispered.

"And because of all that, you've felt really thrown. As if you didn't know who you were anymore."

"Yes," she whispered again, sounding fierce, sounding grateful that he'd listened to her and really heard her.

"Well, this was the point of the blindfold and the unfamiliar place, Kel. No matter what's unfamiliar to you, no matter what's throwing you, I'm here. And I know who you are." In moments, he'd pushed off the slacks, unshackled the buttons of his blue dress shirt.

"Who you are," he said, "is my lover. Just like I'm your lover. And this is the thing." He took a long, slow breath. "I love you, Kelly. I want you. All of you. Whoever you are, whoever you were. I love the before and after. I love the during. I love the everything about you."

She ripped off the blindfold and faced him with

BLAME IT ON PARIS

fierce eyes. Just like that, there was a power shift. He'd tried to direct this whole thing, for her, because he believed she needed to hear not just that he loved her, but that he loved all the incarnations and reinventions of Kelly Nicole Rochard.

Even when she was aggravating the hell out of him, he loved her. She was suddenly winding around him. The seducee turned seducer. The cherishee became the cherisher.

Soft hands stroked him closer. Dark eyes took him in, looking at him—at his face, at his nakedness, at his erection, at all of him. "You are," she murmured, "everything I ever dreamed of in a lover."

Well, hell times three. If she expected him to have any self-control after that, she was dreaming.

But then she didn't seem to have any self-control after that, either. She loved his body as if she owned it, as if she'd never met an inhibition.

An hour later, an eternity later, he lay on the blanket, Kelly curled naked next to him. She'd dozed off like a baby—her own fault, for turning making love into a marathon. He was just as whipped, just as wiped. But he couldn't erase the smile off his face. Didn't want to give in to sleep.

Will didn't care what was rational or irrational, what the world thought or didn't think.

He knew, in his gut, that everything in his world was right as long as Kelly was with him.

Nothing could stop him when they were together.

They could go anywhere, be anything, do anything. He'd gone into this night with Kelly, knowing his dad wasn't going to be laid up forever—knowing that his chances of being able to stay here were steadily deteriorating.

But he *had* to believe Kelly valued who they were together. She'd come to see it his way—that it didn't matter where they were, as long as they were together.

And for the first time in years—maybe in his whole life—he really believed that things were going to turn out okay. They'd go to Paris. Be together. The rest didn't matter; it would sort itself out.

"Will," Kelly murmured.

"Hmm?"

"Go to sleep."

All it took was her permission. He draped his arm and the blanket over her, then dropped off into deep sleep.

CHAPTER FIFTEEN

WHAT WAS WITH this Tuesday? Kelly put down the phone in her office, stared at it for one long dark second and warned the device, "If you ring one more time in the next half hour, I'm going to throw you against the wall."

It immediately rang.

"Yes," she barked into the receiver. "This is Kelly Rochard."

It was the construction guy she'd contacted—one of three construction companies who were giving her estimates. She couldn't very well *not* take the call. She had to hear the price, their terms, get their schedules, their references.

She'd just hung up when Brenna showed up at the door. "There's someone in the lobby who—"

Her phone rang before she could answer Brenna. Her coworker threw up her hands and gestured that she'd track her down later. Good thing. This call was from a painter, who was prepared to come in and start the job as soon as this weekend.

Only Kelly couldn't start that quickly. She had to

pick out new counters for the bathroom first. And she was a *long* way from settling on colors.

"But I thought you wanted it done fast, and I got an opening—"

"I do, I do, and I'm grateful you could squeeze me in." Her mom had given her the reference, so she knew the painter was trustworthy. Only holy kamoly, did everything have to hit on Tuesday morning?

She finished the call and pointed the royal finger at the phone.

It didn't help. It rang again.

"My heavens, I've been trying to get you all morning," her mom said. "I'm sorry to call you at work, honey."

"That's okay." It was. Somehow just airing all the old history about Henri Rochard had brought her closer to her mom. For all the turmoil, all the worrying that her relationship with her mother would be scarred in some way, the opposite seemed to be true.

"Well, I needed to know for sure if you could come early on Saturday. They're claiming this block party is for me, but you know how it really goes. Everybody helps set up, and I'm stuck working late on Friday—"

"I'll be there by nine-thirty. Is that early enough? You want me to bring anything?"

"Nope, just yourself. And the time's perfect. Thanks, sweets."

The phone rang again almost as soon as she hung

it up, but this time she ignored it. She *had* to get some real work done, and that included the project she was doing for Will. The hunt for John Henry, his mystery employee, hadn't required tons of time, but she wanted the job completed faster than yesterday.

Brenna showed up in the doorway again, but before she could say a word, Kelly said firmly, "There isn't a client I haven't spoken to this morning who should need me for *anything.* I just need a few minutes without interruptions!"

"But—"

"Five! Just five whole minutes! Hold the calls!"

She turned back to the computer. It bugged her, the house Will had thrown so generously in her lap. In fact, a lot of things had been bothering her since the weekend.

Will was a darling. He couldn't help that. But it troubled her that she hadn't been pulling her weight. No, she didn't have money like he did. But he'd asked for help, tracking down his employee, and that *was* one thing she should have been able to do for him.

Will's father was going to be on his feet in another week or so. At that point, Kelly knew perfectly well it was time to sink or swim.

Go with Will to Paris.

Or stay here.

"No," she muttered to herself. "You're not going to think about that now. You're going to…" She narrowed her eyes at the figures popping up on the screen.

She'd become an expert at locating people who didn't want to be found, but people living right out in the open were notoriously harder to trace. They actively and regularly covered their tracks and all their personal histories. Real people, of course, didn't have blank spots of years. When someone had a blank spot, they'd been somewhere and done something.

Like John Henry. A blank spot of five and a half years, to be precise.

Will was right. His employee had something to hide. She just wasn't positive what it was yet. Down the pike, she could call a cop friend if she needed to. Sullivan wouldn't give her confidential information—even though he was practically her godfather and she'd babysat his firstborn—but he would confirm information if she already had it. And then there was Father Donovan, who always, always honored the sanctity of the church, but he did like his gin and tonics, and he happened to have access to Catholic university alumni records.

Their boy, J.H., had been to a Jesuit school.

Just a few more minutes....

Brenna showed up in the doorway again, this time looking peeved. "*Don't* tell me to go away again. There are three women in the lobby to see you. They don't have an appointment. They know that. But they're absolutely positive you'll be happy they're here."

"Right," Kelly said ironically, but she rose out of her chair. "I'm sorry I've been a bear."

"You have been," Brenna concurred.

"And I'm sorry you had to put them off if they're for me."

"You should be."

"Two Hershey's dark chocolate do it?"

"Three." Brenna sniffed.

Peace again. Kelly rounded the corner into the lobby and then stopped in surprise. The three blondes waiting for her were Martha, Laurie and Liz—Will's sisters.

"Well *hi!* I'm so sorry—I didn't realize you three were out here. I was so involved with a project that I wasn't listening—"

"No problem, no problem."

The three of them looked like an advertisement for Saks. Martha looked like an urban young mother, arched collar, blue skirt, hair perfect for any weather. Laurie was wearing blue, too, but an artsier batik watered silk skirt with a white silky top. And Liz looked totally hip, her tank top dipping low, brand sunglasses used as a headband, her denim skirt from the top-of-the-brand heap.

Martha swiftly took the conversational lead. "Will said you'd been working incessantly. We thought you might like to go to lunch if you had time. We know you have to be back soon, but there's a place just a skip from here, Barney's, that serves the best lobster salad…"

"We all decided at the same time that we'd like to get to know you better, and we'd been talking about going to Barney's…and then we thought, why, your office is just around the corner, Kelly, so…" Laurie filled in.

By the time they were seated in Barney's, Kelly knew perfectly well she was being suckered. She didn't mind. Why turn down a lobster salad and a raspberry iced tea? She liked Will's sisters, wanted to know them better, and frankly, she'd have done the same thing in their shoes—vetted their brother's girlfriend.

The questions were subtle, buried in girl talk about shopping and brands and school history and movies. And Will. They readily volunteered little tidbits about Will. The beat-up dog he'd brought home when he was eleven. The girls who chased after him in his high school football days. The time he'd driven their dad's prize antique Morgan into Julianna Raymond's swimming pool—after a National Honor Society induction, besides—and Will had his clothes on, but Julianna sure didn't.

In the meantime, Kelly filled them in on her background…her school, her single mom, the whole nine yards. No point in pretending she came from blue blood. No reason to. Will knew it all, and she was proud of who she was, just as she was. They'd never get along if she felt she had to put on a mask around them. Eventually, though, they ran out of personal questions and moved tactfully toward more serious material.

"Your dad…" Kelly propelled into the conversation.

"Yes. That's one of the reasons we wanted to

talk with you." The three of them sobered fast, but Martha was the one who answered. "Dad's getting better, but I have to say, we all believe he *has* to slow down. His blood pressure's out of control. He and Mom want to do some traveling, not just vacations, but really see something of the world while they both still have the energy and the health. But there's no way he'll even consider retiring...unless Will stays."

Laurie shook her head. "He's tried to leave the place with managers before. They're always good people. And he'll plan to take three or four weeks off with Mom, but he never makes it more than a few days. The only one he actually trusts with the company is Will."

Kelly was starting to worry whether the lobster salad was going to stay down. "And how do you all feel about that?" she asked honestly.

"We can't intervene," Liz said bluntly. "Getting in between Dad and Will is like being between a lion and a tiger in the same cage. We love Will. He needs to do what he needs to do."

"Yes," Martha agreed. "We all feel that way."

Now Kelly knew she was going to have trouble with the fabulous salad, and man, she loved lobster. It was so unfair. But the three of them were too ready with their lines, too prepared. She knew something was missing—just not what that something was.

"So..." she said. "How do the three of you feel about the company? Have you ever worked for your dad? Have you any interest in a particular job there? How does it all work in your family?"

None of them had any business sense, they freely admitted. But they were in the middle of exciting lives, doing things they loved. Family came first, of course. Which was partly why they wanted Will to come home. They loved him. They needed him. He was critically important to all of them.

Martha had plans to buy a cottage on Lake Michigan. Kelly had already been on the boat, right? So she'd likely seen the place. Everyone in the family could take advantage of it in the summer, all the kids could congregate there, learn to sail and swim, be together. Will was probably the only one who could make that happen, because his vote in the family could sway it into happening.

Liz had a different agenda. "I'm trying to get out from under my dependence on Dad. I finally got my degree in interior design. I told Will my plans." Liz, all animated, relayed her plans to open an interior-design studio in Chicago. She didn't want to need Maguire's anymore, wanted to stand on her own. Will understood, Liz claimed. She just needed a stake to get her business going.

And then there was Laurie. So pretty. Closest in age to Will, Kelly knew. She was the one with classy, quiet looks, a sweep of blond hair, no bling, just elegance in the way she looked and spoke and tilted her head. "I have no plans to move away. I want to live here, by my family and friends, have a quiet life. Will knows I've got a guy. He's a fabulous, fabulous artist."

"He is," the other two sisters agreed.

"Naturally it's hard for an artist to get started, but I don't have to live expensively. He's so wonderful. Will's going to meet him at Mom's birthday party a week from Sunday. I'm hoping you'll get a chance then, too."

Kelly was still smiling and waving goodbye when the sisters dropped her back at the office, but her smile died the instant their Pacifica was out of sight.

She stood in the heat, feeling hugely sick to her stomach.

Every time...every darned time she started to really believe she and Will could make it, something happened. The other night, at the house, the way they'd made love, the way they'd talked, Kelly could feel it again. Not the fantasy of Paris. But the plain old, real wonder of love. She adored that man. He seemed to adore her right back.

And she'd come home from that believing that surely the love they had was strong enough to survive and solve their complicated family problems.

But now she thought...not.

The problem was that she was plenty tough, but Will wasn't. He thought he was, but the wrangling with his dad tore him apart, sliced at his ego and his heart relentlessly. And now Kelly saw how it was with his sisters.

She liked all three of them. They were fun and funny and smart. But they were also so determined to get what they wanted. They'd set up the lunch to lay out their agendas. Of course they wanted Will home. Martha wanted her house. Laurie wanted her guy subsidized, and Liz wanted stakes in a new business.

In many ways, they were totally wonderful. But Will had tried to tell her they were on the spoiled, self-absorbed side. She hadn't believed it before. Now she understood that he really was trapped here. Possibly so trapped that there simply were no answers except getting out and living elsewhere.

What was she supposed to do? If she loved him, really loved him, would she let him go? Or follow him to a life in Paris, where nothing important to him—or her—was resolved?

Damn it all. She'd found her knight, so how come there seemed no possibility whatsoever of a happy ending?

"WILL?"

He heard his father's bark from the library just as he reached the front door. He backed up, carrying a fresh mug in one hand and a wrapped present in the other. The day outside was a steamer—the first of the summer so far—with the threat of storms later in the afternoon.

The threat of storms was already prevalent in the cool, quiet library. Will took one look at his dad's face and could smell ozone. "How you doing today?" he asked.

"Pissed off that my ankle isn't better. Frustrated to be cooped up at home. But fine. You got a minute?"

"Sure," Will said.

His dad still hadn't regained his normal ruddy coloring. Ironically Will wanted Aaron to be his usual tyrannical self. He was doing fine. Just sitting. But Will couldn't remember a time when Aaron didn't charge around full bore, both at work and at home. "Sit," Aaron said, and motioned to the chair across from the wide leather couch.

His dad had the bad ankle propped on a pillow on the coffee table, his cane by his side, an untouched tray of a very fancy lunch on another table nearby. "Your mother's driving me crazy," he confided. "Going to no end of trouble, cooking me all kinds of stuff. My God. Eggs Benedict this morning, with crepes and fresh pineapple. Now a fresh crab salad and some kind of cucumber soup and this strange-looking thing." He shook his head at the unidentified plate. "I've been trying to coax the dog in here to eat every morning so she won't know I didn't eat it myself."

Will actually relaxed and smiled. "Hey, you could try a few bites." Something in him was hungry. Not for the gourmet tray, but to share a simple, honest smile with his dad. How many years had it been since they'd had a conversation? A normal, everyday, no-porcupine-barbs conversation?

"I *do* eat. But I'm not getting any exercise because of this goddamn ankle. How can I work up an appetite? And she's making enough for ten men." Aaron shifted position with a grimace. "Were you going somewhere?"

"Yeah. A friend's birthday." He didn't mention the birthday was for Kelly's mother. No reason to hide it, but so far, they were talking fairly easily and Will didn't want to invite any prying.

"Well. I won't keep you long. I just wanted to tell you, son, you're doing an outstanding job. I keep getting reports from the plant, from the office, from everywhere. You took over like a lion. I knew you could. I knew you would."

"Thanks. When you get back in the saddle, I'd like to think you won't have any extra worries. Things are going fine. A lot of great people are helping me. But everyone misses you."

"I doubt that. I know perfectly well they call me a slave driver behind my back," Aaron said wryly. "But I was hoping your doing this would be a good thing for you."

"I'm glad to help out." Will could feel himself getting stiff, in spite of his resolve.

"I don't know how long I can keep control of this helm, Will."

Will nodded carefully. "You've built an extraordinary empire. But one advantage to that, Dad, should be having the financial freedom to make whatever choices you want to. Slow down, when you want to slow down. Sell, if that's what you want to do. Keep it all under your own wing, if that's how you want it to be."

He didn't mention the one choice he knew Aaron wanted—for him to take over. And for once, that moment passed without a fight. Aaron studied him, but he didn't take him on the way he usually did. Just smoothly moved into another subject, and Will relaxed again, thinking damn, he was home free. They'd actually managed a whole conversation without being inclined to strangle each other.

"Your mother's sixtieth party is a week from Sunday. Arrangements at the club are all finalized. Think we'll have better than three hundred."

Again Will shared a smile with his dad. "That sounds like hell and a half."

"You said it. And white tie besides." Aaron groaned. So did Will. "At least you're the one who'll have to dance with her."

"Everyone will dance with her, but you know I will, too. Having a car accident's a hell of a way to get out of it, though," Will teased.

"That's what your mother says." Aaron added quickly, "She'd like us all to go to church together that morning. It would mean a lot to her if you'd attend."

Will could feel his smile slip, his stomach start to clench. "You know I'll be there for the party, and anything I can do to help ahead of time. But I don't know about the church part."

"Would it would kill you to go to church? For your mother's sake?"

"It wouldn't kill me, no. But I can't adopt a religion as a birthday present to Mom." He heard the snap in his voice, tried to erase it. "I know Mom wants me to believe. But I don't. Pretending would just be hypocritical on my part."

"Hypocritical? I'd call it respectful. Respecting your mother."

Like he'd ever failed to respect his mom?

Twenty minutes later, Will was still breathing smoke when he stalked out to the car.

Still. As he drove toward Kelly's mother's house, he realized the rotten truth that he wasn't mad at his father but himself.

Maybe Aaron had initiated the fight, but that was always true. Aaron was still under the weather, his ankle still causing him pain and frustration. Further, for Aaron to be housebound for the past couple weeks was absolute hell for his dad, and Will knew all that, which meant he should have kept his cool.

They'd had a peaceful, productive week together. Will should have known it was too good to last. Only now he felt lower than dirt. He could have done better with his dad, and he knew it.

But as he turned onto Char's street, he closeted

that problem. The immediate challenge facing him was going to take his full concentration.

Kelly didn't know he was showing up, had verbally fretted that he wouldn't be received well because of her ex-fiancé. He understood that, but he'd caught enough clues to realize she was worried about how friends and family were going to treat her.

It just wasn't right, letting her face a tough family situation alone.

Now, though, he started to get a picture of what he was walking into. Char's house was located near the end of the block, where neighbors had roped off the street and taken ownership. Picnic tables were set up right in the road. Smoke billowed from a half dozen barbecues. A handful of bullet-shaped, grandpa-aged men supervised the two kegs parked in the back of pickup trucks. Dogs of all sizes chased kids of all sizes, everybody shrieking and yelping as they ran through sprinklers. Babies were parked in the shade, either in strollers or buggies. Adults milled everywhere. People were talking and shouting and singing.

In fact, the noise level rivaled the decibels of a Saturday-afternoon football game.

Will had assumed a block party meant a few neighborhood couples coming over to share a birthday cake, not a free-for-all that involved hundreds, food, booze, gambling, and—in someone's front yard—dancing. The dancing was as crazy as the rest of it—the music changing from the ancient "Tennessee Waltz" to an old Police rock song while Will was walking from where he'd parked the car.

He searched the crowd, seeking Kelly. In a blink, he'd summed up the chaos as pretty damn great. Maybe a little rowdy, but the family feeling and natural camaraderie were unmistakable, and not for the first time, he recognized what strong emotional, healthy ties Kelly had here.

Ties that he would deprive her of, if they took off for Paris.

That thought put another whump in his mood, so again, he tried to shake it off. He located a picnic table, which was mounded with presents all wrapped in comics, added his to the heap—although his looked out of place with its pink wrapping and bow. He thought at the time he'd gone the long mile for a guy, but now he could see that Sunday-funnies and gag gifts were more the order of the day, not something pretty for a pretty lady.

Since he'd done everything else wrong so far today, he figured he might as well look for more trouble. And almost immediately he spotted Char—dressed to hold court in white shorts and a white top with a child's gold crown perched on her head, her laughter peeling out through the crowd.

He was aiming for her when he finally caught sight of Kelly. She was wearing a red polo, white shorts, her hair clipped up and out of her way, carrying a tray of drinks that looked bigger than she was.

He turned toward her and tried to wade through the sea of moving bodies. Several people glanced at him. Some did a double take, and even a triple. A couple shouted out a hi, as though they thought they knew him. A few others gave him a startled, long stare, as if they knew of him—but that was probably just some latent paranoia showing up.

"Why, Will…" Kelly's mom caught up with him before he could reach Kelly. Char greeted him with a deliberately big hug and a welcoming hello, which gave him a chance to wish her happy birthday. As if sensing he needed a hero—or a heroine—Char grabbed his arm protectively and started introducing him around.

His head started buzzing. There was a Mary, and an Aunt Willa and an Aunt Suzanna, then a bunch of people whose last name was Matthews—he gathered they were ex-in-laws—and then came a Pete and a Bill and another Bill and a Steve who-used-to-play-football and another Steve who-was-just-divorced.

There were too many names. He felt himself scrutinized on a par with a piece of meat at a butcher's, shook more hands than he could count, took on chitchat, all the while trying to find Kel in the crowd again. Still, it was an easy crowd to work, people just looking to have a good time, and yeah, curious about an outsider, but there was nothing weird about that.

Someone named Gaynelle was introduced to

him—a lady about Char's age, who heard his name and promptly flushed red. But the minute she turned away, Char just said kindly to him, "No help for that, Will. Oh, and here's Uncle Fred…"

Fred pumped his hand like he was a faucet in a drought. "You're one of those Maguires? I'll be damned."

It was going okay—except for not finding Kelly— until Char suddenly turned to him, something different in her voice, and said, "And, Will, this is Jason White. Jason, this is Will Maguire."

And that was it. All the noise, all the laughter, all the pushing, slightly sweaty bodies seemed to fade out like a bleached wash.

"So…you're the son of a bitch."

The man's voice was pleasant enough, but the content made Will think of acid rain.

So, Will thought.

So.

He had about a millisecond to form impressions. Her ex-fiancé was about what he'd expected, since Kelly would never have picked a loser. The guy had decent looks, plenty of IQ in the eyes. He was a little round-shouldered, Will thought critically, but that judgment might have been colored by his searching hard for a fault. Jason, similarly, was looking him over as if examining roadkill.

"I was wondering if I'd have a chance to meet you," Will said, with no inflection at all in his tone, or he hoped there wasn't. If he'd ever aspired to being onstage, which he hadn't, this was certainly his moment. There didn't seem to be a soul in the whole circus-sized crowd who didn't know that Will was the one Kelly had left Jason for—at least as far as they knew.

"I can't believe you'd show up here." Jason, wearing a white polo and shorts, was a few inches shorter than Will, which made Will extra wary. Short guys always had more to prove in public.

Will had plenty to prove, too, of course. That Kelly didn't have to worry anything would happen if he showed up. That Kelly would know she had a support system here if anyone was unkind to her. That Kelly would know he could handle tough situations without bailing.

Which meant he couldn't punch out the bozo, no matter the provocation.

"I didn't come to cause anyone a problem, Jason. I wanted to bring Char a present. To meet more of Kelly's family."

"Yeah, right. Did you imagine you'd find any friends here? Everyone in this whole crowd has known Kelly and I since we were kids together."

"Yes, Kelly told me that." A little late, Will realized he could smell alcohol on Jason's breath.

"You thought you'd be welcome?"

Not that Will could feel a trickle of sweat snaking down his spine, but he was pretty sure if he said anything wrong, anything at all, Jason wouldn't mind taking a swing at him. It wouldn't be about who won or who got hurt. It would just be for the joy of Jason getting to throw a punch.

Will understood the dynamic. He had the same Y chromosome, after all.

But he *had* to come through for Kelly in this. That was it. There were no other choices. He had to be the guy she needed him to be. Period.

"I didn't think about being welcomed or not," he said quietly. "I just wanted to know some of the people in Kelly's life. Actually, that includes you. I never met her until she was going through hell and a half after the mugging in Paris."

Jason either didn't hear him or just wanted to bully through his own agenda. "If you think Maguire money's going to make you look good here, you'd better think again. Seduce another guy's woman. You're in the dirt class and there's no shovel deep enough to get you out."

My, this was pleasant.

Will swallowed bile, swallowed some more bile, then swallowed again. It'd be so easy to answer that. So easy to defend himself, to get angry, to take on the battle Jason was inviting. Instead he said, "I'm sorry you lost her."

And then thought, uh-oh. Jason opened his mouth, closed it, didn't seem to know what to say or do.

Will figured that was it, he was either going to get

punched out or things were going to calm down. Given that he'd screwed up absolutely everything else today, he figured it was going to go the wrong way.

CHAPTER SIXTEEN

"KELLY..." Her mom shot in the back screen door. "You were right."

"About what?" Kelly was in the kitchen to grab a fresh roll of paper towels and a new tray of brownies.

"He's here."

This batch of brownies was sticking harder than the last. Kelly had to dig in the spatula at the edges. "Didn't I tell you he'd come?"

"Okay, yes, you did." Her mom leaned against the counter. "He's a good guy," she said slowly.

"I told you that, too."

"Yeah, well, you came home from Paris all different. Some of it *had* to be him. Maybe I didn't want to believe it was about me and your father so much. It was a lot easier to believe that Will was at fault."

Kelly glanced at her mom again. "And now? Do you still feel that way?"

"Now, I guess I wouldn't have any trouble loving a man who would walk on water for my daughter. Which, just for the record, is exactly what he was doing a minute ago. Jason found him, and I believe

Jason was drinking a fair amount before he showed up this afternoon. If Will were my boyfriend, I'd probably go out there and find some subtle way to rescue him."

"Holy kamoly, were you waiting for an invitation before telling me?" Kelly left the brownie tray and the paper towels and galloped outside.

She had no problem finding the guys. The neighborhood, being the neighborhood, was never quiet at a gig like this unless there was something fascinating worth being quiet for.

Under an old elm tree, near the birthday present table—and in the shade of one of the noisier poker games—Jason was sprawled on the ground, Will crouched next to him.

No one was going anywhere near the two except for Kelly, who hadn't run faster since high school track.

Will felt her shadow, looked up immediately with panicked eyes. "Kelly, I never touched him. I think he'd had a fair amount to drink. And he was standing in the sun. And—"

"I'm guessing that's right. He never could handle much alcohol."

"He's having a real tough day," Will said.

"Aren't we all?" Any other time, a dozen people would have helped them. Instead, both families watched the two of them shift Jason over to a cool grassy spot in the shade.

"Need a lukewarm damp cloth. Maybe a thermometer. If this is just passing out from drinking, it's one thing," Will said. "But if it's heat related, we'd better figure it out pretty quick."

Will took his pulse. Kelly wanted to shake her head, not surprised Will was taking charge even with her pistol of an ex. Minutes later, Jason's face and neck were being sponged down with lukewarm water. His pulse and temperature revealed nothing out of the ordinary. The diagnosis was too much beer too early in the day, for a guy who was already hot under the collar.

Jason's sisters got around to moving in, then. A measure of their acceptance of Will, whether Will knew it or not, was their exchanging some basic dialogue with him, even a second of laughter.

"Come on, you," Kelly ordered Will, once the crisis was over and Jason was in his family's hands. In an ideal world, she'd serve him a glass of lemonade and hang out at the party with him, but nothing was ideal today. Everybody brought food and drink to these neighborhood parties, but kitchen detail—since it was her mom's birthday—fell on her for this one. There was no end to trash pickup or delivery of more food.

Since she was doing it, Will was doing it. The chores were a major comedown for a guy from the other side of the tracks—mopping up spills, serving the seniors, picking up paper plates and pop cans, carting trash. But Will never left her side.

"Don't be angry," Will said. "I know you told me not to come."

"It's all right. I knew you would, and I really need to talk with you besides. I found the guy you were looking for, Will. It just came together this morning, in fact."

"Wait. *How* did you know I'd be here? And what guy?"

"John Henry." They both had to stop in front of the seniors. Anyone over sixty-five expected to be waited on in this crowd, even if they could outrun and outdance the younger generations by miles. Beer, lemonade, pop and ice water were delivered. Will brought up the rear with a trash bin.

"You were right about him, Will. There are missing periods of time. It seems he wasn't John Henry when he started out in Peoria, but Jackson Henry. Jack. Went to Northwestern, like he told you. Majored in economics, mastered in business. Aced the school thing, just like he claimed."

"*How* did you know I was going to be here?" Will persisted.

She ignored him. His employee problem was of real importance—for him and for her, she thought. "But he took a job with DynCal. You must have read their story. Not at an Enron level, but upper management was still scooping in profits, making their report to stockholders sound better than it was. Your John Henry was fired. Disappeared. Then reinvented himself."

"Wait…" Will was trying to carry two filled trash bags at once. He stashed them in the party garbage containers, then caught up with her at a breakneck pace in spite of the heat. "So. You knew I'd come…"

Kelly was well aware of the family and neighborhood watching Will breaking his butt, doing all the cleanup. "Apparently your John Henry changed his name—legally—when he moved to South Bend. He's doing a good job for you?"

"Too good. Something just didn't seem real. That's what made me nervous." Will finally gave up and pursued her topic instead of his—at least for now. "You do damned good work, brown eyes."

"I know I do." For that smug comment, she got a kiss. On the nose. Which was better than no kiss, but only by a hair. On the other hand, she figured Will realized that PDAs on the home turf in the presence of Jason's family was never going to sell too well. "So what do you think you're going to do about this John Henry, Will?"

"Fire him."

By then they had returned to the kitchen. She was handing him a tray of cookies and another of brownies to take back out, but now she frowned. "Wait a minute—"

"Kel, a soft heart doesn't work in business. The guy lied. He's responsible for money. I can't have it."

"But he didn't necessarily do anything wrong in that company. Maybe they fired him because he wouldn't play crooked ball. Or maybe because he discovered what was going on. I haven't found any evidence he was part of it. And, Will…"

"What?"

She heaped another tin of cookies on top of the ones he was carrying. "I don't think it's weird or wrong that he tried to reinvent himself after making a mistake. Don't we all do that?"

He stopped. So did she. They were outside by then, both their arms full, the sun beating down on both of them, but he seemed to realize, as she did, that somehow the conversation had turned into something a whole lot more serious than the Maguire's employee. And Will tackled it head-on. "You didn't reinvent yourself because of making a mistake, Kel. You didn't make a mistake. You didn't run away and try to hide out from your problems at all. It's not the same thing."

"In a way, it is. I was about to make a mistake— by going along with lies. Lies about who I was. Lies about who I was expected to be, in a marriage I was expected to want. And I didn't know how to get out of any of it. So I left, to give myself a chance to think and change." She cocked her head and said gently, "You did that, too, Will. Left South Bend because you couldn't figure out how to make the situation better with your dad. That wasn't a crime. You were trying to find a way to cope."

"It's not the same as John Henry."

"No," she agreed softly, and wondered how long they were going to stand there in the sun, dying from the heat, but both of them seemed to simultaneously realize that worries had been festering for both of them for too long. Maybe it wasn't the right time or place. Maybe there was no right time or place. "What's the same, though, Will Maguire, is that neither of us admires someone who can't find a better answer than running away."

"You're implying I've been running away."

"No. I thought that when I first knew you. Not anymore. When I was researching this John Henry for you, though, I kept thinking about us. Your employee ran away from his problems. I've been trying to come to terms with my father—you've been trying to find a way to come to terms with yours. Neither of us are runners. But neither of us are the kind who can just happily move on until we've crossed our t's and dotted our i's."

Will started to look annoyed. And hot. "Okay. Just spit out what you're trying to say. Do you even know where you're going with this?"

Well, she hadn't known until that moment. Until the ball in her stomach turned sharp and scary. She faced him with her heart in her eyes. "I'm trying to tell you that I'll go to Paris with you, Will. Or anywhere else in the universe that you want to go. If you resolve your relationship with your dad first. No matter what you have to do. Find some way to fix it."

"Kel. Don't try that kind of ultimatum thing. Not with me."

She said softly, "I'd never do the ultimatum thing. With anyone but you. Because I love you, Will."

"*Now's* a hell of a time to tell me. Hundred people around here, most of whom are watching every step I take, hoping I trip."

She cocked her head. Until that moment, she hadn't thought he was aware of how intensely he'd been scrutinized. "I don't know how to tell you this, but you've been passing every test."

"Only because I haven't tripped yet."

"No. Because you're a good guy and you keep showing it."

He put down the brownies and the cookies. Right on the ground. Walked her into the shade of her mother's young maple. "You love these people," he said.

"I do. They've been part of my life forever. They're full of faults. And sometimes they're intrusive and annoying. But they've watched out for me. I've babysat their kids, had a bleacher seat to the rise and fall of some marriages and divorces. They're good people, Will."

"Yeah. I can see that."

"And I hate to tell you this," she murmured, "but you had a great time this afternoon."

"Picking up trash? Carrying stuff in the sun? Hauling your ex-fiancé under a tree? Being grilled and sniffed at and pried into by complete strangers?"

"Yeah, all that. You liked it all."

He opened his mouth and then said, "Well, hell. So I did."

She laughed. So did he.

But she was thinking her heart was feeling so full that it could pop like an overfilled balloon if she wasn't careful. To lose Will now would hurt more than she could bear.

But they really weren't in Paris anymore. And somehow, as hard and fast as they were both moving, trying to change things, trying to fix things, they weren't finding the answers that would enable them to be together.

And they were running out of time.

WILL STOPPED by Kelly's house Wednesday at lunch. She had left a phone message, asking him to make some decisions before she pushed ahead on some renovation projects. He couldn't carve out more than an hour, but he'd shucked his suit coat and was carrying a fast-food hamburger as he waded through the sea of vehicles on the street.

He charged up the walk and poked his head in the door. "Kel?"

He could hear a buzz saw upstairs, the sound of hammering and sanding coming from the kitchen, but Kelly must have heard him above the general din, because she came bounding out of the kitchen area, looking very happy. "You're here! I'm so glad you could make the time. I've got a bunch of stuff to show you."

"I'm okay with your judgment, you know. Told you that already. Your taste's better than mine."

"Well, yes," she teased. "But it's your money, hotshot, and I don't want to waste it."

Mentally he'd been holding his breath when he charged through the door. The whole party for her mom on Saturday was still fresh in his memory. He'd wanted to come through for her. And he thought he had. After all, he hadn't punched out Jason and he seemed to have been grudgingly accepted by her wild clan of friends and family.

That was what he'd hoped for.

But he wasn't a man with any tolerance for ultimatums, especially regarding his father. He'd wanted to hear that she'd come back with him to Paris, but not with strings attached. And hell and a half, but the string that frustrated him wasn't her ultimatum business. It was seeing how happy Kel was *here*.

She loved the damn place. She *was* loved.

Kidnapping her to Paris sounded romantic and wonderful and perfect. What the hell did they need anyone else for? They had each other.

One look at her and he knew that was true. She was what he needed, all he needed.

"Hey," she fussed, "are you listening?"

"Of course I'm listening." She was herding him from project to project at the speed of sound.

First, she'd shown him the hardwood floors—newly sanded, ready for a choice of finish. She'd chosen a finish, wanted him to approve. It wasn't the cheapest, but she'd done research and believed it was the sturdiest. That was a yes.

Then she'd picked out models for a new fridge and dishwasher—more easy yeses. Then to the bathroom. She was showing him samples of tile colors.

"So pick," she said.

"One of those blues," he said. "Whatever you think."

"They're all blue, Will. You're not going to be any help to me at all, are you?" It was a rhetorical question, he figured, since Kelly was already moving on to a new subject. "I can't *tell* you how thrilled my mom was with the present you picked out for her. When did you get so brilliant?"

"She liked it, huh?"

"Are you kidding?" The present had been a gift certificate to a florist, where two coral rosebushes were being saved for her. "My mother was beside herself. You won fifty million brownie points with the neighborhood, besides." She frowned when she heard a noisy engine sound outside. "UPS, it sounds like. I'd better—"

"Of course, go...."

Actually it was FedEx, and when she came back in moments later, he started with another subject they had to cover. "Kelly, I'm stuck on Sunday for my mother's birthday party."

"Well, of course you are. I'm going. All three of your sisters called me. I'm picking you up before church."

"Um, problem there, because I'm not going to church. Which the family knows perfectly well." He could smell his sisters' interference. Kelly would have no reason to know his family had set up her "picking him up" as a maneuver to get him to church. Kelly undoubtedly believed she was helping in some way. He would have explained the situation, but he suddenly caught her expression.

She'd opened an official-looking envelope, looked at the contents and suddenly her face lost color.

"What's in there?" he asked.

"Nothing. Just the lab results." She tossed the paper into a patchwork basket of other toss-out mail by the door.

"What lab results?"

"The DNA test. I had it done when I got back from Paris. I told you about it. I told the lab to send the results to my father's address, not to me. I didn't want or need to see it. I couldn't care less," she said swiftly.

"Whoa." She'd dismissed the report as if it were nothing, which it most certainly wasn't, emotionally or legally, for her. But she moved on as if determined to stick to her conversational agenda.

"Anyway, what if I pick you up, say around quarter to ten on Sunday…because if you're at your mom's that night, then you wouldn't have to drive me home later. Besides, I don't know if you want me to stay through the whole day."

"It's white tie." Will lifted his voice to be certain she heard this devastating news.

She only lifted a brow. "I've never worn ties. I'm guessing they'll let me in in a dress."

Then he remembered that she wouldn't likely be allergic to dressing up the way he was. "I'll pick you up," he said.

"But it'd be inconvenient for you," she argued.

He was suddenly aware they were arguing about who was doing the driving, and somehow the fact that he wasn't about to attend a mass had gotten lost in the scuffle. So had everything else. And someone had just turned on a noisy power drill upstairs. "Wait a minute. This lab report you just got—that means your dad now knows for sure that you're his daughter?"

"Will, I told you I've been e-mailing my dad ever since I got back from Paris. He hasn't returned a single note. Not a word. He either doesn't want a daughter or he doesn't want me. If he actually needed DNA as proof, then as far as I'm concerned, he can jump in the pond...and I mean that big pond between the continents. Now about the electricity—"

"Kel. No one was talking about electricity."

"But we should have been." She motioned vaguely toward the kitchen. "The guys blew a fuse when they first started working. I just put in another one, but it kept blowing, and the house is of an age, you know, so I called an electrician, asked him to check out the electrical system. Now, I can't imagine you wanting to spend any money you don't have to, but if this were my house, I do believe you should—"

Her cell phone rang at the same time someone knocked on the front door. She threw up her hands at the same time he threw up his. "You get the phone," he said, "I'll get the door."

He glanced at his watch before pivoting around. Almost one. He *had* to be back for a meeting at one-thirty. They hadn't finished up all her house questions; he'd had no chance to tell her what had happened with John Henry at work. He had a whole lot more to say about her dad situation, and she probably wanted to know more about the party arrangements on Sunday. And all that was just life stuff. They hadn't had two seconds to talk about *them*.

She'd said she'd go to Paris with him. She really, really had. Obstacles or no obstacles, surely they'd get a chance to talk about the one subject that mattered?

Impatiently he answered her front door, only to find the lunkhead, alias Jason, who was close to the last person in the universe Will had the patience for right now. And he could hear Kel on her cell, her voice tone indicating she was dealing with a business call.

It looked like dealing with Jason was on him.

Oh well, Will mused, and stepped outside, meticulously closing the door behind him. As kindly as an old friend, he greeted Jason with, "Hey, I'll bet you had the mother of all headaches last Saturday."

Poor guy winced. "I did. That's what I was here about. To talk to Kelly."

"She's tied up. We're both about to head back to work." Jason didn't look like such a hothead by bright sun in the middle of the day. He looked more like, well, just a decent guy. Buttoned down, for sure, but nothing really wrong with him except that Will noted the fresh haircut, the crisp look of a new shirt. That wasn't for a Wednesday workday. The dude was spiffed up for Kelly.

Not gonna happen.

Jason seemed to finally realize something along that line too, because he said gruffly, "I guess I owe an apology to you, too."

"No problem at all," Will said genially. "I'm glad we met. I know we'll run into each other again. Your family's important to Kelly. You both share a lot of friends."

"We do."

Jason stood there, as if wanting to push for another chance to see Kelly, but eventually he started shifting his feet. When Will failed to offer more conversation, he scratched the back of his neck, checked a button on his shirt. Finally, he worked up the guts for a blunter approach and said straight out, "Are you and Kelly..." but then couldn't seem to finish the question.

"Yes," Will said, which covered the complete answer as far as he was concerned.

"She'll always be my first girl," Jason said, with the same note of beer-courage stubbornness he'd tried out on Saturday.

"I know she will. And it's a good memory for her, hope it is for you. But she'll be my last girl, and I like my place in that line." Will didn't make it sound like a challenge or a warning. He just stated it like the eternal, irrevocable, irrefutable, undeniable fact that it was.

"Yeah. I get that feeling." Jason's voice was barely audible. "Well, tell Kelly—"

"I will. She'll be relieved you were okay after Saturday."

"I don't want her thinking that I wanted to make a scene," Jason said.

The hell he didn't. But Will, because he was practicing restraint brilliantly at that moment, didn't push. "Hey, it's okay," he said magnanimously.

A moment later, the front door opened with Kelly looking bewildered, as if she'd been searching all over for him and couldn't imagine where he was. Jason was pulling out of the driveway and Will was waving goodbye to him.

Kelly took one look and started giving him that foot-tapping, hand-on-hip type of posture.

"What?" he said. "I was totally, one hundred percent nice! You can ask him!"

She said nothing.

"I mean it. Kel, it's obvious he's a decent guy. He was embarrassed about Saturday. I tried to make him feel better."

Kelly murmured, "In a pig's eye." But she kissed him. He'd been good as gold, maybe better, and yet he somehow got a kiss when he lied to her? And it was a good kiss.

When she leaned back and opened her eyes, she was smiling, their pelvises still glued together. "Why would I bet a week's salary that he won't be back?"

"I have no idea. Since I was so nice to him. But I do think it's conceivable that this is the last time he's going to try seeing you alone the way he did today." He added, "That's just a guess, of course. I have no basis whatsoever to think that, really. I just—"

"We're on a front porch in the middle of a busy neighborhood, so quit being so damned cute. I can't seduce you here. And we both have to be back at work besides."

"I was being cute, huh?"

"When you're not being a male chauvinist egomaniac, you can be a little cute," she qualified.

"And you were thinking about seducing me, huh? Right out here in the open?"

"Would you quit sounding so delighted?" But just then, one of the workers yanked open the door with a question, effectively interrupting them as nothing else could have.

KELLY THOUGHT later that she should have known she was inviting trouble. It was the same-old, same-old with Will. They had fifty million things conspiring to keep them apart. His dad. Her dad. Both of their nosy, interfering families. In her case, an insane work schedule, complicated by trying to live in a house with a half dozen construction projects going on. And in Will's case, being swallowed by the magnitude of handling his father's business.

But somehow, when they managed even a few minutes together, they seemed to have fun anyway. They seemed to feel fierce, wild, wonderful desire anyway. They seemed to laugh anyway.

So it was extra frightening, when she heard stones hitting her window at four o'clock on Friday morning, that she wasn't even thrown. All right. She was a *little* thrown. Bleary-eyed, she crawled out of bed, grabbed her cell phone, punched in 9-1- and then peeked out the corner of the window to see what was going on.

And there was Will, standing in the dew-soaked grass. He was wearing a suit, as far as she could see in the dark—a serious going-to-work suit. And grinning up at her like a hyena.

She threw open the sash—no easy thing to do on the old windows in the upstairs bedroom—and leaned out. "You're mad. Stark raving mad. And I'm having you committed." First, though, she clicked off her phone.

"Can you come down and play?"

"Of course not. It's Friday morning. I get two more hours of sleep before I have to get up and work all day. Do you have anything against rest? Sleep?"

"This is important. And it includes breakfast."

She sighed. "Give me five." She closed the window and got in gear—splashing water on her face, brushing her teeth, throwing on gray slacks and a pale blue top, hardly a great work or play outfit, but who could think at four in the morning? She was lucky she remembered shoes, and was still brushing her hair when she jogged outside.

"I don't talk this early, and for damn sure, I shouldn't be expected to be nice," she warned him.

"I understand."

"You'd better have a good reason for this."

"I understand."

"And I haven't even put on makeup, so don't be looking at me."

"Yes, ma'am. I won't look." He added hastily, "Although you don't need makeup to enhance your extraordinary beauty, anyway."

"I'm not receptive to malarkey this early in the morning, either."

He made the childish gesture of zipping his lips, making her want to laugh, but she didn't. She held on to her cranky mood for at least four more minutes. Maybe five.

"What in God's name are you up to?" she demanded when he pulled up to the Notre Dame football stadium. A light rain had started up, which made the golden dome glisten bright and magical.

Will looked up at the rain, though, and muttered, "Hell. This may not work out quite as planned."

"In case no one ever mentioned this to you, the stadium's locked. You can't just walk in there at all hours."

But somehow or other—Will wouldn't admit how, which made Kelly fret that the means might not be kosher—he produced a key. By the time he was maneuvering the lock, he was also carting a monster-sized box and an umbrella. Naturally she grabbed the umbrella. It was obvious he couldn't juggle everything at once.

"Okay," he said. "This was the plan. Remember when we were on the boat, and you wanted to seduce me in broad daylight?"

"It wasn't *quite* like that," she defended.

"Close enough. And because I thought it was such an excellent idea, I thought I should enable you. I mean, if you want to get into this sin and fantasy thing, you should have a willing accomplice. It's the guy's job in a relationship to help the woman achieve her dreams. My sisters read that to me from a woman's magazine, so I know it must be true." In the middle of that nonsense, he suddenly sighed and turned serious. "Only damn, Kel. The forecast was for overcast skies, not *rain*."

The stadium was…well, all theirs. The only times

she'd been inside, the place had been packed for football games. The inner corridor was ghostly cool and dim, and once Will led her out to the stands—to the fifty-yard line, to be precise—the wide empty space seemed to hold all the echoes of exuberant yelling and happy screams and devoted fans. Will, however, looked more and more distraught.

"I checked the forecast an hour ago, and it was supposed to be cloudy this morning. Just cloudy. No rain. *No rain.* You know what?"

"What?"

"Maguire's has a box. But I didn't bring *that* key because I didn't think we'd need it. The whole point was to be out in the open air."

Holy smokes times ten. While she held up the umbrella, he opened the massive box he'd been carting around. First he withdrew a navy-and-gold blanket, then French crepes packed in a heated container. Out came more treasures. A carafe of French coffee with gold-rimmed demitasses. A blue-and-gold flag. Sterling forks and white linen napkins. A vase with blue and gold carnations. The water had spilled out, but the flowers were still fresh, and certainly happy enough to sit in the rain.

She looked at Will as he withdrew all this stuff, all these details that he'd planned for her, the whole Notre Dame theme, all the French foods, all the elegant little touches...and felt her heart melt like chocolate in heat.

The rain sluiced down harder, no longer light, but

pelting in a harsh, beating assault. The umbrella covered some parts of their bodies. Not all. Will looked more and more miserable, and Kelly kept thinking that she needed to say something to make him feel better, but her throat felt so thick, so full of emotion that she couldn't seem to say anything at all.

Will seemed to interpret her silence as agreeing with his responsibility for this major screwup. "Okay, okay, I admit the plan was flawed and on the impulsive side. But neither of us can seem to scare up an ounce of free time—at least not for each other. I know we're seeing each other Sunday, but that's about my mom's birthday, it's not *us* time. And yeah, I admit I thought you'd get a charge out of having breakfast at Notre Dame. And I wanted you to remember Paris. I wanted a chance for both of us to *be* like Paris again, even if we could only catch an hour before real life—"

He looked up, as if hoping she'd interrupt him. She didn't.

He started again. "I guess the chances of your seducing me on the fifty-yard line are pretty slim, huh? On the other hand, it's a thought that'll hold. There'll be other chances. There could be some terrific warm morning sometime next week. You could just forget that this particular morning turned into a complete and total fiasco."

"Will?"

His shoulders relaxed. She was willing to speak to him.

"I love you," she said, softer than a whisper.

His grin started to show up again. Just a rise of the corners of his mouth, but it was coming back.

"If you want to make love, right now, in the pouring rain—it's okay by me."

There now. His eyes brightened right up.

"But it looks as if a maintenance guy just showed up. At the top of the stairs? So it'd seem to be kind of iffy to pull that off right at this minute."

Will's head shot toward the uniformed man—then two men—and he swore. "They're not supposed to be here until seven. Could anything more go wrong this morning?"

"Well," she said as she finished the last crepe and rather hastily started gathering their gear together. "We could get arrested. That'd be pretty awkward. But I have to tell you this."

"What?" he demanded, shooting to his feet as he saw the two maintenance men had suddenly noticed them and were walking in their direction.

But she didn't tell him her thought—they had to move too quickly to get everything together, to peel out of there, hopefully without the maintenance men calling the cops on them, hopefully without both of them getting completely soaked in the downpour.

They reached his car, gasping for breath, both of them hopelessly laughing. Will didn't want to, but even he had to give in to the humor of the situation. And that was the first time she had a chance to say what she'd wanted to earlier.

She kissed him in the damp car, on the cheek, both of them shivering like crazy. "You're going to do it, aren't you?"

"What?"

"You're going to find a way for us to be together. Because your dad's going to be well soon. And that means you'll need to be making decisions about what you want to do."

"I know what I want. I want you with me, Kel. That's all that matters. The rest of it—I just don't care."

"Oh, yes you do," she whispered. "You care terribly, Will Maguire." And she felt her heart thud like a dropped ball bearing. It had taken her all this time to figure out what she needed and wanted in her life—who she was, and who she wasn't.

She was the one who had started out confused.

But it was Will, she understood now, who didn't know himself. And she couldn't make an overwhelming life choice for him.

No one could live a fantasy forever.

CHAPTER SEVENTEEN

"QUIT LOOKING so grumpy," Kelly scolded him as they marched up the church steps. "You're not going to die if you spend an hour in mass."

"I could."

She patted his behind—discreetly—just as they reached the holy water, which she used and he didn't. He got another scolding look when he failed to genuflect. His family was already there—his dad and mom in a pew up front, his sisters and various other family members filling the next couple aisles. Will figured if he got to sit by Ralph, the little squirt would act up, and he'd get to take him out of church. They could play on the lawn or something.

As if Kelly suspected he had nonreligious intentions, he got another pat—this one close to a pinch—as she herded him into an aisle behind the family.

"Unka *Will!*" Ralphie shrieked, making Martha turn around and roll her eyes for attracting the baby's attention.

"I'll take him anytime," Will mouthed back to her. The rest of the family, alerted to his presence, turned around like a practiced choir and sent Kelly smiles. Kelly, not him. Kelly was getting all the credit for his attending mass.

Kelly, who was pinching and patting and prodding him every time he looked sideways.

"What?" he demanded when the service was finally over and they could escape back to the car.

"You and I are going to get this religious business out in the open. Get in, buster."

He did, although getting into her car was like a bull trying to fit into a thimble. She drove, looking damned gorgeous in an ivory top and a skirt that swished around her bare knees. She was wearing the scent he'd gotten her in Paris, and she'd put a couple clips in her hair and pearls in her ears. It was a good-girl pure-lady look, and just made him want to strip her right there and then.

Instead, she picked up take-out coffee and drove him to a spot on the river, where she parked and handed him his cup.

"This whole church thing," she told him. "You're being downright dumb about it."

"Excuse me?"

"You stood there in church like a lump. You know perfectly well what to do. If you don't believe in the religion, that would be one thing—"

"I don't."

"What a fib. The truth is that your dad pushed religion down your throat, so you took off in the other direction. He wanted you to be devout, so that's the last thing you were willing to be."

"Kel. Try waking up. I'm not the devout type."

"Horse spit." She slipped out of her sandals, lifted her legs over the gearshift and plunked them in his lap.

She seemed to think she could yell at him and get her bare feet rubbed at the same time. The woman had no end to her illusions. It was downright astonishing.

"You're not preachy and churchy, Will. But you have a lot of spirituality in you. You stand up for people. For what's right. You have endless kindness and compassion for those more vulnerable than you. You don't take crap from anyone, but you're not a bully or mean about it."

"You're calling that spirituality?" he asked.

She took another sip of coffee and started in again. "You walk at night for the joy of it, take the time to smell the flowers, get down on the floor to play with your nephew. You're first in line when someone needs help. You try to avoid directly hurting people. I see examples of that everywhere. No matter how much your dad infuriates you, you don't attack him. Or your sisters."

"And you think that's spirituality?" he asked again.

"Yeah, actually. It's just colored in prettier words when you sing it in a hymn."

He couldn't even drink his coffee, because he had to rub her toes, the balls of her feet. When he traced a thumb down that delicate, sexy arch, she purred just like a cat. "Just for the record, why are we talking about religion?"

"Because we have to be sure we agree about what matters, Will. Is it important to you if we believe exactly the same things?"

"No. Not at all." That was easy to answer.

"I agree."

Since she seemed determined to add a complicated, touchy discussion to an already complicated, touchy day, he went along. "Speaking for myself, I think religious and personal beliefs are matters of the heart. They're not up for argument. They're up for discussion, because talking about what matters is interesting and honest. But I don't want to be pushed and I'd never push you."

"Oh God, Will, you said that so well. And I'm totally on the same page." She added, "I think everyone has a spiritual side. The only thing wrong is denying it. If you get a great feeling walking in the woods, then I'll walk in the woods with you. But if I need to go to church, I'd like you to occasionally come with me…or at least *be* with me about what I need to do."

"I am. Okay." He'd given more attention to her right foot than her left, so now he had to make up to leftie. After getting a good long gulp of coffee, he said gruffly, "I think a couple should protect each other's private stuff. I don't mean sex. I mean the kind of things you're afraid of, when you're all alone or in pain."

Slowly she swung her bare legs back to her side of the car and put down her coffee. "Will, you are so good at being honest with me. It's one of the things I love about you."

Like the day at her house, like the failed Notre Dame breakfast fiasco, like this morning in church, Will felt a raw, gut feeling of fear. He sensed that he was a pinch away from losing Kelly, that she wanted something from him and he wasn't coming through.

Only he couldn't seem to pin down exactly what it was. It was as if his whole life could be threatened if he couldn't solve the Rubik's Cube. He had all the colors, all the pieces, but he still had no idea how to put it together.

He grabbed her wrist when she turned the key and started the engine. "If you like it that I'm honest with you, why are you frowning? What was this big conversation about?"

"You're honest with me, Will. But I need you to be honest with yourself."

"What's that supposed to mean?"

"It means that you think you're low-key and laid-back. And you're not. You think you're happy lazy. And you're not. You think you're an ex-Catholic. But you're just a Catholic who's angry about church issues, which isn't the same thing."

"And all this interesting insight is going where?"

"It's going toward your dad." She must have seen a certain expression on his face, because she said swiftly, "I know. We've talked this half to death. But I want you to really hear me this time. I'll follow you anywhere. But you and I can't make it if you've got a raw sore on your heart that you keep pretending doesn't matter."

Oh, yeah. That old song. Will didn't huff, but it crossed his mind again that he *could* have fallen for a woman who'd settle for diamonds and yachts and traveling around the world free as a bird. Instead, he got Ms. Interfering, Bossy, Poke-Into-Deep-Sores Rochard.

She only said one more thing. "When you deal with your dad, Will, get your mind off what he wants. Get your mind on what *you* want. Think about who you are, not who he is. It'll solve everything. I promise."

Apart from trying to reason with the most idealistic dreamer who'd ever been born, Will still needed answers that he had yet to find, no matter how hard he tried.

BIG-BAND MUSIC spilled from the open doors of the country club. Every bush and branch was lit up on the long white patio and steps.

Kelly didn't freeze, though, until she got a good view of the crowd.

She wore a long black dress that she'd thought was downright adorable when she bought it—a clearance $79.99 buy at T.J. Maxx. Now she saw beads and sequins, satins and organza, and the stones dripping from necks were a long way from her rhinestones.

"We just aren't in Kansas anymore, Toto," she murmured.

Will tugged on her arm. "Say what? What's wrong?"

His voice was still laced with aggravation from this morning. Hell's bells, she was just as aggravated with herself. "Nothing," she assured him brightly. "Just can't walk very fast in these heels."

"This'll be boring as hell," Will warned her, "but we should be able to escape in a couple hours. Not until Mom's cut the cake and opened her presents, though."

Another reason to freeze in panic. Somehow she was sure she'd bought the wrong thing. Or an inadequate thing. "Will, what did you get her?"

He was carrying a medium-size box, clearly wrapped by a pro, not him. "My dad and sisters always get her bling and girl stuff. But my mom's actually a techno junkie, so I cater to that. Got her a GPS with her own voice recorded for the person giving directions."

"That's terrific," Kelly said, panic building further. She'd gotten a coffee-table book on fancy gardening, because the Maguire house had been so exquisitely and uniquely landscaped. But that was before.

The Maguires had all seemed so natural. Before. They all seemed to have the usual family squabbles and idiosyncrasies. Before. They all seemed to— likely—spit in the bowl after brushing their teeth, like she did. Before.

Now she smiled blankly as Will climbed the steps,

his hand at the small of her back, and introduced her to a couple. The woman was wearing a designer gown, her shoes costing more than Kelly made in a month.

"Will!" Another couple greeted him, kissed him, teased him about turning into a Frenchman.

He kept her alongside him. Barbara and Aaron greeted both of them—Barbara giving her a giant, warm hug. Ditto for Aaron. The sisters were there, the kids. Kelly understood why his mother had wanted the family to attend mass together that morning. That was the time the occasion would be about family. This fantabulous birthday bash was clearly less about family and more about an excuse to enjoy the bling. The place didn't need to be lit up. There were enough diamonds to illuminate a couple of universes. Chocolate diamonds. Yellow diamonds. One pink diamond.

"Hey." Will cornered her after they'd filled plates with an array of gourmet delicacies. A chef was sizzling salmon flown in from Alaska. A king crab the size of a small room was displayed on a satin-gold plate. Individual chefs manned numerous tables, offering foods from the islands, South America, the Orient. Kelly could hardly take her eyes off the wonders.

"Kel."

She glanced up. Will looked as stunning as she'd ever seen him. The white tux was perfect for his regal bones and ruffled blond hair; he looked a mix of bad boy and elegance. But mostly elegance. He could fit in anywhere, anytime, with anyone, she thought, and his long, lean body was just made for that tux.

"Kelly, wake up. What's wrong?"

She looked up *again,* and then shook her head with a laugh. "Nothing. The party, it's just so beautiful."

"Pretty stiff and formal, if you ask me. But my mom's in her element. She's loving it."

A woman their own age took one look at Will across the patio and sailed over. "Will!" Apparently Will had gone to school with the brunette, because she acted as if she not only knew him, but had laid claim to him body and soul—especially his body—at some point in the past. She dismissed her husband as if he were a purse on her arm, threw her arms around Will, shot Kelly a hello and then ignored her, and continued to gab for three minutes solid about their shared history.

It hit Kelly like a slam and kept slamming.

His money had never really bothered her, because she'd always felt so natural with him. But this was the first time she'd had it jammed into her face, that this was the life Will was born to, what he was used to. Not just some dumb money, but real wealth. Not ordinary family and friends, but people who'd been all over the world and had power.

And here she'd been telling him what to do from the day she met him. Demanding he figure out who he was, as if she had the intuition to *know* what was wrong with anyone as complex as Will, as if she knew anything about the life he'd grown up in.

"Excuse me," she murmured to Will, when yet another couple ambled up to greet him. She motioned, a universal signal that she was headed for the ladies' room.

She wasn't, but she needed a moment of silence for a minute. Around the corner of the long patio and lawn, she found a swimming pool—lit up and surrounded by more guests—but past that, she found a little corner of quiet. A nestle of trees provided a privacy border for the pool area, and no lights intruded into the warm shadows. There was a walkway, cement benches, probably leading to a golf course—Kelly didn't know or care; she just sat down for a second, and tried to draw a couple deep cleansing breaths.

She'd never had a panic attack before, but she was pretty sure this was one. Her heart kept pounding as if a sniper threatened her at gunpoint. Her palms were damp and her stomach was twisted like a rope. She couldn't seem to catch her breath.

"Hey, Kel…" Liz, Will's youngest sister, showed up under the tree, and abruptly spotted her. "You needed to escape from there, too? When they started up with the big-band songs, I had to catch some air."

Liz plunked down on the bench beside her. "My mom's having a blast. Definitely her dream of a party, but it sure isn't mine. Too many canapés and Chantilly and pink rouge, you know? Not that Mom is that old. There's just a heavy focus on investment strategies and retirement homes and grandkids in every conversation. A major whew."

Liz, thankfully, seemed oblivious to Kelly's freaked-out mood, and just having her there helped Kelly get a grip.

"You've never lived anywhere but South Bend, have you?" Liz was happy to gallop in any conversational direction.

"Nope. Born and raised here."

"Yeah, me, too. That's why I'm dying to get out. I'm so hungry to move to Chicago. Someplace with life and lights and things to *do*. People with energy and ideas. People with some edge, you know?" She stretched her long legs, then glanced at Kelly. "You don't agree?"

"Well, I loved trekking into Chicago. Love traveling whenever I can afford it, too. But I have to admit, I always love it here. It's just *home*."

"You don't ever get bored?"

"Sometimes. But it seems like, well, I'd love to travel to glamorous places, do glamorous things. But over the long haul, this seems to be a good place. The kind of place where you feel safe, where people know you, where you'd want to raise your kids because there's such a strong sense of family and all that. Sounds boring to you, huh?"

"Maybe it won't later," Liz said, clearly seeking to find a tactful response. "I just need out of here for now. I'm not ready to settle down— Hey, Will!"

Kelly turned swiftly at Liz's delighted greeting.

She'd had no idea that Will had walked up and found them, or how long he'd been standing there. He answered his sister immediately, but he wasn't looking at Liz—he was looking at her.

He stepped closer, reached out a hand, his expression looking absolutely grave.

"What's wrong?" she asked immediately.

"Nothing," he said quietly. "I just heard you talking."

She searched his face. She couldn't imagine anything she'd said to Liz that was odd or that he'd have objected to, but something happened, because his expression echoed a man who'd been hit hard with the wrong kind of surprise.

The band suddenly picked up the happy birthday song. "Mom's going to open up presents," he said. "We'd better get over there."

"Sure," she said. But she suddenly wasn't even remotely sure of anything.

THREE AFTERNOONS LATER, Will sat in Dr. O'Malley's waiting room, waiting for his dad to come out. Aaron claimed the visit was unnecessary, since he already knew he was going to get a completely clean bill of health.

Will bought that like he bought into fairy tales. His dad would never have asked Will to drive him unless he feared hearing a medical verdict that he didn't want the rest of the family to know.

Will also figured his dad was going to turn this

JENNIFER GREENE   361

into another effort to manipulate him into taking on the business. But Maguire's, right now, wasn't remotely on his mind.

Kelly was. He'd been shaken ever since his mother's birthday bash.

Kel didn't want to live in Paris.

She'd never wanted to live in Paris.

She'd said she would. She'd said she'd come with him. He knew she meant it, and he'd believed she'd *wanted* to go to Paris with him, wanted to be with him. He'd believed she wanted everything they'd had in Paris together, that the only reason they were both in South Bend was to resolve family problems, after which, they were both free.

"Mr. Maguire?" The nurse standing in front of him looked impatient, as if she'd been trying to get his attention for some time. Possibly she had. His father answered to Mr. Maguire. He never had.

"Your father would like you to join him in the doctor's office," the older woman told him, and ushered him into a room at the end of a long hall.

Will walked in and immediately noted his father's pale complexion and angry eyes.

"Aaron's ankle has healed well," Dr. O'Malley said pleasantly. "In fact, he's fully recovered from the accident. We're pleased with all the X-rays and tests in that regard."

"He's trying to put a 'but' in there," Aaron growled to his son.

Dr. O'Malley ignored him, something he'd probably learned to do a long time ago when dealing with certain impossible patients. "However, his blood pressure is through the roof. It would help if he'd quit sneaking the occasional cigar, but that really isn't the issue. His blood-sugar levels are too low. He's got a building hiatal hernia, as well as ulcers. So far, the ulcers have been controllable with medication, but the best we can say is that they're not getting worse."

"He's making a lot out of little things," Aaron said to Will. "You grow older, your body starts to wear out. It's annoying as hell, but it's not like any of this is a surprise."

Will looked directly at the doctor. "He needs to cut down on work."

"It's so nice to talk to someone who can add two and two. Your father certainly can't. In an ideal world, he could just cut down, but your father doesn't seem to be able to do that."

"I could if I wanted to," Aaron interjected.

"And that's the thing. He doesn't want to. So if he continues on this pattern, he's headed for some serious health repercussions. Since I can't get him to see reason, Mr. Maguire, I'm hoping you can."

"Poppycock," Aaron grumped when they climbed into Will's car a few minutes later. "And don't tell your mother any of that crap. She's on me all the time about traveling and getting out of the business and doing things together." He shot his son a sneaky glance. "Of course, we'd be able to do those things if you'd come on board."

"All right."

"Don't waste your time saying no. I've heard it all before. You act like I'm torturing you, offering you a chance to climb into a successful business that's done well by all of us. I raised you to care about family, so I've never understood—"

"I said I'd do it, Dad. And I will. If we can come to terms."

"—why you wanted to take off, live in Paris. Kicking around's one thing, every man needs to sow some oats. But you're getting near thirty now, I think...." Aaron stopped talking. Stopped moving. They were at a stoplight on Grape Road that stayed red and stayed red and stayed red. And when it finally turned green, Aaron said, "*What* did you say?"

"I said that I'll take over Maguire's. If you and I can come to terms."

Back at the house, Will asked his mom to come through with a couple sandwiches and iced tea, then to leave them be in the library for a while. Barbara looked as if her son had given her gold. She didn't know what the specific discussion was going to be about. Didn't care. Typical of his mom, she could smell something good in the air.

She danced in with the sandwich tray and tea, bussed both her men on the forehead, swore no calls would get through unless there was a fire and closed the double doors to give them privacy.

"You may not be willing to live with my terms, Dad," Will said frankly.

"Maybe not. Let's hear what you have to say." His father leaned forward, and damnation, but if he didn't shock Will by listening.

CHAPTER EIGHTEEN

KELLY YANKED off her gardening gloves, swatted at a mosquito and stood up. The two peony plants were planted. Now she just had to mulch and water.

Ideally, she wouldn't have chosen to garden at seven-thirty on a hot, muggy night in the silk shirt and skirt she'd worn to work, but she was an emotional basket case. No point in denying it. She probably should have asked Will if he wanted peonies planted in the backyard before going ahead, but what the hey. The yard needed color; peonies were going to look gorgeous in that northeast corner, and she had to do *something* to calm herself.

Coming home from work, she'd picked up the mail and found the letter.

The letter sitting in the front hall right now.

She knifed open the first bag of mulch and started mounding it—another action that drew every mosquito from here to Indianapolis. She wasn't crying. It wasn't that kind of upset. She was thinking about crying, nonstop, but mostly she was festering on the inside. The letter was huge, but it wasn't the whole crisis.

Will was the whole crisis. They'd barely shared two seconds since his mother's party, and even though he was busy, Kelly knew perfectly well he was avoiding her. She didn't know specifically why, but she could guess. She'd pushed him too far. She'd nagged and badgered him too much. When it came down to true, clear thinking, she'd lost him because she couldn't get her shit together fast enough.

That wasn't counting that she probably didn't measure up when he'd seen her next to all his old, gorgeous, rich girlfriends at his mom's party—but that was just a detail, and she knew it.

She sniffed, opened the second bag of mulch, wiped a grimy hand on her Banana Republic outlet skirt, and almost jumped five feet when she suddenly saw Will striding toward her from the corner of the house.

"I rang the bell but couldn't find you. The house was open, so I figured you had to be around here somewhere... *Kel.* That's way too heavy for you." He jogged forward and grabbed the bag of mulch. The idiot was wearing a suit, the jacket open, but still a suit, which meant he immediately got mulch dust all over him.

She opened her mouth to yell, but couldn't because she was drinking him in. Something was different about him. Maybe a look of freedom or confidence or something, probably because he'd come over to formally dump her—but whatever it was, it looked good on him. Sexy. Compelling.

He wasn't meeting her eyes, making her feel even more tied up and freaked, but his hands did happen to be occupied, shaking out the mulch in a circle, so it was possible he didn't mean to be ignoring her. "Peonies?" he asked.

"Yeah. I know I should have asked you first. But that corner doesn't get a lot of sun, so…"

"They'll be perfect here." He added, "My mom never stops talking about gardening, so that's how I knew the plant. And just so you know, she was nuts about the gardening book you bought her."

"Was she?" Kelly thought her voice sounded pathetic. She'd really wanted to give his mother something that everybody else—everybody *rich* else—wouldn't think of.

"Beside-herself happy. She's got gardening books, but none about the history of design. She's crazy about it. You've got a hose close?"

"Yeah, I'll bring it." It was one of those old hoses, heavy to lug, and when she put the nozzle on, a wee bit of it missed and zapped him in the side.

He yelped, then laughed as if everything were perfectly fine between them, when they both knew it wasn't. Yet he just stole the hose from her and watered in the new plants, while she picked up the mulch bags and started the cleanup, moving slowly. As the sun dropped, the temperature cooled and the bugs got worse, yet she didn't want to hurry. She would likely have done anything to postpone the conversation she feared was coming. The dread thudding in her pulse seemed even worse, because Will coming over and joining her, the way they always seemed so naturally comfortable together, only invoked another sharp pang of loss.

"Good and watered in," he announced, and walked over to turn off the water. And just like that, the fun was over and her worst fear began.

"Kel," he said lazily, "we're not going to Paris."

"I knew you didn't come over here to hang, much less to mulch. Believe me, I knew, Will."

"Huh?" Momentarily he looked confused, then motioned toward the house. "Let's go in and clean up, okay?"

"No." He looked at her in confusion. "I can't go in the house for a few more minutes. Just let it go, all right? There's something in there I can't face for a while. Can we sit out on the steps?"

Naturally, Will, being Will, had to amend the plan. After rinsing their hands under the hose, *she* sat on the steps while he went into the kitchen, emerged with two dripping-cold cans of pop and a damp towel to wipe off their faces and necks. They both hunkered down on the front step, watching some neighborhood kids play kick ball at the end of the road.

"I had a long conversation with my dad," Will said. He was next to her, hip-touching close—but not. Not touching anywhere.

"Your dad?" She'd been so certain a breakup

conversation was coming that she had to struggle to change mental gears.

"You were right, Kelly. It was on me to figure it out, not him. And you had the key, not me." Will sighed, stretched out his long legs. "I hate it when a woman is right."

"What is this humor? Tell me what happened!"

"Wellll." He told her, about taking his dad to the doctor's, hearing the doc's prognosis, then cornering his dad. "You told me I loved the company, Kel. But I've been so busy hating it for so many years that I never opened my stubborn eyes and looked. My whole life, I've actually been into business."

"I didn't think you'd ever see it."

"Well, that was the thing. Separating what I hated from what I loved, and figuring out how I could fit into it. So I told Dad I'd take it on, but on certain terms. I'm not supporting my sisters, not like he does, treating them like princesses with no brains of their own. So I told him I wanted a salary and stock in the company, a formal payback plan. My sisters can either take a job or a minor share of stock—not enough to give them voting rights over me. Anything else Dad wants to settle on them is fine, just as long as it isn't on me."

"How'd he take that plan?"

"He poured the whiskey. You can probably smell it on my breath." He leaned forward, close enough to kiss her, but he didn't.

"No smell of whiskey," she murmured, seeing his

blond chin stubble, the tired lines around his eyes now. A dog barked in the middle of the street. She didn't look up.

"Well, we only had a sip. Dad shouldn't have had any, and I knew I was driving. Here." He scooped a curl off her forehead and tucked it behind her ear. "I also told Dad he'd never make it as a retired layabout, and we needed to face reality, because we'll never be able to work together. So I offered him a job doing PR if he wanted it. He knows everybody in the business. They love him. He could do that totally separate from me so we wouldn't clash. If he doesn't want to, that's fine, too."

"How'd he take that?"

"He wanted more whiskey." He sighed. "Then we went out and told Mom. And she wanted to have a bunch of toasts, too. Mostly they both wanted to call you so you could have toasts with us, because they knew perfectly well you were the one who brought me on board."

"It wasn't me," Kelly began.

"Yeah. It was. It always was. My sisters may not be terribly thrilled with the deal, but it's not hurting them. And actually, they might like the chance to be involved—or to have their own nest egg to invest or spend their own way, instead of always having to ask for it. And that's enough on this. My family issues have dominated our time way more than enough. It's time to get back to *us*."

She was just lifting the cold pop to her lips. Now she set it down again. Her fingertips were suddenly frozen, and not because of the temperature of the can. "Okay," she said carefully.

"I needed to find a way to resolve the deal with my dad. But the motivation was you, when I realized that you really didn't want to live in Paris."

"I told you I would—"

"Yeah. I know you did. But I also heard you talking to my sister about how much this was home for you. It wasn't what you said, it was the tone in your voice. How much it means to you. I didn't realize, I swear, Kel. I thought you'd love it in Paris."

"I'd love anywhere we were together. I told you. I meant it." Love ached in her voice. "It was you. I wanted you to be happy. And at first, I thought you were so *dumb,* Will. You couldn't see it, how hard you were working in Paris, how readily you found business work there, because that's *so* who you are. Maybe you wanted to think of yourself as not driven or ambitious, but I have news—"

"Well, maybe I am. Just a little."

"But en route, I got so confused. Because when we got back home here, I saw how it was with your sisters, your dad. They never let up. So then I thought maybe you *were* better off in Paris, and I'd just thrown an apple in the orange bin by pushing you so hard to settle things with your dad."

"Apple in the orange bin?"

"Whatever. I can't do metaphors right now. I'm having a major blond moment, and never mind that I'm brunette. Anyway. I'm just trying to say I didn't think you'd be happy until you figured it out. It wasn't even about your dad or about where you lived. You can live anywhere. You can do anything. But I really believed you needed to know the kind of work, the kind of life, that would make you happy. You needed to know *you*."

"Hey. You were the one who lost her identity."

"I did, I did. But maybe that was when I recognized the lost soul in you, Maguire."

"Nah. I wasn't a lost soul. The minute I found you, I was never a lost soul again. Just because it took me a while to put the pieces together, I knew what the finished picture had to be, Kel. You. With me. Forever."

Oh, for God's sake. She thought she'd lost him. Her pop spilled and so did his when she hurled herself at him. Her mouth found his like a bee finds honey, knowing what she needed, knowing where exactly to find it. He tasted…oh, yeah. Just like her magical Will, the lips smooth and tender, that tongue of his wily and wet.

His shirt crinkled when he wrapped his arms around her, taking her in, holding her close, rocking her. "I never wanted you to give up anything for me, Kel. It made me feel good that you loved me enough to do that. But it made me feel awful as hell to think you'd leave something that really, really mattered to you to cater to me."

"I'd be happy to cater to you." She stopped to kiss him again, on the throat, on his cheek. "I just didn't believe you'd be happy, which meant that I didn't believe we could be happy as a pair unless both of us were very clear about who we are. What we need. From each other. From ourselves. I was afraid."

"I don't want you ever afraid again."

"I was afraid you'd always feel dissatisfied. Kind of trapped if all that stuff about your father was hanging over your head."

"Well, it's not hanging now." He stood, pulled her up and leveled a slow, hard kiss on her lips until they were both out of breath. "I've got something in my pocket for you."

"I know."

"Not *there*. My *real* pocket. The right one. Feel?"

Since he asked, she voluntarily groped and probed. "I'm finding two hard things. One is harder than the other. But one definitely seems to feel like a small square box."

"Yeah, that's the one I was trying to tell you about. The other thing's for you, too, but I think we'd better go inside first, don't you?"

She did, but suddenly remembered what was inside the front door, and froze.

"WHAT'S WRONG? What's in the house?"

"A letter," she said. "Actually a letter and a check. Or an international money order, to be precise, rather than a *check*-check. Not that I've seen anything like this before, but—"

"Kelly, spit out what you're talking about." His arm protectively around her, he determinedly led her inside now. Lawn mowers were still droning in the distance, a few kids in the street playing kickball, but the sun was dropping like a stone.

Inside Kelly's front door, Will switched on the overhead, which happened to be an old brass chandelier, and immediately smelled fresh paint, dried fresh varnish. The front hall looked extraordinarily different, with crown moldings and gleaming wood floors. She'd done wonders, which didn't surprise him. The only things out of place were the two torn pieces of paper on the floor.

"It was for…well, I had to convert it from euros. But I think it was for about a half million dollars. And believe me, I couldn't wait to tear it up," Kelly told him.

He saw her eyes. All the hurt, all the fury. Another time, he would have pressed a hand on his heart to make sure it didn't leap out of his chest, but he needed to clarify the situation before indulging in a heart attack. "You tore up a check for a half million dollars?" he repeated.

"I don't want it! I never wanted his stupid money, Will! I don't want anybody's money! Money is just…" She made whirling motions with her hands.

"I know. It's just money," he said, soothing her, loving her another zillion-years' worth. She really didn't give a damn about fortunes, at least not in the way most people in his life always had.

"He got the results from the stupid DNA test. He also got all my e-mails, all the ones he never answered. But *now* he says he read them. And when he got the DNA results, he sent the check, admitted he was wrong. He should have acknowledged me before. He wants to get to know me now. He regrets not being part of my growing-up years and all that, blah-blah-blah."

Tears spattered from her eyes. Not a gush of them, just a little splash.

"That's what you wanted."

"I didn't want *money*. I wanted him to know me. To *want* to know me. To really believe I didn't want anything from him but to find out who my father was. The check feels like a stupid payoff."

Again Will shot a quick look at the torn-in-two check. At least she hadn't shredded it. It might just tape back together. Not that he was inclined to mention that now.

One of them had to be practical in this life.

Will knew which one of them was going to be. But right now, he locked the door—physically and in every other sense—against any and all intrusions. Including practical ones.

"You know what?" he murmured, and pulled her into his arms again.

"What?"

"Whatever you do about your dad, I'll be standing next to you."

"Whatever you're stuck with, Will, I want to be standing next to you."

The kiss that followed seemed softer than silver, shinier than gold. He gave from his heart, showing her his heart. He'd never done that before…really, truly, revealed his naked heart to anyone. But Kelly knew him, better than he knew himself.

He could trust her, more than he even could himself.

"I'm thinking," he said, "that I'd really like to see what you've done with the upstairs…"

"Brilliant idea," she assured him, and turned toward the stairs. "You want to start with a shower?"

"Yes. Together. But I'd really like to show you the box in my pocket first."

"Oh. Oh, yes, the box." She lifted her head, showing him the mischievous smile, the brown eyes so full of emotion. The Kelly he'd first fallen in lust with. The Kelly he'd later fallen hopelessly in love with.

He dug in his pocket, and emerged with the velvet box. Because she never could wait more than two seconds for a present, she pounced.

She fell silent as she looked at the contents.

"Will," she said quietly, "there are two rings here. Not one."

"I know. The big one—the hussy— I thought you'd better have a three-carat sparkler, so your mom would like me."

Her head shot up. "She already likes you."

"I know, I know. I've been making headway with her, but this is insurance. The other one, though…"

"I *love* the other one, Will."

"I hoped you would. It was my great-grand-mother's. I know, it's not as big. And it's a really old-fashioned setting, but…" He couldn't finish, because she had wound her arms around his neck. *Again.* And just hugged. Fiercely. Ardently.

"Ask me," she ordered him.

"Will you? Be my bride, my wife, share life and love with me?" Hell. He knew he wouldn't say it well. He didn't do emotional stuff well. But he hoped she could hear all the love in his voice. The need, the want, the feeling.

"I will. If you'll be my husband, my mate, my love through life," she whispered back.

Hours and hours later, she murmured from the pillow next to him, "Do you want to honeymoon in Paris?"

He answered with the obvious. "We can, but we don't have to travel to do that."

"Huh?"

"You are my Paris, Kel. You always will be." And he kissed her again, just to make sure she understood what he meant.

REQUEST YOUR FREE BOOKS!

2 FREE NOVELS
FROM THE ROMANCE/SUSPENSE
COLLECTION PLUS 2 FREE GIFTS!

YES! Please send me 2 FREE novels from the Romance/Suspense Collection and my 2 FREE gifts (gifts are worth about $10). After receiving them, if I don't wish to receive any more books, I can return the shipping statement marked "cancel." If I don't cancel, I will receive 4 brand-new novels every month and be billed just $5.49 per book in the U.S. or $5.99 per book in Canada, plus 25¢ shipping and handling per book plus applicable taxes, if any*. That's a savings of at least 20% off the cover price! I understand that accepting the 2 free books and gifts places me under no obligation to buy anything. I can always return a shipment and cancel at any time. Even if I never buy another book from the Reader Service, the two free books and gifts are mine to keep forever.

185 MDN EF5Y   385 MDN EF6C

Name	(PLEASE PRINT)	
Address		Apt. #
City	State/Prov.	Zip/Postal Code

Signature (if under 18, a parent or guardian must sign)

Mail to **The Reader Service:**
IN U.S.A.: P.O. Box 1867, Buffalo, NY 14240-1867
IN CANADA: P.O. Box 609, Fort Erie, Ontario L2A 5X3

Not valid to current subscribers to the Romance Collection,
the Suspense Collection or the Romance/Suspense Collection.

Want to try two free books from another line?
Call 1-800-873-8635 or visit www.morefreebooks.com.

* Terms and prices subject to change without notice. N.Y. residents add applicable sales tax. Canadian residents will be charged applicable provinäal taxes and GST. This offer is limited to one order per household. All orders subject to approval. Credit or debit balances in a customer's account(s) may be offset by any other outstanding balance owed by or to the customer. Please allow 4 to 6 weeks for delivery. Offer available while quantities last.

Your Privacy: Harlequin is committed to protecting your privacy. Our Privacy Policy is available online at www.eHarlequin.com or upon request from the Reader Service. From time to time we make our lists of customers available to reputable third parties who may have a product or service of interest to you. If you would prefer we not share your name and address, please check here. ☐

BOB08

JENNIFER GREENE

77177   BLAME IT ON CUPID   ___ $6.99 U.S. ___ $8.50 CAN.

(limited quantities available)

TOTAL AMOUNT $ _____
POSTAGE & HANDLING $ _____
($1.00 FOR 1 BOOK, 50¢ for each additional)
APPLICABLE TAXES* $ _____
TOTAL PAYABLE $ _____

(check or money order—please do not send cash)

To order, complete this form and send it, along with a check or money order for the total above, payable to HQN Books, to: **In the U.S.:** 3010 Walden Avenue, P.O. Box 9077, Buffalo, NY 14269-9077; **In Canada:** P.O. Box 636, Fort Erie, Ontario, L2A 5X3.

Name: _____
Address: _____ City: _____
State/Prov.: _____ Zip/Postal Code: _____
Account Number (if applicable): _____

075 CSAS

*New York residents remit applicable sales taxes.
*Canadian residents remit applicable GST and provincial taxes.

HQN™

We *are* romance™

www.HQNBooks.com

PHJG0408BL